STRANGE GODS

STRANGE GODS

John Cornwell

SIMON & SCHUSTER

LONDON·SYDNEY·NEW YORK·TOKYO·SINGAPORE·TORONTO

First published in Great Britain by
Simon & Schuster Ltd in 1993
A Paramount Communications Company

Simon & Schuster Ltd
West Garden Place
Kendal Street
London W2 2AQ

Simon & Schuster of Australia Pty Ltd
Sydney

A CIP catalogue record for this book is
available from the British Library
ISBN 0-671-71810-X

Typeset in Trump Medieval 12/14 by
Hewer Text Composition Services, Edinburgh
Printed and bound in Great Britain by
Butler & Tanner Ltd, Frome and London

PART ONE

A Thirsty Man

'Give me a man in love: he knows what I mean. Give me one who is thirsty and wandering lost in this desert.'

Augustine of Hippo [*Sermon on John*]

CHAPTER 1

Here at the outset is a confession, and a coincidence. On the day my Jesuit superiors asked me to volunteer for the South American missions, Jill announced that she was going to have our baby.

That first year of the nineties I had been plagued by coincidences: dreams of prognostication, million-to-one encounters, stray thoughts that fathered events; then, on Easter Tuesday, the synchronicity that brought things to a head.

There I was, sitting in my priestly book-cluttered nicotine-polluted bedsit in the Mayfair Mother House, when I heard the familiar squelch of footsteps on the polished linoleum of the corridor and saw that distinctive manila envelope appearing under the door.

It was the briefest of directives: notice of a change of scene for my pastoral duties, sanctioned by the men in Rome. 'Would you like to consider work,' they said, 'in Latin America?'

So, having spent five years as Director of the Fellowship of the Word, evangelizing the poor pagans of the Third World by dining out with rich Christians of the First, I was being invited to pack my bags to gain some first-hand knowledge of the objects of all the charity I'd harvested (£20 million, to be precise, in the five-year period).

That's how we do things in this post-Vatican Two era: no military-style orders, but *mental* obedience – 'suggestions' to 'volunteer'.

No sooner had I decided to fall in with their suggestion (for reasons I shall make plain), than my mistress, if I might use that quaint term of Jill Connell, my secret woman friend, called me to say that she was two months pregnant. Such eventualities among the Roman Catholic clergy normally happen the other way about: fatherhood first, request to volunteer for the missions second. Small wonder I experienced a sense of synchronicity. But was this the coincidence of God's Providence? Or the malevolence of darker forces? There might have been a rational explanation, of course; I did not suspect that my superiors had discovered Jill's pregnancy ahead of me (although I would never put anything of that sort beyond them), but it occurred to me that they might have known about '*a* Jill'; perhaps they were helping me face the contradictions in my life. Leave and marry! Or get a grip on yourself and behave like a Catholic priest.

Behaving like a Catholic priest, a celibate, 'in the world but despite the world', has never been an easy proposition in the long history of the Mother Church of Christians; in the run-up to the turn of the second millennium (when – according to the Charismatics – Satan is stirred up to new heights of aggression), the proposition may be hazardous in the extreme.

So things had been coming to a head in more ways than one. Here I was, a cleric for our times: a charmer and a chatterer, much in demand as a columnist, a 'talking head', a preacher; always to be depended upon for an instant opinion. Yet behind that mobile, concerned face of mine I was in trouble.

For several years now I had been restless, hypermanic, *uncentred* (in the care-babble of my counsellor at the Society for Priestly Renewal); wracked with sudden terrors, flights of unbidden ideas and mood swings, from brilliant exuberance to dark paranoia. The worst was that interminable period before dawn when I would lie on my bed in the Mother House seized with a fear of this life as well as the next, of daylight as well as darkness. Sometimes in those still and silent hours I would think of a certain bridge where the Tube trains rushed beneath.

I had consulted a psychiatrist, who prodded me and took blood; who told me that I was suffering from 'suspected endogenous manic depression'. My condition, he said, was a result of 'global brain cell dysfunction'. The more he explained, the more it sounded like a root and branch eco-catastrophe in the vast undergrowth of my cerebral cortex.

This doctor, a reputable clinician at the Maudsley Hospital, prescribed Lithium – a multi-molecular warhead delivery system that sneaks through the blood-brain barrier to carpet-bomb the nerve cells with powerful long-life chemicals: a smart drug apt for a psychiatric epidemic of our time. Lithium, it seemed, was to the mantle of my cerebral cortex what the defoliant Agent Orange is to a jungle canopy. Lithium purged me and parched me; it gave me an implacable thirst. I was permanently in the desert, burning and restless. But the therapy calmed the dramatic storms of manic highs and depressive lows, as if the meteorological force fields of my brain were being governed by those unquenchable fires in the cortical foliage. In my wilder flights, I sometimes speculated that the ecosystem of my brain, the pulsing silvery blue-green planet in my skull, was suffering from overheating; that I was destined for a drastic depletion of protective mental ozone layer.

Yet in rare calm moments of recollection I was convinced that my condition was of my own making, that the cure was obvious and ready to hand; that I was reaping the reward of my secret sins. In the early hours I would plead with Him to cleanse me of my hidden sins: against poverty, obedience, and above all, *chastity*. Had He heard?

As a young priest I had pondered, with no small pity and terror, the dilemma of Graham Greene's Scobie. Remember old Scobie. Should he stay away from the Communion rail and proclaim his adultery? Or should he comfort his wife, receive the sacred host in a state of mortal sin, and betray the Lord of all Creation?

Yes, this Catholic Church has come a long way these forty years. A moral paradigm shift of staggering proportions! Scobie's agonizing scruple – driving him to despair, suicide, and everlasting damnation – had become for me, and for countless of my brother priests in this post-Christian era, a matter of daily routine.

My relationship with Jill, a young widow with a small son, had been secret for three years, during which time I broke again and again my vow of chastity, and yet, seldom confessed and seldom shriven, I said Mass and welcomed God into my mouth, into this Temple of the Holy Spirit, while my heart stayed closed against Him. And week after week I would *make* love to Jill Connell; I would kiss her lovely face and breasts, and mouth, and eyes, and enter into her beautiful young body, knowing all the while that my heart, my soul, was clenched against her too – like a hard cold fist.

Most Catholic clerics are familiar with the lusty young woman who prick-teases a priest because she sees in him frustration parallel to her own. In my younger days, I had carefully kept my distance. Was Jill such a woman?

We had met on pilgrimage at Lourdes where she was accompanying her husband Philip, a mournful young Catholic novelist (once promising enough to have been praised in the *TLS* and the *Guardian*), now doomed by the final stages of Hodgkin's disease. I, on the other hand, had joined that Lourdes pilgrimage in the hope, and without much faith, that I might be cured of those psychic peaks and troughs that were threatening to destroy what I ironically called my ministry, along with my sanity. Besides, I found pilgrimages an apt antidote for my capricious moods: new faces, new voices, the distraction of a temporary community on the move.

We found ourselves squashed together in a bar one

sweltering evening where droves of *brancadiers*, nurses, girl-guides, gathered after dark. She was escaping the long hours of accompanying her husband's pain and fear. She was shrill with gaiety; she told me, shouting above the din, she was so bloody hot that she'd taken off her bra. Noting my amused reaction (I asked her to prove it), she told me that she always put on clean knickers before going to Communion. A brazen remark to make to anyone, let alone a Jesuit on pilgrimage. But then, she was trying to 'wind me up', as youth say.

The next day I saw her heaving the stricken body of her husband in one of those hideous adult prams. It was a muggy July day; she was wearing a short summer dress with narrow shoulder straps. Occasionally she rested her weight on the push-bar; she was slender, well made, with sturdy athletic legs. Her body seemed tense under her skimpy dress, and she had a tendency, at rest, to shift her hip and ankle in a way that looked provocative.

I increased my pace and caught up; I was wearing my white sanctuary robe and stole – the picture of a pious pastor. Her emaciated husband lay full length in that litter on wheels; Philip Connell, the dying young novelist, had a tube in his nose and the flies had found his eyes. I was moved almost to tears for them both. He looked up at me and mumbled a brave greeting. I took over and pushed him all the way back to his hostel.

After he had been put to bed Jill asked me if I'd like coffee. We sat opposite each other in the high-ceilinged ward kitchen. She was watching me with those amused blue-green eyes. She had pale skin and auburn hair worn short; a high forehead that receded just before it met her hair line.

She said: 'You look like a druid.'

I took off the stole, then the long white robe, pulling it over my head. Underneath I was wearing a white short-sleeved shirt and clerical black trousers.

'Now you look like a cop,' she said, laughing.

I was trying to smooth down my shock of hair and she was leaning with her elbows on the table, her bare shoulders slightly hunched.

'What are you? Are you a parish priest or something?'

I liked her familiar manner, a change from the grudging respect of most young Catholic lay women.

'I'm a Jesuit. I raise *money*,' I said, signalling what I hoped was a wry smile. 'I try to milk Catholics of their wealth . . .'

'Are you any good at it?'

'I meet my targets.'

'Do you sell favours . . . *spiritual* favours?'

'I'm not *that* depraved; but they all want something back.'

'And what do they get?'

'I tell them: giving is good for the soul.'

'And how would *you* know?'

We were looking each other over, enjoying our banter.

'Well, you're right; but I've nothing to give . . .'

'Why don't you sell off those Church treasures? Give the money to the poor?'

That hoary old chestnut, I was thinking; but I knew that she was more interested in the style of my answers.

'OK,' I said, 'so we sell the *Pietà* for a hundred million dollars; and we give a dollar each to a hundred million of the poor. The next day they'll still be poor; and the pilgrims to Rome will be the poorer.'

'And the Holy Father?'

I was looking at her lips; I had noticed the way she drew her mouth very lightly to one side before delivering a quip. Her skin was beautiful, almost magnolia; she had a noble nose, sculpted, original; it gave her a sardonic air of sensuality and disdain. I felt a compulsion to reach out and stroke her cheek.

'You want the Pope to be poor?' I said.

'No more impertinent questions about his wealth. It might make your milking job more easy.'

I laughed and let it rest. There was nothing earnest about her; just surface play.

'So what brings you to Lourdes?' she was asking. 'Rich pickings?'

I laughed again and bowed my head. I said, 'Oh no, I'm off duty . . . strictly off duty, Jill.

I had not the least desire to unburden myself of black depressions, self-doubts, night fears.

She was silent for a while, gazing at me steadily; she said, 'I was watching you last night in the bar.' She left the statement hanging a moment. 'And you looked *very* off duty . . .'

I took a sip of coffee.

'You were looking at the girls,' she went on. 'Nothing wrong with that . . . only it was obvious. You were *really* looking.'

'Are you suggesting,' I said with mock dignity, 'that I came to Lourdes to pick up a lady?'

'A lady! You wouldn't be the first.'

I blew out my cheeks. 'You *shock* me, Mrs Connell, you really do.'

'I was watching you, Father . . . Nicholas. Can I call you Nicholas? I thought you looked a bit forlorn.'

'And I was watching you *too*, Jill, and you looked very . . . brave.' I said this with an edge of tenderness, as if to convey my desire to comfort her without discussing her husband's suffering; nothing more serious. I was thinking: I want to share something with this woman – but just on this level.

'And how about you,' I said. 'You have a career?'

'I paint . . . I try to paint.'

I was looking at her long, strong, expressive hands; artist's working fingers.

'You paint people?'

'Sometimes.' She put her head slightly to one side, as if she were sizing me up for a sketch.

'You've a good head,' she was saying, 'and you've got . . . sea-grey eyes, very indignant; and extraordinary hands.'

I held out my knobbly, raw-boned hands; I said, 'I inherited them from my mother. She was a Sheehey from Kerry ... The Sheeheys were street fighters, you know! And I've got her hair.'

She was laughing again. I was putting one hand through my shock of frizzy dark hair. I said, 'I'm six foot two; but with this I can look six foot five.'

That evening we met again in the bar, surrounded by the roaring young women; and we drank, and shouted and laughed until midnight. Then I walked her back to the hostel, talking frivolously all the way. For a few minutes, quite naturally it seemed, she rested her hand on my arm; I could feel her strong fingers on my flesh.

She was telling me that she had a small son called Dominic. And as she talked I reflected that there was another Jill Connell: the inner person, the immortal soul, that lurked beyond her skittish, entertaining exterior. I looked at her. She was talking rapidly, and I was wondering: Who is this woman? What is she really thinking? Does she suffer pangs of conscience? Does she spend time carefully weighing moral choices? Does she believe her husband's soul will survive his body? Does she really like me?

I did not want to know Jill Connell that way; nor did I want her to know the soul within *me*, my inner torments and my apocalyptic terrors. I wanted to keep our relationship on the surface of things.

When we returned to England, we kept in touch. Her husband rallied for a while; then he died. After that we spoke almost every day on the phone.

Then, a month or two after his funeral, I asked her out to dinner and she did not hesitate to accept. I worried for a day or two about the venue; then I invited her to the Travellers' Club.

Already out of mourning, she came – wearing high heels and fishnet stockings, and a short dark red leather skirt, showing off her long shapely legs. Her cheek-bones were highly coloured as if from weeping; in the light of the chandeliers, they looked rouged.

Several heads turned when she entered the 'morning room', including old Monsignor de Lacy-Roper, who was entertaining a bishop; they looked up at me bleakly, and I felt a spasm of shame. I decided that I would not ask her to the club again.

She drank two large gins in quick succession, then we went up to the dining room and sat alone at the 'ladies'' end. She wanted to stay on the gin.

There I was, in my smartest charcoal-grey suit and prim freshly laundered Roman collar, nibbling at a plate of smoked salmon, comforting the young widow in the sombre ambience of the club; and all I could think about was whether I was entering an 'occasion of sin'.

She said, 'Is this where priests entertain their girlfriends . . . or boyfriends? Who are those old geezers down there?'

'Not so loud, Jill . . . I'll be chucked out.'

'Why did you bring me here, Nicholas? Don't let's come *here* again.'

I had caught the nuance; I said, 'Can I come and see you at home?'

'Of course . . . it's a long way out, but you can come if you want.'

Several times that evening she touched me, unconsciously, it seemed, as we talked; I looked down at her long, pale fingers resting lightly on my hand, and I was convinced that she was as intent to exploit my companionship as I was to exploit hers. And what was the harm, I reflected, in that?

I was charming and jovial, apparently in control; but I was perplexed as to how I should bridge the gap from priest to closer friendship; how to continue to play the role of pastor on the way to . . . what?

'I'd like to see your little boy Dominic,' I had said.

Later, I murmured, 'You'll meet Philip again, Jill; pin your hope on that. It will give you the strength to pick up the pieces; make a new start . . .'

Even as I said it, I knew I had struck a false note. I had been intent (under what layers of self-delusion?) to separate my 'appetites' from the inner intentions of my heart, by appealing to her loyalty to her dead husband's soul.

'Crap!' she hissed. She was staring at me angrily with those daunting eyes.

The silver-haired members on the centre table looked up.

'Philip's gone. Gone for good ... *that's* what gets me back into life ... nothing else!'

I did not believe her; I was convinced that she was merely drunk and fractious.

A week after our dinner at the Travellers' I visited her her flat on Claybury Hill. Then I started making weekly evening visits, staying later, becoming ever more doting.

I'm not going to suggest that Jill seduced *me*; no. But I believed that her need for sexual satisfaction was equal to mine. I felt at the time, such was my mounting appetite for sex, that I could face neither life nor death without spending one whole night with her naked in my arms. Part of me believed that a sexual experience with Jill would somehow cure me, *save* me. Yet I was convinced that this need to *enjoy* her, to satisfy that exquisite *concupiscentia carnis*, that tendency towards the *flesh*, was to give in to that dark and predatory drive that, Augustine reckoned, appropriated and procured God's creation to 'selfish' ends. I saw her, I knew, as a sexual object: someone, no, *something*, to be had. And yet, I believed that to enjoy only her body while holding back my inner self, my soul, would be a lesser sin than yielding to a deeper love. And all the while I knew that what came between our desire for each other and its fulfilment was the courage to sin.

So I *laid siege* to her. I phoned her day and night; I brought her flowers and champagne and gourmet titbits, and toys for her little boy; I flattered her, laughing at her stories, making her laugh till she wept: then finally I got what I wanted.

12

I slept in her bed, her lovely naked body wrapped around mine. I was forty-seven years of age, she was just twenty-nine, and I had never had a sexual relationship in my life.

I had her on each weekly visit; over and over again.

From the back of Jill's flat you could see the lawns and coppices of a neighbouring mental hospital where the patients shuffled along the gravel paths and mouthed to themselves under the trees. With its perimeter fences, its institutional buildings, its Gothic towers, and the deep-sloping green roofs with their pinnacles and pediments, the hospital reminded me of my seminary, of the monastic formation that moulded my priesthood. Sometimes I stood at the kitchen window, watching those inmates with their interiority, their drab, neglected clothing, their detachment from the world, and wondered whether their predicament described something of my own temperament: that determination to keep my inner distance from Jill. Gazing out of that window there were times when I had longed to return to the disciplines and certainties, the regularity and, yes, the *sanity*, of a religiously ordered existence.

On the other side of the flat there was a balcony where Henry the Jack Russell terrier lived in his kennel. When the first aeroplanes of the day began to circle towards Heathrow, Henry would bark at the sky. I stood there in my underpants stroking Henry's neck, while the aircraft whined and growled and seemed to change gear just over Claybury Hill, filling me, and Henry it seemed, with a primal dread of hovering wings.

On clear days the prospect from the balcony was like a map of my life. There in the suburban streets to the north, on the brooding margin of Epping Forest, were the scenes of my childhood: the tower of the parish church where my mother attended daily Mass until the day she died, and next door the tall house of the Jesuits, the severe role models of my youth; the Jesuits, who were to raise me, take me out of my lower middle-class

13

mediocrity, and show me spectacular vistas of the intellect and the spirit.

A little further north was the Catholic cemetery at Leyton by the Central Line Tube, where my father and mother lay buried; and there in the foreground, among the gasometers of Plaistow and Becton, the first parish, Our Lady of Lourdes, where I endured eight years as curate to Monsignor James Keenan; and on the distant horizon, amongst a muddle of Portland stone, the office where I worked as director of the fund for our missions across the world – the Fellowship of the Word.

Just visible in the foreground was Eastern Avenue and its never ceasing traffic. 'The highway,' Jill used to say playfully, 'that leads you to my heart!' She never knew that on my way up to her heart I often made a detour. I used to drive into the car park of an ugly red-brick Catholic church where a huge hoarding proclaimed a day-glo red message:

GOOD NEWS NINETIES –
DECADE OF EVANGELIZATION!

Sometimes I went in and sat at the back to savour the familiar smell of incense and candle grease and to look up at the sanctuary lamp winking above the tabernacle. It seemed important to me to sit there for a while, trying to sort out my thoughts and my conscience before going on up the hill to spend the night with Jill.

Sitting in that church I pondered all the usual platitudes with which we sexually active celibate Catholic priests salve our consciences: that we are all weak, all fallible, all prone. I told myself that Jill was a temporary companion along the route of life's varied pilgrimage (not for nothing had we met in Lourdes!); that with God's grace I would come out of this affair more human than I went in.

The trouble was, how should I say with conviction that most important prayer in the life of a Christian? How could I utter the words 'and lead us not into temptation', knowing full well that I intended going up to Jill's for one reason alone? I never came out of that church with an easy conscience, but somehow it helped, examining the cracks and fissures in that fragmented self of mine, to know what I needed to do to make my peace with God. I always ended with Augustine's plea: 'O Lord, make me a Saint. But not today.' And I went up to Jill's, comforted by the reserve I had created against her in my heart.

Anybody entering the church and seeing me there, my head bowed in the pew, might have thought me a pretty holy fellow. But nobody came. I was the sole visitor, while the traffic swept by on Eastern Avenue unheeding of the God of all Creation within. With the shortage of priests there was no resident pastor, but my old friend Father Derek Somers had charge of it along with two other local parishes. Derek was a true labourer in the vineyard, a true pastor to his people. There he was with his dyed hair and his pacemaker (three heart attacks already by the age of sixty), still loyal and forging on with seven thousand souls in his care and no one to help him. And he kept the doors of this hideous little church open for the chance visitor to the Blessed Sacrament: me. And yet, I was not, as it turned out, the only visitor.

One evening I came by to find the doors locked. I felt as if I had been shut out. I shook the handle and cursed out loud. Was it an omen? Later I heard the place had been vandalized. Not your usual breaking and entering. Someone had defecated on the altar and broken into the tabernacle and thrown the consecrated hosts all over the sanctuary and pissed on them. A delinquency apt for our evangelistic, Good News nineties! A sign, moreover, for a sexually active celibate priest; an emblem, to be sure, of my own routine acts of Eucharistic sacrilege.

It was then, not long after they locked the doors of the church, that Jill started to lay hints that her view of our relationship and its prospects were different from mine.

I had come that evening via Fortnum and Mason's

bringing caviare, *pâté de fois gras*, Brie, black olives, nectarines, passion fruit, peaches, sweet white seedless grapes, and a magnum of Bollinger.

When I knocked on Jill's door little Dominic came whooping and cheering to let me in. However late, he would rush from his bedroom to greet me like royalty and lead me to my usual armchair with cheers and applause. Dominic was now six years old and had a row of crazy stunted teeth and large blue eyes that started out of his head as if in permament shock at the weirdness of the world. I cherished little Dominic; he was always coming out with something strange and beautiful. 'When I grow up,' he would say, stretching his arms wide, 'I want to be a tree!' Taking off my glasses carefully he would look closely into my eyes. He was curious about my skin's surface. It was as if he were looking for mysterious clues on the surface of my face. He liked to pull and poke it about, examining it minutely for peculiarities, for impurities and odd growths. 'This one!' he would say thoughtfully, pointing a forefinger at a wrinkle, a pimple, or a mole. I found the intimacy of his scrutinies disconcerting.

Later I was sprawled on the sofa, and Jill was lying on the rug below me. She liked to eat with her fingers and suck them as she went along. Sipping her champagne, looking up at me through the glass, she said, 'We'd make a lovely couple, Nick, you and I; I fancy a cottage in Norfolk, near the coast ... You should think of taking up gardening; and writing. Aren't most of you Jesuits artists *manqué*, struggling between surrender to God and the demon pride of the artist?'

I was wondering which particular Jesuit, ex-Jesuit, or failed Jesuit she had in mind. For my part, I had a fleeting image of Joyce's desiccated ascetic in that Dublin lecture room. Not the sinister figment of French fiction, powder glass in one pocket, spiked discipline in the other – but the parchment skull-face, silhouetted against the crossbar of the window frame, a bony hand swinging, beckoning

16

with the sash-cord noose. Then I thought of Joyce, teaching English for a shilling an hour in Trieste.

'I'd *starve* in a cottage in Norfolk,' I was saying, leaving her to load up the significance of 'starve' as she chose.

Then Dominic came up behind me. He had his sticky hands over my eyes, then my mouth; he was pulling my ears and making rubbery kisses on my neck.

'I'd straighten you out a bit if I could get you to the country,' she was saying. 'Now that you've got this far, it's about time you thought of hanging up your hat and your trousers for more than one night a week; sorting out your guilt problems, your *sin* problems . . . what were you about to say?'

'I was about to remark,' I said, 'where would I hang up my soul?'

'You give me the creeps, talking about your soul.'

She was watching me, and I was trying to look elsewhere, tickling Dominic and pulling faces at him. Why was it that she treated my priesthood as if it were a neurosis?

I was thinking too that as belief in the soul evaporated during what remained of this nub-end decade of the second millennium, so would belief in freedom of the will, and the interior life, and the after-life, then the tide of Christianity really *would* be on its final run down the strand. And what would we make of death? Would it be just another illusion, like the soul? Like the self? Would we think ourselves immortal in the same sense as there was no limit to one's vision? Is that how we would finally deconstruct the problem of death?

She had come to sit with me on the sofa. I began to stroke her cheek and tried to kiss her lips, but she raised her head so I couldn't reach; I wanted to change the subject. It came too close to the source of my gravest anxieties. Without the supernatural, the immaterial soul, to fill the huge, mysterious gap of existence, I suspected that I should go finally mad. How was it, I mused, that I could be so closely involved with someone who wasn't equally convinced about the meaning of our human existence!

Jill put her fingers through my hair and kissed me lightly on the tip of my nose; she said, 'Just look at you; you've gone all defensive, all silent and morose. I'll show you where your soul is . . .' And she put her tongue gently, tenderly into my mouth and worked it under my tongue and up the soft sides and across the ribbed roof of my mouth; her tongue was delicious, sweet, soft underneath and slightly furred on the surface; then she nibbled the lobe of my ear. And I was thinking, what if she were right!

She was studying my face now, looking into my eyes with concern. She took a short intake of breath and shook her head; she had an affectionately pitying look that could touch me deeply, and at the same time rouse my suspicion. I was not inclined to believe that any human being could be so interested in *me*.

I might have realized the gulf in understanding that stretched between us, had I hazarded a guess, even then, at her quiet acceptance of my glaring shortcomings: my tendency, on those rare occasions when she cornered me, to intellectualize, to compartmentalize; my evasions, my hypocrisy, my ability to leave a discomforting hint echoing somewhere in the middle air unanswered, all of which seemed virtues to me in my determination to keep our relationship on the surface of things, but which had become, I would see in retrospect, symptomatic of a liaison of selfish convenience on *my* part with every passing week.

'What are you thinking?' she said, her blue-green eyes just an inch from mine.

'About money . . . Today I relieved a pious son of the Church of fifty thousand pounds.'

I liked to talk about my success as a fund-raiser; it was as if I had made the money myself; as if I were sharing the thrill of the wheeler-dealing that generated all that loot. The final gasp of the eighties! Usually Jill would encourage me to tell her the details; she liked to make me happy; she liked to laugh at the foibles of my benefactors. But this evening she did not react. She said, 'I can borrow my sister's house in Scotland . . .'

'You want me to go on holiday with you.'

'We've never spent real time together.'

I was thinking of the commitment of such a move: a week or more of a live-in situation; the long lie-ins, the heart-to-heart talks, the daylight intimacy, with no escape route; the three of us taking trips to the beach, going shopping together; the possiblity of being seen by people who knew me as a priest. Surely, she had not thought it through.

'I'm under a lot of pressure this summer,' I said, stroking the back of her neck.

'You could come up just for a couple of days . . . You might get a taste for it.'

'This is what I've got a taste for,' and I stretched up until my lips reached hers.

So, by a series of stratagems, Dominic having been sent to his bed, I forestalled, and postponed, further discussion of holidays, or hints of a more complicated relationship. And she seemed reasonably happy.

What was the matter with me? Why could I not consider spending a week alone with Jill and Dominic? What was I frightened of?

Bound with the deadly sweetness of the flesh I had been dragging my chain up Claybury Hill, and somewhat else besides, afraid to be set free, and equally afraid of being committed. I had been living on a borrowed conscience.

Not long after we started our affair I went to see a hare-brained Dominican confessor who said: 'Go ahead, sleep with her in good faith, Brother, you're learning something about love!' Then he fathered a child and vanished to join a New Age sect in La Jolla, Southern California. So I relied on occasional confessions to priests who did not know me, and my own inadequate attempts to make private acts of contrition. But even in the liberal climate after Vatican Two no Catholic cleric who wasn't a complete Judas priest, or insane, could settle with an easy conscience for a permanent 'occasion of sin', as we say. Sometimes I was inclined to put the matter more apocalyptically: I was inclined to believe that the failure of the Catholic priesthood and our religious sisterhoods to follow the example of Christ and the Apostles in pursuit of a single chaste ministry signalled the imminent demise of the Catholic Church. What more insidious symptom than the stench of impurity within the sanctuary itself, the horror of which haunted the fitful dreams of Pope Paul VI and prompted him to write that uncompromising encyclical *Humanae Vitae*. No one forced a Jesuit to take his vows of poverty, chastity, and obedience (those inversions of our end of the millennium norms of greed, fornication, and egotism); but the inability of such large numbers of religious to hold firm, once committed, to purity of body, and crucially of heart, was telling us something about our contemporary failure to make the radical, the heroic, gesture for *Him*. The flight from celibacy, from chastity, a mere trickle in the sixties, had become a grand highway for whole defeated, bedraggled armies of clerics and nuns in the seventies and eighties: a final, spiritual retreat from Moscow! One hundred thousand desertions from the priesthood in twenty-odd years, and twice that many nuns. No trivial incident in history, I was inclined to think; no favourable portent for the prospects of Christendom at large. In more pessimistic mood, I would ponder the fate of Holy Mother Church, and speculate whether I was being swept with her as she plunged, along with our traditional Christian values, towards disintegration. How come that even *I*, who had weathered the storms of the sixties and the seventies, had begun to experience the crumbling of my resolve! Was she indeed founded upon a rock against which Satan and the Gates of Hell could in no way prevail? Or was she *heading* for the rocks? Was this colossal establishment, the One True Holy Catholic and Apostolic Church, the world's largest single Faith – one billion souls, the whole ship's complement, cargo and passengers – plunging down the rapids towards a final catastrophic disintegration? And what Abomination of the Desolation, what Dark Age, lay in store for us after the final passing of the protective influence of the Mother Church of all Christians?

In calmer moments I believed that the problem lay entirely within myself. *I* was the problem, and *He*, who had stalked me all my life, was the solution. What I needed, more than confession, and contrition, and prescriptions for smart drugs, was a change of heart! I, Father Nicholas Mullen SJ, seventeen years a priest, and thirty years a Jesuit, was in need of a religious conversion. I needed to rediscover the neglected spirituality of my youth: the disciplines of asceticism, the call of the interior life, the transforming eye of Faith, the stern but exhilarating imperative to imitate *Him*. I needed, in short, to be born again!

What was stopping me?

I enjoyed going up to Jill's; I relished the anticipation, the sheer hedonism, the gorgeous relief of our lovemaking. Jill was talkative, sexy, funny. She made me laugh; and I made *her* laugh. We used to laugh until we fell down on the floor and rolled about breathless. She was a sinewy, energetic lover; *having* Jill Connell – coming inside her, her quivering athletic legs around my waist, her firm shuddering arse cupped in my large hands (anointed for such a different purpose!) – was a prize that outstripped my most far-fetched carnal fantasies. Let's not be coy! What beats it? The Devil's gift, the *summa voluptas*, the *calor genitalis*, the abiding derangement, the demonic intrusion, the rich pleasure, the terrible force of *orgasm*: as beyond the control of the will as the embrace of death – the dark sweetness of the Fall itself! The sex act, the *summum malum* of our fallen nature: the legacy of that shattered harmony of body and soul that had once been ours in the Garden of Eden!

Was there ever a more profound betrayal of my deepest

loyalty? My loyalty to *Him*? Was there ever a more apt illustration of the treacherous allure, the lubricious *lubricum*, the 'slippery' inward sucking of the flesh at the expense of the spirit, so eloquently admonished by Paul, Origen, Jerome, Ambrose, and, yes, Augustine! Augustine, that late developer in the disciplines of chasity, had cried out to the Lord: '*O tardum gaudium meum!*', 'O my late joy!' As for me, I had cause to weep over my late attachment to lechery: *O tardum discordiosum malum!*

One night a week was more or less enough; and although we thrilled to our lovemaking, although we revelled in our laughing and drinking, nothing would have induced me to linger in her flat after dawn, when the hangover and the guilt, the boredom and the post-coital depression, the paranoia and entrapment (occasioned by the mere sight of her knickers out to dry) set in.

Then came the 'suggestion' to go to South America. South America offered the prospect of doing something drastic. I was under no illusions about life on a tropical mission station in one of those vile, violent, and poverty-stricken countries, cut adrift from my comforts: my CDs, my books, my vacations, my golf, my weakness for the odd bottle of claret and a good French restaurant, my Rover with its quadrophonic sound system, and my weekly visits to Jill. South America signalled the opportunity of finding *Him* again, in an act of ultimate self-sacrifice. 'Unless a seed falling to the ground . . .'

Yet no sooner had I called the Acting Provincial and agreed to volunteer, and made an appointment to learn my specific destination, than Jill telephoned to say that she was pregnant: two months pregnant!

After three years' caution we had been occasionally *incautious* for the sheer erotic, inebriated, irresponsible novelty of the thing. Even as she told me – 'I'm pregnant, Nicholas, two months pregnant!' – tearfully, nervously, over the phone, I tried to persuade myself, just to see how it felt, that this was a providential sign, confirming God's will that I should marry her, after all, and be done. But in that selfsame moment I sensed the old abyss opening up. Her pregnancy, much as it alarmed and grieved me, for her sake and mine, only increased my resolve to make a clean break, submit to the South American option, and salvage my religious life.

Enough!

On the night before I was to learn my specific destination in South America, on the night on which I was to talk to Jill about her pregnancy, I drank half a bottle of Teacher's to bolster my resolve. Then I got into my Rover and set out across London for her flat.

Later I found myself weeping, standing in the wind and the rain, my forehead pressed hard against the wall of that locked church off Eastern Avenue. I was going over my lies, my deceptions, my betrayals, my drinking, my lechery; my failure as a lover, as a priest, as a Christian. It was as if I were trying to cool my burning soul on the cold wet bricks.

After a while a young policeman came by in a patrol car. He was slow of manner and had huge forearms which he kept massaging as if getting ready for a struggle. He seemed to think I was planning to get inside the church for a sinister purpose. He asked me a lot of questions about my status and habits. When I told him I was a Jesuit priest, that I was praying to the lonely God inside the church, he looked me over: my drenched-charcoal-grey Austin Reed suit and my clerical grey shirt with its absent Roman collar. He cautioned me gravely, then ordered me to move on.

I left the Rover in the car park and went on up to Jill's on foot.

That evening I played with Dominic while Jill watched us from the kitchen table where she was getting something to eat. My clothes and hair were soaked through, but she didn't say anything. She looked so appealing sitting there in a faded pink T-shirt and blue jeans; with her auburn hair in a pony-tail, her bare elegant arms, she looked like a teenager. She would be thirty-two at her next birthday; I would be fifty.

After Dominic had gone to bed she switched off the television and we sat in silence. She was fingering a magazine. I guessed she wanted me to say that everything would be all right; that I would support her, take care of her. But I was struck dumb. I had no words to tell her that our relationship was finished; that I was going to South America. I could not find the words to talk about her pregnancy.

I knelt beside her. She was trying to look into my eyes; but I avoided her gaze. I kissed her on the cheek and rested my head in her lap. She was stroking the back of my head, gently, as if I were a child. Eventually I said, 'When did you see the doctor?'

'I've known several weeks.'

'You didn't tell me.'

'I was waiting . . . I was frightened.'

'I'm not angry . . . you should have told me straight away.'

'I was frightened of what I always guessed. You don't love me . . . I'm bearing the child of a man who doesn't love me. You don't love me, Nicholas . . .'

'Of course I love you.'

'You've never said that . . .'

My mind was frozen. I said: 'What will you do?'

'I won't cause you trouble.'

'We're tired. Let's go to bed; we'll talk in bed.'

In bed I snuggled against her back. She was wearing an old shirt of her husband's, always an unspoken signal between us that she could not, or would not, have sex. I pulled up the shirt tail, put my hand on the warmth of her belly. I should have told her about South America; but my mind was on other things. I ached to make love to her, and I was thinking, yes, that this was the last time I would make love. I was thinking of Augustine's howl from his very cock and testicles: 'Are you dismissing us? . . . From this moment, will we never be allowed to do this, or to do that? And, O my God, what was it they suggested in those words, those *thises* and *thats*!' I wanted her to look up at me – her eyes glaucous and vacant with desire in the dim orange glow of the street lamps. Lying there with Jill snuggled into me I began to stroke her, reaching down towards her neat hips and the soft bush of her pubic hair; but she pushed my hand away and pressed her heel sharply into my shin.

She knew the depth of my betrayal.

I moved away. I lay awake looking across the room, shaking with frustration, breathlessness. Jill did her painting in the bedroom and there was a smell of oil paint and turps which gave me a touch of asthma. In the half-light I could see her still-life paintings stacked against the wall. In the past few months she had been painting bottles – green bottles, grey bottles, blue bottles; she was fascinated by glass, its translucence, its luminosity, the mystery of its smooth interstices and irregularities. The sight of those shapes in the twilight, gleaming, erect, excited and aroused me.

She began to cry.

I lay listening to her crying for an hour or more. It was a deep, inward sorrow that shook her whole body.

I had diverted my gaze from the paintings to take my mind off sex. I was looking at my suit, my charcoal-grey trousers and jacket, my clerical-grey shirt, draped over a wicker chair. It seemed strange, I thought, how our clothes – for a priest so much a part of the persona and which, in my case, snap and crackle with static as I take them off – lie limp and dead through the night, waiting to resume life in the morning.

She said, quietly, miserably: 'I dreamt last night you'd fallen in love with someone else . . . Just admit there's someone else.'

I remained silent. There was somebody else all right, I was thinking. There was *Him*, still drawing me like a gravitational force, despite of everything; despite the feelings that were beginning to stir within me that night: Jill, with my child inside her, reaching out to envelope me with the tenderness of her inner self.

I could not sleep, and I could not speak. Eventually, as if controlled by an exterior force, I rose from the bed and started to get dressed. I began to put on the public badge of office of my priesthood, my damp cold clerical clothes, and I fumbled with the buttons, with the sodden laces on my black clerical shoes, shivering in the semi-darkness.

She was saying softly: 'Please stay with me. Please talk to me . . . Nicholas . . .'

I was on my way, and she was saying, 'Nicholas, I love you so much; and you're going to be the father of my child . . .'

The words shocked me. I, who had been called 'Father' for half a lifetime, was struck with terror at the very sound of the word – *Father*.

Then I heard myself rasping, as if it were someone else: 'Don't ask me, Jill . . . it would kill me!' I was hastening down the hallway in a panic of fear and vertigo, slamming the door behind me, heading for the lift. As I reached the road I could hear Henry the Jack Russell terrier whimpering and barking at the sky.

CHAPTER 2

O'Leary was at his usual table in the panelled comfort of his favourite restaurant, the Savoy Grill, sipping a glass of champagne; perusing the wine list, a preoccupied gleam in his eye.

'God bless you, Father,' he said, rising to clutch my hand with a smooth grip.

He always said that 'God bless you . . .', as if to lay claim to the spiritual conspiracy he perceived to lie between us and the Lord.

O'Leary, exquisitely dressed, with immaculate cuffs and plump gold links, his face rounded and lineless, his eyes intensely blue, seemed to notice my rough appearance (I had dried out my suit on the radiator in the office and I was in need of a wash and shave). But he decided to ignore it. 'The *Maître d'* tells me,' he murmured, on resuming his seat, 'that the lamb is especially fresh and succulent; so I'm contemplating a Château Lafite sixty-one. How about that, eh, Father? Does that put heart into you?'

He ordered twenty-four oysters for himself, and for me some smoked salmon with a little Beluga caviare, and a 'decent sancerre' to begin (I'd swear he said 'dacent'). 'Just to keep our spirits up, eh, Padre?'

It seemed important to him to manoeuvre me with nuances of diction. Our relationship, which went back to the beginning of my stewardship of the mission fund, was complicated. I had never believed he gave his money out of untainted altruism. As I saw it, his generosity towards the mission had a price: O'Leary was smart, and he was very powerful, but he was the victim of a delicate Jesuit-schooled conscience.

I understood his predicament all too well; the entrepreneur, after all, has need of specialist pastoral care. How should a little Father McGinty from Skibereen give competent spiritual direction to a Stoneyhurst educated financial magnate like O'Leary? How should he provide opportunities for what, in the business, we call *condign* satisfaction – gifts to a good cause (and with tax incentives), in penance for all those fiddles and scams that got Mike O'Leary into the club of the top One Hundred?

O'Leary had told me over tête-à-tête dinners (naturally, under the seal of confession) how he had amassed that fortune. He had confessed his sins over dinner and lunch in the Ritz, at Les Ambassadeurs, at Le Gavroche, at White's, and, most frequently, in the Savoy Grill. Those informal unburdenings told of deception, manipulation, hypocrisy, disloyalty; nothing that would have landed him in a court of law, nothing unusual among his peer group, but *crookedness* by the standards of his sensitive Jesuit-nurtured casuistic scruples.

'I want to share this with you, Father Nicholas,' he would say (oh, that powerful uplifting buzzword, *share*).

Then he would go on to share with me, eyes aglint, and an ear for the atrocious mixed metaphor, how he had 'stitched up' a vendor with some 'fancy legal footwork' in a major acquisition secured with 'junk bonds' and a 'reverse takeover bid'. Or how he had 'massaged' share prices by whispering a bit of 'piss and wind' into the ears of 'media chums'.

'Nothing to be done, *now*, Father,' he would say with a sigh. 'It was all so long ago. But I want to make my peace . . .'

He would be looking at me expectantly, hungry for the soothing word.

'First, Michael,' I would begin, my voice mellow, 'I want to thank you for *sharing* with me these very honest

28

reflections on your past life. God', I would go on, head bowed, hands joined, 'God, Michael, does not ask us to punish ourselves by dwelling on our sins . . . God, Michael, expects us to put his love and mercy at the centre of our lives. And you know, Michael, sometimes it may be necessary to cut a few corners. Sometimes it may be necessary, swimming in those shark-infested waters, to be a bit of shark yourself. The important thing, Michael, is to tell God, who loves you, that you are truly sorry for your failings, and to give back a little bit of what you gained. Ours is not a god of vengeance, Michael, but a god of love.'

Michael, by this time, would also be bowing his head and wringing his hands, eyes shut tight, waiting to be stroked just a little more.

'The thing is, Michael,' I would go on, 'you are not at all a bad person. I think, in fact, that you are a deeply religious man at heart. Why else would we be sitting here, you and I, breaking bread, sharing? You've been generous in your giving; you will be generous again. And these gifts, Michael, are valuable in the sight of Almighty God, a token of your desire to make satisfaction for those occasions when you were tempted perhaps to take the shortest way.'

It was still not time for the check, nor indeed, and more to the point, the cheque – the fat cheque. To be sure, here was the wine waiter bringing the brandy, and the *Maître d'* with his cigar box.

Now was the cue for Michael O'Leary's 'personal situation', that is, his personal *sexual* and domestic situation. O'Leary was two years into an affair with a woman thirty years his junior, with two failed marriages behind him: the first, the Catholic one, which had produced five children, annulled, the second, with two further children, still officially on. Michael O'Leary, in other words, was living in sin; he was also, like ninety-nine point nine per cent of Catholics in the civilized world, practising birth control; but his delicate Jesuit-trained conscience wanted someone to tell him that it was all right; not only that he was justified, saved, destined for heaven, but that he could go to sup at the table of the Lord and feel good about it. Michael O'Leary wanted me to tell him that it was OK for him to go to Holy Communion.

There was a time, when I was first ordained, when a priest went into the confessional with a comprehensive rule book in his head on matters sexual and marital. We quoted the rules and expected complete submission. No firm purpose of amendment: no *absolution*! Now all that had changed; one was encouraged to apply 'pastoral' solutions to a penitent's problems; 'internal forum', we called it. One was encouraged to listen carefully for indications of 'good conscience' transcending the details of the case. I could, if I so desired, take the full weight of Michael O'Leary's thumping fat sins on my own already staggering conscience. Small wonder by the age of fifty I was going mad and taking Lithium.

'Well, now, Michael, I hear what you are saying,' I would begin. 'I know that your situation, your problem, gives you anxiety. Which is a good sign, you know, Michael. For Holy Mother Church has a way of making us face up to the lack of integrity in our lives. But the truth is as you've said before, Michael, mistresses have rights too. You've been living with this woman for several years and you're not about to throw her into the street; and I want to take into account your own sense of conscience in the matter . . .'

'Ah, but there's the rub . . .' says Michael

Indeed! There was the rub. Michael O'Leary was not going to let me get away *that* easily. He was not going to allow me pass the buck back to his own exquisite conscience. *That*'s why I was there, sipping Cognac and puffing on a Cuban cigar, instead of sitting in some dark musty confessional and telling him where he got off.

'OK, Michael,' I say soothingly, 'I hear what you are saying; I know where you are coming from, dear fellow. I understand it all too well. I am *telling* you that I am going to give you absolution for these and all your other sins, right here at this table, and I want you to go to Holy Communion this Sunday, because I know that in your heart you have done your very best and you mean to follow a good life.'

With this I put down the brandy glass and with the Havana in my left I make an imperceptible sign of the cross with my forefinger, there in the Savoy Grill, with the *Maître d'* fussing around and the roar of the fat-cat lunch clients all about us. 'I absolve you, Michael, in the name of the Father and of the Son and of the Holy Spirit, amen . . .' And because I am equally capable of a spot of banter, I raise my glass to him and whisper: 'Now drink up, my son, and praise the Lord.'

O'Leary is sitting with his head bowed, his face aglow with a pink smile of contentment. And I, Father Nicholas Mullen SJ, am feeling like a piece of shit. But what the hell! This generous son of the Church, over cigars and Cognac, has signed cheques these past five years worth more than two million pounds to support our missions. And while it has no bearing whatsoever on my pastoral attitude to the man, he has been more than generous to yours truly: he it was who insisted on purchasing for my sole use that Rover 2300; opened an account at Austin Reed's ('Rich people,' he said, 'don't give money to men in baggy suits'); paid my sub and tabs at the Travellers' Club, and arranged for me to sign the bill at Mon Plaisir, Simpson's in the Strand, and the Connaught Hotel dining room. Then there were the golfing holidays at Sandy Lane, Barbados, and the regular cases of vintage claret. So what right had *I* to read the riot act about mistresses!

And that's how it went, more or less, over lunch that day at the Savoy Grill; except that before cheque-signing time, I had a little confession of my own to make; a small request of a personal nature that Michael O'Leary might consider money well spent in the discharge of his condign satisfaction.

I told him about my posting to South America. Then

I raised the matter of Jill and her pregnancy – not the full details, to be sure, but enough to explain my predicament; enough, without being explicit, to demonstrate my urgent need of funds for this unfortunate woman and her unborn child. How difficult it was to think of it as *our* unborn child.

Michael O'Leary was very still, very attentive; he sat with his eyes fixed on my face with a peculiar absorption. When I had finished he was silent for some minutes more, puffing on his cigar and looking away into the middle distance of the restaurant; I, all the while, in an agony of anticipation and no small discomfort at the inversion of our roles.

He turned to me, the faintest of smiles on his thin lips.

'Is she pretty?' he asked.

'Is she pretty?' I said. 'Yes, very; I can confirm she's pretty.'

'How old?'

'Thirty-two next birthday.'

'You did quite well,' he said. 'And is she good in bed?'

My anger, which can be dangerous, was fast mounting. I was thinking of all those years supporting O'Leary's Jesuit-trained conscience. But a lot was riding on this conversation.

'We had a most enjoyable time,' I said tartly.

'How often do you see her?'

'How often . . .'

'And how many times do you do it in one night?'

Was he mad?

'Michael,' I said, hearing my own voice crack and fail, 'is this inquisition *entirely* necessary?'

'You do it on top? Or what?'

I had just confessed this man and absolved him.

I sat, as he had often sat, my head bowed and my hands joined tightly together. Very tightly indeed, for those knobbly, raw-boned Sheehey fists were itching to fly up and clock him one, there and then in the sedate Savoy Grill.

I sensed him watching the angry workings in my face.

'And how, Father,' I heard him say, 'how do *I* fit into all this?'

I sat there, wringing my shaking hands, leaving the initiative with him – for better or worse.

'Well, I can imagine where I am supposed fit in . . . And how much are we talking about?'

'I'd like,' I said in a whisper, 'to give her, I don't know, twenty . . . thirty thousand pounds . . .' I hated myself for putting a price on it.

He was pursing his lips in a silent whistle.

'Well, don't let's sell her short,' he said with mild disdain. 'Don't let's fob her off! But let's just understand the situation, Padre, shall we?'

I looked up at him. He was relaxed, totally in control, actually enjoying himself, it seemed.

'All this time you've been acting as my spiritual director, talking religion and giving me absolution, you've been having it off with your floozie. I don't wish to pass judgement. How could I? But you're expecting *me* to donate money for this . . . floozie of yours so that *you* can wash your hands of her. And the implication seems to be that this is on a par with my giving money for the missions . . .'

He took a puff on his cigar and sipped his brandy.

'Now give me just one reason, Padre, why I should do a thing like that when I already pay high taxes to encourage sexual irresponsibility in the form of income support for single-parent families?'

A hit. A palpable hit! An observation fit for a Jesuit-schooled mind all right.

I felt like rising from the table and throwing the contents of my coffee cup into his fat face; but the thought of Jill held me back. I decided to play it cool, to attempt to appeal to his sense of loyalty to the priesthood and Holy Mother Church, that all-purpose standby, avoidance of *scandal*.

'Michael, you owe me nothing,' I said, my voice trembling with barely controlled fury. 'And I'd be the first to admit that I've no one to blame but myself for the mess I'm in. But I've come to you for help for the simple reason that I've nowhere else to turn. You don't need me to tell you that I have nothing, no resources whatsoever. I could give up the priesthood, try to get a job; but it would solve nothing. In fact, I'm asking for this money to save my priesthood, and to avoid the considerable *scandal* that's likely to follow.'

He was looking at me with mild contempt; and how could I blame him? He was playing with his cigar. There was, once more, a long silence between us as he sipped his cognac and contemplated the taxis coming and going on the other side of the plate glass windows.

'You want *me* to save *your* priesthood!' he chortled. 'I'll tell you what I'll do, Padre, I'm going to teach you a lesson about charity.' He was taking out his cheque-book, unscrewing his gold and jade fountain-pen.

'I know what you think of me,' he was saying. 'I know that you see me as a soft touch because of the weight of guilt I carry. But what do you know about motives for giving, Padre? All you've ever had to do is accept the cheques and put them in the bank.'

His pen was hovering over a blank cheque. 'Have you ever wondered, Padre, why I've given so much money to your foreign missions rather than the multitude of deserving causes here in Britain? The homeless, the hungry, the sick, the dying, the educationally disadvantaged . . . the list is endless, eh?'

He was staring at me with those cornflower blue eyes. 'You're a manipulative bastard all right,' he went on, 'but if you think I've given to your fund because of your skill at shoehorning money out of me you're wrong. I'll tell you why I've donated a fortune to your cause, Padre . . .'

He put the pen down and joined his hands; his neck was tensed.

'Many years ago,' he said in an almost inaudible voice, 'when I was a schoolboy at Stoneyhurst, a Jesuit missionary turned up. His name was Father Christian; Father Christian

O'Rourke. He was at home on leave from somewhere, Africa, or the Far East, and he came to give a talk in the school. I had a problem, the usual sort of Catholic adolescent thing, and I went to see him in confession. I felt wretched, guilty, and the Jesuits in the school had made me feel worse; in fact, they'd made me feel damned. But when I came face to face with Father Christian, I met for the first and only time in my life pure boundless love and holiness. Father Christian was a Saint; and he gave me a taste of God's love and compassion. When I came away from Father Christian I was walking on air. I've never set eyes on him since; he went back to the missions, where he's still working to this day, according to my information.'

He was looking at me with almost crazy intensity now.

'I've given two million quid to your bloody missions because I know that whatever my faults and failings I've had a share in Father O'Rourke's life and work.'

As he finished, I was thinking: Oh, that word 'share': so many subtle shades. All those spiritual stocks and investments! Yet, despite the unworthy thought I sat amazed at his vehement declaration. Here was something that he had never 'shared' with me before, and I felt almost chastened by its implicit reproof of my secret denigration of him.

But I was astounded nevertheless by another curious coincidence. I had not thought of Father Christian for years; and yet, when I had decided to 'volunteer' for South America, his face, his towering presence, had flashed instantaneously across my mind. Why should I have thought of Father Christian O'Rourke, involuntarily like that? Was it that I knew he was now on one of our missions in the depths of the Peruvian rain forests? Or was there something more providential, more mysterious at work?

O'Rourke, that byword of exemplary priesthood in the Society of Jesus, had been known to me all my life. I had sat at his feet as a boy. He had preached in the novitiate and in the seminary on fleeting visits from the mission fields.

In those far off pre-Council days he was the focus of pious gossip and adulation among the young Jesuits throughout our Province: for his asceticism, his missionary odysseys, his holiness of life. But he had not returned home in recent years, and his reputation had been fading in our memories. Father Christian O'Rourke. A Jesuit of the old school: humble, pious, pure of heart, brave; Christlike. He was the living exemplar of an uncompromising imitation of Christ. In our post-Council days of 'progressive' priests, of lax and agnostic priests, of gay priests, and priests who had mistresses and drove Rover cars, Christian O'Rourke had been forgotten, bypassed; yet, for all of my generation who had remained within the Society, he had continued to exert a quiet influence: a star on the distant horizon of our consciousness. It was good to know that Father O'Rourke was still with us, still at work, somewhere in the world.

I was nodding my head acquiescently. With the emotional confrontation, the sancerre, the Lafite and the cognac, I was beginning to feel agitated; I wanted to get out and take a stiff walk, swing my arms, sort this out in my head.

But O'Leary hadn't finished with me. He was filling in a sum of money on the cheque in front of him: '£100,000 only'. Only! Then he passed it across the table and waited for me to pick it up.

'This cheque, Father,' he said quietly, 'is not made out to anybody or anything. You can spend it on a deserving cause; or you can spend it on the fruit of your irresponsibility. I leave it to *your* conscience to decide. And you will have to live with your choice. Just fill in the name and the money will go through.'

I sat with the cheque in my hands staring at the amount.

At length he summoned the *Maître d'* with a wave of his hand; turning to me he said quietly, 'There's just one thing that's bothering me ... What makes your superiors think that you could be God's gift to those poor bastards in Latin America?'

*

Out in the keen Easter air I headed for Admiralty Arch, marching with an exaggerated stride, swinging my arms strenuously like a Guardsman, leaping off the pavement to avoid the troops of lunch-time shoppers, dodging through the taxi rank outside Charing Cross, until at last I gained the freedom of the tree-lined gravel beneath Carlton Terrace on the Mall.

Turning up the Duke of York's steps, I came face to face with a denizen of cardboard city, a youth in greasy jeans and sweater, a filthy blanket over his shoulders, a skinny hound at his side on a leash of binding twine.

'Help me, Father,' he said, hand outstretched, 'I'm hungry.'

I stopped and looked him over. He seemed in good shape, if a trifle grubby and stinking of booze. I tried to make past, but he was blocking my way. I was sizing him up. The Roman clergy are always fair game for accostings: I've been spat upon, tripped, punched, pushed, verbally assaulted, stoned even. But I've given as good as I've got. Well, I could have knocked this weedy fellow to the ground with one blow of the old Sheehey right fist; but he looked benign enough.

I had nothing in my pocket save O'Leary's cheque, so I said with all the sympathy I could muster: 'I'm sorry, my friend, but I've nothing to give you.' i was ducking and weaving; I wanted to continue my career up the steps.

'God bless you, Father,' he said, standing aside promptly. 'Thank you for speaking to me.'

I marched on past the Atheneum, round the corner into Pall Mall; I was still wondering whether the young beggar's remark had been sarcastic as I entered the friendly portals of the Travellers' Club.

In the smoking room I ordered a glass of water from the steward and sat myself down at the escritoire beneath the garden window. Popping two Lithium tablets into my mouth, I swallowed them down. Where prayer, Lourdes, antidepressants, t'ai chi, and the Alexander technique had failed, Lithium could put me almost on an even keel, but the thirst of Lithium is the thirst of purgatory; my tongue, my lips, my throat, my whole soul, was parched: burning.

Taking a piece of Travellers' Club writing paper and picking up a pen, I pondered the ethical conundrum set me by my benefactor. So I had this fat cheque to spend as *I* pleased. I saw myself standing with £100,000 worth of twenty-pound notes in the midst of a deserving rabble: the homeless, the starving, the maimed, the sick, the unemployed. And there, amongst them, our unborn infant in her womb, was Jill.

I was thinking of O'Leary's test of my moral integrity. Could I justify the gift of this huge sum to Jill? Should I be assailed with scruples?

If it came to that, could I justify any of the decisions of my priestly vocation these recent years? How had I justified dedicating the prime of my life to fund-raising for our foreign missions? Running around the country, begging and cajoling cash, covenants, and legacies with every kind of spiritual and psychological blandishment? Had I done it as a free moral choice? Or had I done it out of mere 'mental' obedience?

There had been a time when I longed for nothing more than the ministry of a parish. I had come out of the seminary like a young stallion out of a stable. I had started in Plaistow with a thirst for souls. But eight years at Our Lady of Lourdes had pushed me to the limit of my spiritual resources. While poor old Monsignor Keenan sat solacing himself, curtains drawn, with his video-recorder and the convenience of canned Guinness six-packs, I took on the work of us both. I was out all day long, and half the night, in the schools, and the hospitals, in the hospices, and in the prisons. Masses twice a day, and four times on Sunday; funerals, baptisms, confirmations, anointings, benedictions, home visits, instructions, marriage counselling; schools, youth clubs, Bingo; converts, newly-weds, unmarried mothers, the bereaved, annulments, separations, the sick, the dying, the old, the young; the committees – for finance, new buildings, renovations . . . And in the midst of this I was up till the early hours trying to finish a doctoral thesis on Christology (the meaning of Christ) – 'Who do you say that I am?'

Eight years in Plaistow had left me emptied, sterile, approaching burn out, incapable of uttering a single satisfying prayer: ever more remote from Him. The harder I worked, the more distant He seemed. Eight years on the parish in Plaistow, eight years of public solitude and lonely gregariousness, taking in the dirty washing of five thousand souls, had taught me one thing: that I had failed to find Him for myself. My people were crying out for bread, and I was giving them stones. When they asked me to become director of the mission fund, I did not hesitate. I felt like the fly escaping from the bottle.

Once again my energy seemed inexhaustible, my purpose invulnerable. I had thought nothing of driving a thousand miles between Monday and Friday, preaching, cajoling, imploring. I had a gift for charming money out of both the rich and the poor. I was a natural promoter, an impresario, a publicist in the cause of the Word of God to the people that dwelt in darkness. Yet, as I met my targets, my hundreds of thousands, then my millions, had I got any closer to Him?

Then the disillusionment. What did *I* care for these contemporary 'missions' to the Third World (so remote, it must be said, from the saintly evangelism of Father Christian O'Rourke)? What did I really care for my confrères' socialist enterprises in the name of Christ the Poor Man, their 'base communities', their Liberation Theology, their Marxist jargon, their 'conscientizing of the rich', their 'contextualizations' and 'praxis', their so called 'option for the poor'? Incapable of solving our problems at home (not least the mass apostasy of our Catholic youth), were they not losing themselves in the problems of others, where they could achieve little good, and considerable mischief?

So what price the justification of a free moral decision?

My five years running around begging for money for Third World interference, my decision to take up their suggestion to escape to South America, had little to do with a free moral choice, an option for charity and evangelism. And yet I had begun to yearn for my *own* freedom, the freedom to make that huge change of heart, that *metanoia*, that discovery of Jesus and what it meant to be a Christian within the depths of my own being, my *self*.

And what of my self-abasement before O'Leary to secure this £100,000? Had it been a free option for Jill and our unborn child? A token of my responsibility for their future lives?

Jill's Catholicism was tenuous to say the least; she had not spoken of terminating her pregnancy, nor had I given her an opportunity to discuss the matter. But as I took the cheque from my pocket, I knew, in the depths of my conscience, that this charity was to set *me* free from the trap of that potential dilemma. If financial provision should be a factor in Jill's decision to lose the baby, then on that score, at least, my conscience would be clear.

Was it as straightforward as all that? No; I knew that had O'Leary denied me the money I should have left the priesthood, done any job I was capable of, to avoid being party to an abortion. But I wanted it both ways; and O'Leary, it seemed, had come to the rescue.

Sitting at the escritoire in the smoking room of the Travellers' Club, I took O'Leary's cheque and, without further scruple, made it out to Jill Connell. Then I began to summon, at last, the words of my farewell.

> Darling Jill,
> I should have talked to you last night, but I had no words to explain myself. I know that what I am doing looks like wickedness, or sheer madness. I have been a bad priest, and a selfish and inadequate lover. And now it seems I am throwing away the one chance I'll ever have of becoming a decent husband and a father.
> I am devastated by the thought that I have misled

you. Please forgive me. Believe me – if I thought it could work, I would ask you to marry me. But I can't extricate myself from this vocation which has been part of me from my childhood.

I might have tried to muddle through, but my people have forced a decision on me. They are sending me to South America.

You will have to decide, Jill, whether to keep the child, or whether to have it adopted. I have a responsibility towards you to make the years ahead less difficult, and I am enclosing a cheque, the free gift of a benefactor.

I shall write when I arrive at my new posting. Please let's keep in touch. Over the past three years I have become deeply attached to you and Dominic.

Would that things had been different; but it's like wishing that my whole life had been different.

With much affection, and sorrow
Nicholas

CHAPTER 3

Father Eustace Proctor, the Acting Provincial of the British Province, greeted me in his book-lined office high up in our imposing red sandstone headquarters in Mount Street. He was a small man with a white goatee beard and fierce black eyes behind heavy bifocal horn-rimmed spectacles. His face glowed with the ruddiness of a fresh-air fiend.

Father Proctor was a marathon runner, a karate black belt, and a keen squash player. He was an expert in Oriental languages, a specialist in modern communications and information technology. He was also, in spirit if not in avocation, an agnostic.

With his telephones, his faxes, his telexes and winking computer terminals, Proctor was the modern Church bureaucrat; his asceticism was clerical super-efficiency; his deepest conviction was pragmatism; not the merest hint of piety, a picture of Our Lady or a small crucifix, marred the atmosphere of soulless, passionless, hi-tech professionalism in his office. Compared with his, I sometimes believed, my sins were minor.

He leaned back in his office chair a little. He was getting a waft of my Lafite, charged with cognac and cigar fumes.

'I'm eager to learn my South American destination,' I said at once, leaning forward earnestly.

Father Eustace leaned back even further.

'Well,' he said, a trifle solemnly, 'that's excellent. But we have a condition that I hope you won't find onerous.'

The point of his angry little beard was jutting towards me and he seemed to be looking over his monstrous spectacles with all the severity he could muster.

'Things,' he went on, 'have not been going all that well, I'm afraid . . .'

He had no need to expand on the matter; he was, after all, responsible for the 'morale' of the House. We were highly trained Soldiers of Christ, not schoolboys; we were expected to be self-disciplined; but my behaviour within the community had been outrageous, even by my own bizarre standards, and I was aware of certain exaggerations that take hold in all-male all-celibate houses like ours.

There had been rumours circulating: that I had not just one but two or three women. There had been questions about my conduct of the fund's accounts; the amount and nature of my expenses. I had not been joining in our occasional community liturgy. I had not been able to sustain a conversation with my brother priests for more than half a minute. They had all suffered the sharp side of my tongue. All of this, it had to be said, was uncharacteristic of the Nicholas Mullen of former years.

I sank my head; I said gruffly, my voice catching with emotion: 'My behaviour, I know, has been far from exemplary . . . but that's all finished.'

I was feeling mawkish, unreal, as if I were acting out a charade; I thought I might even shed a few tears.

Father Proctor was looking at me strangely. 'Oh, no, I'm not alluding to your *behaviour*, Nicholas . . .' he said, his voice suddenly gentle with concern. 'Oh, no . . . we all have our difficulties; we accept you, my dear Nicholas, as you are. *Heavens*, no! When I say that things are not going well . . . I am referring of course to our missions in Peru.'

We all have our difficulties! Christ Almighty! What a Church we were living in! Nuns with vibrators; Monsignors who peddle drugs; archbishops who dabble with the Mafia; paedophiliac priests; priests with floozies. What did one have to do to incur the displeasure of a contemporary superior in this post-Christian era! Light one's cigarette on the sanctuary lamp? Screw one's mistress on the high altar?

But was this merely a disarming tactic? A move in a determined strategy to get me off their hands without a fuss?

'But my condition,' continued Father Proctor, 'you may find somewhat harsh ...' He was gazing at me, eyes stretched, as if anticipating a dismayed reaction. 'We think it best that you don't delay ... there are connections tomorrow at noon, to Iquitos, via Miami and Lima ... It's a long journey ...' His voice trailed. 'It's very far away.'

So they wanted me off the premises: immediately, *statim, extemplo, quam celerrime!*

'Fine, the sooner the better,' I said. And I added jauntily, as if in celebration of my future Latin American career: *'No hay problema!'*

But I was thinking furiously – Iquitos, Peru, why the hell do they want me in *that* armpit of the universe? Why there? We had houses in Salvador, Guatemala, Guyana, Brazil, Colombia, Ecuador, Chile ... Nowhere in Latin America was particularly safe or cushy: but *Iquitos!*

'Only for a few weeks, so that you can get acclimatized in our House there with Father John and the others, start to learn a little Quechua, brush up your Spanish, get settled in. Then we want you and John to go west to the highlands, the Selva Alta on the borders of Ecuador ... I don't have to tell you that it won't be a tea party up there. The assignment is not for the faint-hearted ... We want you to join Father Christian O'Rourke at Aranuba.'

Clapping my hands I gave a short high-pitched whoop which nearly caused Father Proctor to fall backwards in his chair.

How could he have known? How could he *possibly* have known? There was a synchronicity for you! First O'Leary, then of all the 26,000 members of our Society I had been selected to work with this one priest in the entire world who, I was convinced, could secure a change of heart in me. Had their stratagems even accounted for this?

I was already imagining a peaceful, traditional mission

in some sunny forest upland, a spiritual retreat under the personal guidance of Father Christian O'Rourke! Was that not an extraordinary act of Providence?

Father Proctor was gazing at me unsmiling, perplexed, fingering the file that lay on the metal desk before him. He said, 'I don't quite see the point of the hilarity . . . I only hope that you are not under any kind of illusion about Aranuba, Nicholas, or life with Father Christian.'

Father Proctor was pursing his lips; he had paled a little, as if in anticipation of his next announcement. 'Father Christian has just lost two of members of the Society and two nuns . . . Peru, Nicholas, is a dangerous place.'

'Lost?' I said. The ridiculous phrase *lost in transit* had flashed across my mind.

'Yes, Nicholas,' he went on, cautiously. 'They were killed, you know.'

'An accident?' I asked, almost hopefully.

'Oh dear, no, Nicholas . . . They were brutally murdered, although its's uncertain whether by terrorists or government militia . . . No doubt you will be able to shed more light on the matter when you reach him.'

Well, it was sobering me up like no amount of Lithium to hear *this*.

Father Proctor handed me a file. I flicked through it: air tickets, travel itinerary, traveller's cheques, and a photocopy of an agency news report. By the look on his face it might have been a death warrant. He said, 'It didn't make the newspapers, except a line or two in the *Guardian* and the *Telegraph* . . . People are getting inured to the idea of priests and nuns being killed out there . . .'

I took the file and stood up.

'You'll have a lot to prepare, Nicholas,' he said without a trace of emotion (our Jesuit style). 'I should travel light if I were you.'

'*No hay problema*,' I said again; this time with less vim.

'Perhaps we should have a farewell drink tonight, with a

few of the brethren, after supper,' said Father Proctor. 'You may be gone a long time . . . Perhaps, Nicholas, you may want to stay on, you know, indefinitely . . .'

He had no need of finishing that sentence. I gave him my nonchalant smile; but my mind was in turmoil.

I went down in the lift to my own current quarters, my Edwardian cavern with its fancy cornices and coping, its vague smells of socks and stale cigarette smoke, housing my accumulated bachelor clobber of the past five years.

There was a time, during the long sojourn of my early training and young priesthood, when I kept my temporary quarters (in Oxford, Heythrop, Rome, Fribourg, London) in monastic austerity; no clutter, no ornaments; just my favourite icons lit by votive lamps.

This room in the Mother House revealed something of my state of mind in recent years: drifts of yellowing newspapers and magazines along the sides of the walls; piles of old and unwashed clothes; stacks of unreturned library books chaotically filling the book cases; clutches of liqueur and whisky bottles on top of the filing cabinets; my complicated hi-fi equipment surrounded by hundreds of open, dust-laden CDs. Only one item, standing among the ashtrays and dirty coffee cups on the mantelshelf, spoke of my religious status: a sepia reproduction of a sixth-century icon of the Christ from St Catherine's monastery on Mount Sinai, looking out at me with curious eyes that seemed to say: 'So what are you going to do next?'

I sat at my desk and opened Father Proctor's file, taking out the photocopy of a UPI report, datelined Iquitos. It was just a week old.

Two Jesuit missionary priests and two nuns were yesterday reported killed on a tributary of the River Napo 200 miles east of Iquitos. First reports suggest that the priests and nuns were murdered by the Maoist terrorist group, Shining Path. The head of the Aranuba mission-outpost in the region, Father Christian O'Rourke, has paid tribute to the missionaries. He said: 'These brave men and women were martyrs who gave their lives for the Christian faith.' The victims were tortured before being taken into the jungle where they met their deaths. Their bodies have not been recovered. Father O'Rourke, Irish by birth and a Jesuit of the British Province, said that the deaths would not deter missionaries from continuing their work in the region.

I sat staring at the piece of paper, my head throbbing with alcohol and Lithium. I had wanted an opportunity to make a new start, to suffer and make satisfaction for my sins, and of course I was aware of the danger of our Latin American missions. But deliberately to court martyrdom? And what the hell was the saintly Father O'Rourke up to anyway, getting our priests and nuns killed out there? My Lithium-coaxed brain had shadowy recollections of an extraordinary scheme, appropriate for no one but a madman, or perhaps a Saint.

As director of the Fellowship of the Word I had read hundreds of reports each year from our priests around the world. They told of developmental and educational projects, irrigation and agricultural schemes, their successes and failures. Most of them wanted four-wheel-drive pick-ups, Rotivators, water pumps, mechanical shovels. Their appeals for equipment were supported by graphic descriptions of urgent need, useful sermon fodder as I travelled up and down the country vacuuming up the money from the faithful. But I was remembering that Christian O'Rourke had asked for an item that had provoked puzzlement: a replacement for a crashed *seaplane* – a request that had been promptly turned down.

I went to my box files and pulled out 'Peru – Correspondence and Allied Documents'. Riffling through the yellowing reports I came to a copy of Christian's last letter. It was hand-written in green ink on airmail paper with plentiful literals, archaisms, and pietistic reflections. The saintly Father Christian O'Rourke, that legend of the Society, had told us how he had set his heart on bringing

Christ to the Mekroti people, a lost community in a remote forest fastness on the borders of Peru and Ecuador.

The Mekroti, so he claimed, were a precontact Amerindian people lost in an impenetrable region of the Selva Alta; according to O'Rourke they were probably the last remaining 'lost tribe' on God's Earth; to bring them salvation, he urged, would be a fitting tribute to the Lord at the approach of the completion of the Second Millennium.

Besides, he was deeply 'convicted', as he put it in his Irish manner, that, as Scripture tells, 'the Second Coming cannot transpire until the Gospel has been preached to all peoples upon the Earth . . .'

'When this last tribe has been exposed to the word of God,' he had written, 'His kingdom may come quickly, and He will be glorified by every people and nation with a single tongue until there is but one flock and one shepherd.'

There had been difficulties and hardships. 'As time passes,' he went on, 'we have suffered one set back after another, and in consequence I am convicted that our project is confronting more sinister enemies than mechanical failure, sickness, rapids, and the vast malevolence of these forests where the standard of Christ has yet to be established.'

He now set out a catalogue of accidents, including the loss of a voluntary worker, and the destruction of the mission seaplane, the use of which had been crucial to their plans. Returning from a reconnaissance of the Napo's western tributaries, one of the plane's floats had struck a submerged tree. The pilot's seat came adrift and he died instantly, smashing his skull on the windscreen.

'My own head hit the instrument panel,' he wrote, 'and I bled from the forehead until my cassock was caked in my own blood. The starboard float, which was punctured, sank as if it had been pulled under by a diabolical grip; the aircraft heeled around, ripping the fuselage away from the float-frame and plunging the hissing engine into the river.'

O'Rourke had gone on in his letter to describe how the

local Arabela Indians launched a flotilla of dug-outs to the rescue. The oarsmen had paddled frantically to reach the machine against adverse currents. 'Only the port float of the aircraft, which kept the wreck buoyant for an hour,' he wrote, 'saved me from the shoals of piranhas that were gathering as if scenting the smell of my blood.'

I read through all this with new eyes, and considerable self-interest. Such missionary adventures had been remote, unreal; now they were coming home with a sense of hasty imminence. Rifling through related correspondence, it seemed that the Provincial had pleaded with him to come home; how wise! But O'Rourke was adamant; he believed that although Satan was arrayed against him, he could not fail with Christ on his side. 'I have before me,' he wrote, 'many edifying examples of the heroism of past members of the Society; and nothing so prepares a pagan soil for a rich harvest than being soaked in Christian blood.'

I was flying high despite my ration of Lithium. Confronted with O'Rourke's extraordinary scheme – to bring about the Second Coming no less by evangelizing some highland jungle tribe – I was buoyed up with a fatalistic sense of exhilaration. There was no going back. Father Nicholas Mullen had embarked on this adventure, perhaps his last (I told myself, a trifle melodramatically), and he was going to see it through.

Sitting at my desk I was penning a short note to the Procurator. I wrote: 'Give all my stuff away: Father Nicholas.' I took out the keys to my Rover 2300 and placed them on top of the note.

PART TWO

Land of Unlikeness

They had dignity and respect in the Land of Likeness because they and the land were made in the image of God. How could they have known that this Land of Likeness would become such a Land of Unlikeness – alteration, destruction, desolation: paradise to hell.

Bernard of Clairvaux
[*Sermon on the Song of Songs*
XLII 'Regio Dissimilitudinis]

CHAPTER 4

Our house on Avenida 28 Julio in Iquitos was a two-storey building faced with cracked blue and white tiles, its secretive windows protected by heavy iron-wrought grilles. The terracotta flooring had been sealed with beeswax, the walls were whitewashed; a statue of Our Lady of Guadaloupe – the Virgin of the Americas – occupied a niche in the hallway. Our chapel was a bare room with half a dozen raffia-seated chairs; a crude table, a cheap wooden crucifix, an oil lamp, an unadorned wooden tabernacle; outside the cries of children and women vendors in the warm rain.

My room was a damp, sweltering cubicle with a camp-bed and an upright chair. During that first week I had lain sleepless, drenched in sweat, watching the mosquitoes gathering around the dim naked light-bulb, the impressions of my arrival in Peru still fresh as a lucid dream. The travellers at Lima airport, moving restlessly, watchfully, in flocks along the departures concourse; mean-faced teenage soldiers with automatic weapons; bomb scares and threatened machine-gun attacks; power cuts and distant explosions rattling the plate-glass windows through the night. The turboprop aircraft shuddering and circling over the jungle city of Iquitos, with its floating settlements and tall ruined churches, its tentacles of jerry-built huts disappearing into the swirl of the surrounding rain forest.

Descending the aircraft steps and walking across the concrete runway to the arrivals building I had looked up at the columns of baroque silver clouds rising to a vast sky, my head swimming under the pounding tropical sun, my body enveloped by the warm, wet air of the Amazonas.

At the gate I had been met by Father John Williams, a contemporary of my novitiate days. He wore old-fashioned steel-rimmed spectacles, a grubby off-white safari shirt, dark-blue workers' trousers and threadbare canvas shoes. He gave me a brief bony hug and helped me with my bag. A rusting Volkswagen mini-van waited in the car park.

Time and Peru had not been kind to Father John. He had a moist pallor; he was stick-thin and heavily lined about the eyes and the mouth. His hair was pure white at fifty-one, and he was somewhat stooped. Driving the three kilometres into town through sporadic downpours and water-logged potholes, he asked about mutual friends in London, making polite, self-effacing rejoinders. On the surface there was still the disciplined Jesuit of pious disposition, of clerical demeanour; but twenty years in Peru had hardened Father John into a wiry, hungry drudge. He lit up a cheap-looking cigarette and smoked it dangling from his lips; I noticed that his fingers were nicotine-stained as was the skin above his mouth. His eyes were sorrowful, weary; I had seen that suffering look in the eyes of our priests on leave from Ethiopia, the Philippines, Biafra, Central America.

Our community met for evening meal at eight o'clock, summoned by the sound of a hand-bell from the bottom of the stairs. We ate at the kitchen table, just three of us; Father John and myself and a black-bearded Irish priest called Father Felix MacDonagh. There were three other absent members of the community – two Peruvian Jesuit brothers and a Basque priest, away working with groups of Indians further up the Amazon.

Supper, cooked by Father Felix, was a bowl of rice and a few curried vegetables; there was a jug of boiled tap water on the table. We ate in silence.

After washing our dishes we went upstairs to the 'common room', a parlour with six old plastic kitchen chairs and a beaten-up coffee table. A bottle of pizco, the brandy of Peru, went round and around until it was empty.

On that first night Felix said, 'So you're going with John

to join Christian O'Rourke ... Christian may be a Saint, but he's mad. We've no business sending more priests on escapades to evangelize Indians ... Our work is here, among this lot on our doorstep.'

John looked uncomfortable. He tried to ease the atmosphere by asking me if I had ever been acquainted with Guarani, the Indian language of the region, or Quechua, which we would encounter in the Selva Alta. He told me that he had organized lessons for me in both languages with an instructor from the local national college. Turning to Felix, he said evenly, 'Don't let's jump to conclusions about Christian, Felix. He's doing God's work ...'

The same old John: the measured diction, the goodness, the loyalty to superiors and elders and to fellow members of the Society of Jesus.

Felix snorted and took out a pack of cigarettes. Offering them around, he said, 'Well, Nicholas, and what do you think of going up river to evangelize the last lost tribe on Earth?'

Accepting a cigarette, I laughed without conviction; I said, 'I feel like a novice in this missionary game.' And I said it without guile.

Over pizco and instant coffee my new confrères would tell me stories about their community work. They talked eagerly, with a vein of anger and frustration; but their preoccupations seemed unreal to me, as if I were a reluctant eaves-dropper in an alien world.

John had been working with the people of the floating city of Belém, the cholera-ridden slum of houseboats and rafts on the margin of the river; he was distributing dried milk and millet, attempting to set up a hygiene system, with fresh water and sewage disposal.

Felix told me with a hint of defiance that he was running a health education class, an informal birth-control clinic with provision of caps and condoms and sex instruction for women and men.

55

One evening during those first days Felix and I were taking a stroll along the street after supper. There was a tension between us; to lighten the atmosphere I said teasingly that our benefactors would be delighted to learn about the distribution of French letters.

Grabbing my arm he led me into a street bar and ordered two beers.

Taking a swig, he held up his shaking hand as if to dissuade me from explaining that I had only been joking. His eyes looked crazed.

'No, no, I understand what you're saying, Nicholas,' he said brusquely in his strong Dublin accent, 'very amusing and all that; but I get sick to the back teeth of the fucking Pope and those poofter curial bastards in Rome, prancing around dressed up like something in *Star Wars*, and all the crap they're teaching kids in school and the seminaries with no bearing on the real world, *real* moral dilemmas . . . Sexual morality doesn't dictate that the only place for sperm is up a woman's unprotected vagina in the middle of her month . . . I tell you, this is not a time for dawdling among the fucking flying buttresses and fingering the bloody theological frets; the Church is here, *Christ* is here; this is the place to be, this is where we get near Him, see Him at his wood, watch him bleed and sweat, hear the hammer on the nails.'

I was looking at him, amazed at his anger, wondering whether it could be entirely sincere.

'You won't find Christ in the Vatican,' he went on 'and He's not in some enclosed monastery or nunnery; and He's not up a bloody creek somewhere with Christian O'Rourke packing his bags for the Second Coming! So don't give *me* your knowing, sophisticated quips when you've only just climbed off the fucking plane . . . Welcome to the fucking Third World, chum!' And he raised his trembling glass at me.

The humid heat of the tropics, the initial culture-shock of a strange continent, had depressed my mood; but Felix's uncouthness and aggression was pumping up my lurking manic potential a few notches. In any case, it wasn't in the nature of a Mullen to sit like a bucket and have another's views and prejudices poured into him unchecked. And I was annoyed by his criticisms of O'Rourke: hadn't I pinned all my lingering hope for a conversion of life precisely on those values of piety and loyalty cherished by the old missionary priest?

'With respect, Felix,' I said, trying to control my own trembling hand, 'it's you who are talking crap! We can't all come down here to Iquitos! . . . And it's all very well making up your own version of sexual morality, but the Church hasn't survived these two thousand years with à la carte doctrines . . .'

I was beginning to gabble; I was hating myself for my excitability; and I was giving him just what he wanted, a wide-open target for his further anger and indignation.

'Listen, my friend,' he interrupted, 'the phrase à la carte is yours not mine, and it has to do with restaurants where you've obviously been spending a lot of time in recent years . . . I'm not picking and choosing the doctrines I fancy, I leave that to the ivory-tower theologians back home. What I'm telling you is a bit more basic. Who cares a damn fart up the Mersey Tunnel whether Christ is present in the sacrament of the Eucharist through the theory of transubstantiation, or by some other ingenious fucking rationalization, when our people, and I mean these Peruvian Christians, are being routinely machine-gunned and dynamited in the streets for their religion!'

'Bullshit!' I shouted in return.

The bar had fallen silent; the patrons were looking at us with blank wonder.

'Christians,' I went on, 'have died for their faith everywhere and throughout our history.'

He tossed back his beer, slammed the bottle on the bar, and marched out leaving me to finish my drink alone.

*

57

I had been assigned a language instructor called Adolfo Pasco who worked in the ethnology department of the local national college, a row of modest, tiled buildings known by the grandiloquent title of 'The University of the Peruvian Amazon'. Felix had told me wryly that a male instructor was obligatory since more than half the new missionaries in recent years had disappeared with their female instructors.

Adolfo, a slightly built mestizo with a great mop of white hair, was compiling a dictionary of local Indian dialects. He had been brought into the ambit of the Jesuits through their association with the university where Father John was teaching a course in liberation theology.

Pasco had looked at my height and garb; I was dressed now in casual clothes, a golf shirt and pale-blue slacks; I was wearing a pair of Reebok trainers and sported on my wrist a fat Rolex watch. On my head I wore a pale-yellow bush hat. At first his face was wide-eyed, alarmed, then he burst out laughing – a raucous, mocking cackle. Brewing up coffee in the cubicle which served as his office he said he welcomed teaching me because it meant that he could practise his English. 'You will not succeed in comprehending Guarani or Quechua in four or five weeks,' he said, shaking his head, 'you'll just find yourself more obfuscated . . .'

My daily lessons with Adolfo were slow rambles, *'peregrinaçiones'* he called them, around the promenade of the Plaza de Armas, and along the Avenida Fitzcarald with its high pavements and open sewers. Adolfo was smart, and eccentrically educated – never having left Iquitos in his life except to travel up the tributaries of the Amazon collecting Indian vocabulary. In his ecclectic pursuit of knowledge he had plundered the private and public libraries of the jungle city, and collected drifts of damp, dog-eared paperbacks discarded from incoming flights and off the boats that sailed up the Amazon from as far away as New York and Liverpool. He was obsessed with the political future of Peru, although he was not active in politics, preferring to write up Utopian schemes in a low-cost quarterly magazine called *Macondo*. His ambition was to turn Iquitos into a Platonic *polis*, an Athens of the Amazon. He grew excited when he talked about this scheme and would slap me repeatedly on the wrist.

Our daily rambles took us around the city centre, with stops for iced lemonades and coffees and pizco sours. On these perambulations I came to meet Pasco's circuit of friends, the intelligentsia of Iquitos: chess players, journalists, artists, 'political theorists', who spent their days arguing and smoking in the Café de Venezia on the Plaza de Armas. Among them was Augusta, a robust native Peruvian in her mid-thirties, with tow-thick hair, a powerful jaw, and narrowed eyes – usually hidden by dark glasses. Augusta wore tropical fatigues and invariably carried a fat book under her arm. She had a peculiar self-possession and spoke English perfectly with an American accent and an air of solemnity. She said she had studied philosophy of science at Columbia University in New York City. Whenever we met with Pasco she scrutinized me in silence.

One afternoon on my way back to our house she came part of the way and invited me to take coffee with her in a bar. She wanted to talk about the Jesuits. She quizzed me about the Society; its finances, its aims, and its methods. She seemed obsessed by my Jesuit status, as if I harboured a secret. When I asked her if she was a practising Catholic she laughed and shook her head, looking up at the old mechanical fan that whirred away on the ceiling. Then she became moody; she took a Marlboro from the top pocket of her fatigues and lit up, smoking vigorously.

Eventually she said, 'Why do they send people like you out here . . .? You won't do anything here. Get out of Peru; get right out of South America while you're still in one piece.'

At that moment her advice echoed my strongest wish: to take the next plane out. It had taken me no more than two weeks to grasp that I loathed Iquitos; I did not belong in South America. I had no vocation for missionary work, nor for social work.

Despite the drastic decision to set myself free of Jill and my old life; with eight thousand miles between us now, I was longing for her face. Only the vague hope I had pinned on my encounter with O'Rourke had prevented me asking John for my fare home.

After that, Augusta began to waylay me. As I returned from my language sessions I would find her leaning up against the wall of a laundry at a crossroads on the Avenida Fitzcarald, arms folded, smoking a cigarette. She would wave and invite me for a beer or a cup of coffee.

As we sat opposite each other in a bar near by I would raise a variety of subjects, but she was happiest talking about the Society of Jesus and its evangelization plans in Latin America.

One day she said angrily, 'It's four hundred years since Pizarro launched the holocaust of the native peoples of this continent, and the oppression and conquest goes on. You're despised even by those who profess your religion. You are *pistacos*, white monsters who drink our blood and eat our flesh . . . But why do you keep coming? Tell me, Father Nicholas, why do you keep coming?'

Her outburst had shocked me into silence.

'I'll tell you why you're here. You want to discover how we see you; you want to know who you are in the reflection of our eyes.'

She had taken off her eyes shades. 'What do you see, Father Nick?'

I could see nothing but the reflection of my own face in those pools of darkness. Unnerved, I looked away. Then I got to my feet and left.

Another day she brought a newspaper into the bar and sat alongside me. 'None of us sleeps safe in our beds, Father Nick,' she said in a dramatic whisper.

Opening the paper she pointed to a headline which told of the deaths of three missionary priests murdered by the

Shining Path in Chimbote, two hundred miles north of Lima. Their throats had been slit; one of them was found with his eye plucked out and a cork stuck in the socket, a *Senderista* calling card.

I was looking over her shoulder at the paper, but I could understand little of the article. She was touching my arm with her forefinger. I felt a mixture of sexual arousal and dread.

'Our missionaries have brought compassion and peace to this country,' I said numbly. I was thinking of the practical social work of John and Felix.

'That's worse. The *Senderistas* accuse you of promoting imperialism – making the people dependent.'

Finding her earnest politicizing tedious, I made an excuse and left.

After that I tried to avoid her; but she sought me out a few days later where I was working in the library of the university. She leant on the carrel and talked to me quietly as if there were an intimacy between us. After a while she invited me to come for a walk. '*Please* walk with me. Be *simpatico*, Father Nick!'

We left the building and strolled in silence until we reached the Plaza de Armas. She asked if I would like to come back to her room for a beer. I felt a spasm of excitement; I was feeling lonely, depressed: I felt a faint intimation of sexual adventure.

She lived in a room above a barber shop. There was a hammock strung up to the ceiling and stacks of books in primitive bookcases. The walls were decorated with political posters including a familiar portrait of Che Guevara. When I remarked on it, she gave a low laugh; she said. 'Che was just a choirboy!'

The surreal impact of the comment made me uneasy.

We sat on a mat and drank bottled beer which she brought from the refrigerator in the communal kitchen down the corridor. She was watching me from behind her dark glasses and sipping her beer straight from the bottle.

The sound of the radio in the barber's below and the noise of yelling children on the street lent a peculiar atmosphere of tension.

At length she said: 'Would you die for your beliefs, Father Nick?'

Was she tormented, I wondered, by some internal struggle to do with her courage? Courage to do what?

Without thinking I gave her an orthodox answer, straight from the textbooks of my youth; I said, 'Christians believe that martyrdom is a grace, a grace only given at the appropriate moment . . . the choice between death and betraying Christ. It's impossible to predict how you might behave . . . We're not all called to be martyrs.'

It sounded crass, hackneyed; my words seemed to carry no conviction. I fell silent.

'I think,' she said in a low voice, 'that the spilling of one's blood is the ultimate test of belief . . . the Shining Path guerrillas and the Jesuits have a lot in common; but the *Senderistas* I think are more prepared to shed their blood . . . they *seek* torture and imprisonment, persecution, martyrdom, as the Jesuits *used* to seek it. Nowadays you people only die by accident.'

'Why are you telling me this, Augusta?' 'Are *you* a member of the Shining Path?' I asked nervously. 'Are you trying to convince *me*?'

'I am a *student*, a student of philosophy, a student of politics and science. I am a thinker, an intellectual . . .'

'But the Shining Path are guilty of the deaths of thirty thousand people; how can you justify these killings?' I said it with vehemence, but it sounded forced; unreal. What did I really care? She leaned back on her ankles. 'Just listen to yourself. You, a Catholic gringo priest, are telling *me*, a native of this continent, about atrocities? It was a priest just like you who had the Incas butchered because Atahualpa dropped a prayer book! You gringo priests, you Jesuits, you've spread your religion of oppression through *lakes* and *rivers* of blood; so why are you surprised that the Apocalypse leading to the final world revolution will involve bloodshed?'

I felt weary, agitated, and I felt instinctively frightened of Augusta. I left my beer and got up to go. I left her squatting on the floor looking after me.

That night I sat up late drinking pizco with John in the common room. My conversation with Augusta had been worrying me. I asked him about the *Senderistas*.

'It's the Way of the Cross,' he said drily, taking a pull on his cigarette. 'They creep at dead of night into a remote town. They kill the police, then they order the people into the square. They tie up the mayor, spit at him, beat him; shoot him in the head. The government anti-terrorist squads arrive in time to see the dead being buried. The red flag has been raised; so the people are guilty of giving succour to the guerrillas! They torture and kill the "ringleaders". They drink every last drop of booze in the bar and gang-rape every teenage girl. But is that the end of it?

'Several weeks later the Shining Path is back. They're hungry and angry. They kill and eat all the edible livestock. The proprietor of the bar is decapitated for 'collaboration', they play football with his head in the square and throw it to the dogs. Several young girls are taken out and shot in the head for "fraternization" . . . And so it goes on and on and on, throughout this vast country, along the coastal plains, and the margins of the deserts, in the hills, and the mountains, along the rivers and in the jungles. And soon it may spread throughout the whole of South America.'

Before we retired to bed, John asked me to come down with him to the chapel. John and Felix had long ago given up the recitation of the Office, or any sort of devotion save for Mass in the base communities they served. We just sat there in silence gazing at the tabernacle.

CHAPTER 5

On my arrival in Iquitos I had written to Jill asking for a letter by return to confirm that O'Leary's cheque had gone through. A few days before my departure for Aranuba her reply came.

I took the letter up to my cubicle and lay on the bunk. Opening the envelope and seeing her handwriting I sensed her presence with me in the room.

She had received the letter, and the cheque – which had been 'stopped and returned by the bank'. But the money was now of no consequence, she went on. 'I have terminated this pregnancy, Nicholas, and set us both free.'

She explained that it was not the money. 'I could not bear to bring a child into the world whose very existence would be denied by its father.' She realized that I would be shocked by the abortion, 'but you must not feel guilty; it is my decision'. And now she did not want to hear from me again. 'I am seeing someone else,' she ended, 'and I think it is going to work.'

Hour after hour, until sunset, I lay in that sweltering cubicle gripped by a cold, black hatred: for O'Leary, for myself, for my whole life.

Every so often I got up as if deciding to do something. I picked up my things and packed them; then I unpacked them again. I picked up my breviary, turned the pages, then put it down again.

I sat on the bunk. I was remembering how we had gone down the Thames in the cool glow of a November afternoon, looking out at the passing landscape of rooftops and steeples and tall trees. I had felt her arm resting on mine and I had been struck by the intimacy of our just being together. Moving away a little from her, I had rejected the moment.

Sitting on that narrow bunk, gripped by hatred, and guilt, and now jealousy for that 'someone else', I had an intimation of another rejection, deliberate, wilful, through all eternity.

I raised my hands in the twilight, these hands with their peculiar lineaments and contours, their unique tricks and gestures; they looked strange to me now, as if belonging to another.

After dark I got up and went out of the house. I walked down a street where I went every day to the university; where the inhabitants knew me well enough to acknowledge me with their secretive eyes.

I had noticed the woman dogging my footsteps, a crazy woman dressed in a flimsy cotton frock. She cried out: '*Gringo! Pistaco!*'

She was following me in half-circles, approaching on my right and then on my left. '*Hola Gringo! Pistaco!*' she called out.

She began chanting the words now in a high singsong, looking about her as if appealing for support from the neighbours who were sitting out on their steps. '*Diabolo! Pistaco!*' she was calling.

I fetched into my pocket and handed her a note. She spat at it and turned away. '*Pistaco! Gringo!*'

When I reached the corner I saw Augusta; she was leaning up against the wall outside the entrance to the barber's shop, her arms folded.

She asked me up to her room.

We sat together in silence on the floor for a long time, drinking *agua viva* and smoking Marlboros.

The radio in the barber's shop below had been turned off, the street had fallen silent. I reached out and touched her face.

65

She moved closer. She was stroking the inside of my thigh; she was unzipping my fly. 'Father Nicholas, *gringo* Jesuit,' she murmured.

Now she had taken off her fatigues and she was climbing on top of me, wearing just a T-shirt. She took me straight in; I caught a stench of alcohol, menstruation, the jungle.

Her square Amerindian head framed by the halo of tow-thick hair was jiving above me. She was still wearing her dark glasses, and I could see my own face – pale and distorted, dancing rhythmically in their reflection. 'Fuck you! Jesuit *gringo*!' she rasped. 'Fuck you! Fuck you!'

We were coming together, and I could feel her contempt and anger rising to meet my self-loathing.

I cried out, in pain and emptiness, and I saw, as in a fleeting vision, the bloody image of a life – forfeited for my soul's freedom.

When I reached our house in the early hours I found John in the common room, a brandy bottle empty at his elbow.

Kneeling at his feet, I confessed my sins.

CHAPTER 6

The late afternoon sun breathed and pulsed above the western edge of the jungle canopy like the open mouth of a blast-furnace as our chartered Cessna banked on the river bend and drifted downwards. Skimming across the blood-red waters I remembered O'Rourke's description of the crash that had killed his pilot and braced myself for the landing. Then I saw the mission-station on high ground above the river; a simple cabin with a rusty corrugated-tin roof surmounted by a cross and a ramshackle lean-to chapel constructed of palm leaves and poles. In a circular fenced enclosure between the house and the margin of the forest were a few chickens and pigs and a vegetable allotment. About two hundred yards from the door of the house, on the lower ground by the water's edge, was the local native settlement, a cluster of sagging shanties made of a rejected flotsam of kerosene cans and discarded industrial packing cases.

The man who helped us down from the plane at the landing-stage wore a baseball cap with the peak back to front, a Coca-Cola emblem T-shirt gleaming with grease; I could see his testicles through the holes in his jeans. He grinned at me through two rows of coal-black teeth, his breath reeking wickedly of tobacco and booze. Then I was hit by an overripe bittersweet stench from the settlement, with its smoking fires and rotting offal, where the Arabela native Amazonians were staring gloomily towards us; these recent objects of Christian evangelism were dressed in an outlandish assortment of native costume and bedraggled Western garb, fashionable two decades back

— bits of feathered head-dress, flared jeans, floral shirts with long collar points, charitable cast-offs from First World charities.

After disembarking we were taken with our bags straight up to Christian O'Rourke who was standing looking down at us from the doorway of the cabin, a primitive structure built from breeze-blocks faced with rough plaster. I had not seen him for more than twenty years, but his physical stature was more impressive than I had remembered it: a big man with the shoulders of wrestler, even in his seventies, his torso bursting out of a sleeveless filthy black cassock. He held his grizzled head to one side; his face huge, craggy, deeply lined, haggard as if with sleeplessness. He had grown a great grey beard, matted and impenetrable, which fanned out across his chest and shoulders. He was gazing at me and John affectionately with red-rimmed, bloodshot eyes; as we approached he leapt forward, grabbing us together in his huge arms, hugging and kissing us with jerky movements. As he did this I caught a foul body odour; O'Rourke's holiness did not run to the odour of sanctity, and Aranuba evidently did not boast a shower.

He hurried us into what passed for a living room in the house, a general-purpose chamber for cooking, eating, paperwork, and recreation. It had a mud floor, a few pieces of tubular and plastic furniture, and a primitive kitchen.

O'Rourke was pacing up and down, all consideration and kindness; despite his physique and the uncouth circum-stances of his life; he made delicate gestures with his hands and inclined his head in a refined and gentle earnestness of compassion.

He wanted to know about our journey, about Iquitos, about London. He gave each of us his whole attention as we spoke in turn, devouring us with concern, nodding and shaking his head with impatient assent. But I sensed that his affability was by dint of effort rather than by nature. Much as he professed to know us both, I was convinced he had no recollection of me. He evaded Father John's questions about the circumstances of the deaths of the missionaries, but immediately turned everything back to the expedition in hand, the journey to the Mekroti, attempting to draw us without delay into this single fixed idea and purpose.

What had happened to the peaceful, recollected, holy Father Christian of my memory? With every passing minute his agitation, his inability to answer a straight question, or put us at our ease, was keying up my manic potential. And we had not been offered even a glass of water.

John went to boil a kettle on the kitchen Primus stove while I sat on a crude chair looking out through the window. I could see across the broad brown river half a mile to the further shore which was etched on the horizon by a low line of jungle; above was a vast peacock-green sky. Down at the landing-stage the Cessna was preparing to take off before the light failed; the Arabelas were squabbling among themselves about some tobacco they had traded from the pilot, their voices blunt in the humid heat. Now that I was here, now that I had at last encountered the exemplar of our youth, my spirits had plunged. I felt nothing but anxiety and a terrible thirst.

O'Rourke seemed to sense my mood; he said with what sounded like forced enthusiasm: 'We've a good chance of reaping a large harvest of souls when we go up to the Mekroti now, Nicholas. They live in a sedentary community and there's every prospect of settling with them for several years.'

Several years!

His speech was clipped, nasal, rapid; an Irish idiom I associated with Celtic tension.

He declined Father John's offer of a mug of instant coffee, and he looked on disapprovingly as we lighted up our cigarettes; he said, 'It's important we reach the Mekroti before the Protestants or the prospectors . . . I truly believe that Satan is striving to forestall our success . . .'

I bowed my head and took a deep drag on my cigarette; I did not know whether to laugh or to cry at the explicitness

69

of such a statement in that jungle wilderness, divorced of
even a hint of irony; had it come from any other priest of
my acquaintance, save for some over-zealous Charismatic,
I should have taken it for a piece of weird humour. As I
looked out of the window, to avoid O'Rourke's bloodshot
gaze and to hide my confused emotions, a woman came in
through the door from where she had been working on the
smallholding.

She introduced herself as Anna, a Sister of Charity from
British Columbia; she briefly shook hands, turning away
from us as she did so. She was small, about forty, with
neat features, blonde hair, and fierce blue eyes. She looked
wiry and energetic; but she was shy, constantly avoiding
eye contact. She wore a simple blue cotton dress and
had her hair cut short to the nape; the silver cross
around her neck confirmed her religious status. She started
to interrogate us for news of the outside world, but
she had hardly got one question out, listening to no
more than half a sentence, than she asked another, then
another. When John asked her about the dead priests and
nuns, she burst into tears and hurried behind a screen
that divided the living room from the sleeping area.

I exchanged looks with John.

Meanwhile O'Rourke was shaking his head and making
an assuaging gesture with his hand; he said, 'Don't worry
now, Fathers, she'll be all right.'

He told us that she had been there almost two years with
no visitors and sporadic mail. Because of illness she had
been left behind on the last, fatal attempt to make the
journey up river, and she was still grieving for her dead
companions.

Then a Quechua Indian, tall, and dressed just in shorts
and sandals, appeared at the door. He was the very picture
of the 'noble savage'; handsome, athletic, with narrow
hips, his limbs perfectly proportioned, his skin smooth
as burnished bronze, his forehead brooding and solemn
like a dark cliff face. He stood leaning against the door

jamb, his expression enigmatic. He was fixing me with his Asiatic-looking eyes, the bevel of his nose slightly raised, as if his flared nostrils were picking up subtle messages. I found his brooding taciturn presence irritating.

O'Rourke introduced him as 'Turn'im-talk', meaning 'interpreter' a pidgin survival of O'Rourke's missionary days in Papua New Guinea; his name was Luis, and O'Rourke said that he was 'the mouth and ears' of the mission.

We had barely finished our coffee when O'Rourke announced that we should go into his private chapel to say the Rosary in thanksgiving for our safe arrival. Despite our evident reluctance, he took our coffee mugs from our hands and shepherded us along, brooking no delay.

The private chapel was a grass-walled cubicle with a statue of the Virgin on a pedestal. There was barely room for the three of us to stand, and the heat and the smell of body odour made me want to throw up. We knelt on the hard mud floor and within a few moments I realized that O'Rourke was bent on going through the whole of the fifteen mysteries, an exercise that might take as long as an hour. As I knelt there in the humid heat, pestered by flies, the sweat rolling off me, my throat and tongue parched, my knees and haunches collapsing beneath me, I reflected that the transformation I had sought under the spiritual direction of Father Christian O'Rourke had only just begun.

The Rosary took an hour and a quarter, for he added a full litany to the Holy Mother, a 'Regina Coeli', and a 'Te Deum', which he sang in Latin in a quavering off-key reedy voice.

To forestall further devotions I staggered out of this stink-hole gasping for air even as he sang his 'amen'. But no sooner had I emerged from the front door of the house than O'Rourke came up and clutched me by the sleeve, taking me down the hill a little way. I could feel the strength of his grip as if I were being held with a steel claw.

The sun had set and Anna was lighting the hurricane lamps in the kitchen; the fires of the Arabelas were burning on the lower ground. O'Rourke gazed at me intently in the twilight.

'I've not been absolved, Father, for many months,' he hissed, 'and I've a very difficult confession to make.'

'Surely,' I said, 'tomorrow . . . and I think Father John, who is senior, might be better . . .' I was quaking at the idea of confessing Christian O'Rourke, the rumoured saint, the paragon of my youth.

'No,' he whispered emphatically, 'young John might be compromised by what I have to say . . . we don't see eye to eye . . . Anyways, it's you I want, Father, and you'll not deny me. I long for absolution.'

His wide-stretched eyes were glowing in the darkness, and I had a sudden fear that he might offer me violence there and then if I cavilled a moment longer.

'All right,' I said, my voice shaking a little with exhaustion and nervousness.

'Not here, not here . . . Come . . . come with me.'

Grabbing me with his painful grip he led me across the clearing and pulled me a little way into the jungle undergrowth until we stumbled on a fallen tree. I was almost overcome by the heavy, fertile, fermenting stench of the forest.

He indicated that I should sit down on the tree; then he fell on his knees and put his face into his hands, groaning deeply and raising his arms to the sky.

This was getting too much even for me, a master of the manic performance. Perhaps there wasn't much wrong with me that wasn't equally wrong, or worse, with Father Christian O'Rourke. Had all those years of toil, all those struggles across desert wastes and mountains and through swamps and rain forests to spread the Good News finally unhinged his mind? Or was this crazed disinhibition par for the course with a genuine servant of God!

'Look, Father,' I said firmly, 'I'm very tired. Now, please, make your confession.'

I made the sign of the cross over him and said a brief prayer.

Clutching me by the knees, and with much groaning and sighing, Father Christian O'Rourke confessed that he had told a lie – 'a deliberate and odious lie in the sight of God!'

'Could it be so very terrible, Father?' I asked him, looking at his dark shape below me.

He was beating his breast one moment, clutching me painfully by the knees and the thighs the next.

'It was not the guerrillas who killed my two nuns and my two priests.'

He fell silent, and I could hear only the menacing rhythm of the creatures of the night.

'Then how *did* they die?' I asked him numbly. 'How did the those priests and nuns die, Father Christian? Did they die accidentally?'

'No, Father,' he said, quietly now, 'it was the Father of Lies himself. It was *Satan* who contrived their deaths.'

That night I had retired to a hammock in the dormitory situated between our chapel and the common room. O'Rourke and John and I were divided from Sister Anna by a flimsy partition made of woven grasses. I could sense the others, like me, sleepless and suffering through the long blackness.

The night was infested with predators, humming, squeaking, and swooping. We had mosquito nets but this gave me little comfort as O'Rourke had warned me about rabies-infected bats that bit through the netting. Outside, in the squawking, honking, sweltering night, I imagined a host of other predators: the prospectors who hated evangelizers of every species; the Shining Path who would torture and butcher us if they came our way; and the military of the region who suspected us of giving succour to the guerrillas. After years of those manic-depressive terrors of the mind, I found myself enveloped by the imminent reality of *actual* violence. On that first night, as I pondered O'Rourke's confession, I heard the sounds of a woman being beaten in the encampment below, her screams intermixed with the hideous thud of wood on flesh and bone.

But what could compare now with my fear of O'Rourke?

After I had succeeded in calming him, O'Rourke had told me through profuse tears the true story of his last expedition.

Following the accident with the seaplane, he and his companions, two young Jesuits, two Sisters of Charity, Luis 'Turn'im-talk' and a group of Zapara guides, had departed for the Mekroti country in dugouts and timber plank-boats with outboard motors. It was a week before the rainy season was due; by his own admission, the most hazardous time to make such a journey. A week after their departure one of his priest assistants had been bitten by a snake; O'Rourke might have called off the journey there and then, but trusting to 'Providence' he had decided to proceed; a day later the priest had died of blood poisoning. Then on Ash Wednesday O'Rourke's boat was holed on the reefs of a remote arm of the Napo and they had lost a precious cargo of fuel and supplies. Yet he had persisted with the journey, and continued onwards even after one of the young nuns fell ill with suspected appendicitis. The way up to the Mekroti had been a desperate scramble through rapids and heavy rains. The nun had died in agony while being carried bodily around a treacherous torrent. The remaining priest and nun had pleaded with O'Rourke to return, but he was adamant that they should go on. At length they had abandoned him and started back on their own, without supplies and without guides. O'Rourke watched them go, then, after several hours, had second thoughts; with a heavy heart he decided to go back down after them. He and Luis found them a day later, washed up on the outcrop of an island in the torrential river. Luis had buried all four religious in shallow jungle graves, and O'Rourke had confabulated a story to account for their disappearance.

'Why,' I asked him gently, 'did you not tell the truth?'

'I was afraid,' he whispered, 'that I would be forced by the faint-hearted to abandon this mission.' Clutching my hands, he said, 'Satan has been determined to prevent my mission to the Mekroti; he *knows* that this mission signifies the dawn of the Second Coming of our Lord and Saviour Jesus Christ ... Oh, yes, he *knows*; and he's used all his wiles ... but he must not prevail ... There are times, Father, when it is the lesser of two evils to tell an untruth. And as for those poor dead souls, they died, did they not, true martyrs of God's holy Church? Is that not so? But still it must be confessed, because a lie is a sin and an imperfection in the sight of God.'

Stunned by what he had told me, I had retired with the others that night with no more to eat than a cup of tea and a dry biscuit.

Lying awake in my hammock I thought about O'Rourke and the dilemma he had posed me by relating in confession details I could not act upon. By the strict standards of the sacrament I was obliged to put the story out of my mind. To consider for one moment, even to myself, the implications and further consequences of his admission would be to break the seal of the confessional.

In the mean time I could not sleep. I was hungry, but I dared not think of food. Sister Anna had asked me not to smoke in the dormitory, but I lit up all the same. Within a minute or so I could hear her snorts of disgust on the other side of the partition. Soon my cigarettes would be gone, then God help me! Then it dawned on me, ominously, just how superficial was my notion of poverty; how much, even in Iquitos, I had taken the least of our luxuries for granted: a bed, running water, varied food, alcohol (O'Rourke ran a dry ship). Why had I not listened to Augusta and packed my bags for Europe? But the worst of it, on that first night in Aranuba, was that time had slowed down to an unbearable duration

in which the passage of an hour in that tense darkness seemed like a month; the passage of the night, a
whole year. Time had become a malignant unfathom-
able pool.

CHAPTER 7

In the eerie silence of the tropics just before dawn on that first morning I heard O'Rourke stirring in his private chapel, muttering and whispering his prayers, pouring out his heart to a God more real to him (as was Satan) than the people of flesh and blood with whom he lived and had his being.

As the sun came up in a brassy sky, I heard him calling out the Litany of the Saints as if inviting us to rise from our hammocks and present ourselves for the spiritual duties of the day.

Over a frugal breakfast he talked without pause about the proposed mission to the Mekroti. He told us that he had been waiting ever since the end of the rainy season for the arrival of a party of Zaparas to take him up to the Mekroti country. With each new day, from dawn to dusk, he said, he had been storming heaven.

'When they come,' O'Rourke said excitedly, 'there will be an advance party of one or two canoes, singing and calling out with upraised oars. Then as many as a dozen canoes may appear. They're a timid people, Nicholas, ready to turn tail if they're frightened . . . you must be gentle with them and kind.'

After what he had told me under the seal of confession I was filled with foreboding. It was as if O'Rourke had entirely wiped the confession from his mind; I guessed that he sensed that I was suffering because of the climate. Over breakfast he tried to cheer me up with remarks that would have been funny had they not been so near the mark. He intimated breezily that we were leading a life of unparalleled luxury compared with what lay ahead, especially when we should begin living with real Indians. He said, 'Our isolation in prospect, Nicholas, and the opportunities for self-denial, will be good for the soul.'

And wasn't this, I reflected ruefully, what I had come to South America to discover under his tutelage?

Walking alone down by the river, I meditated on the drastic privations that lay ahead, with the prospect of torture and violent death. Why did I think these privations were good for my soul? Was it because I believed, still, that I was a spiritual essence just a little less than an angel, trapped in a funnel of clay, imprisoned in this miserable valley of tears – the world? Was I really full of shame and resentment, restless and unhappy at being obliged to live an alien existence in a physical universe? Was my soul somehow separate from this life? Forever restless, restless to be disembodied and with Him?

I wanted to talk with somebody about this; perhaps with John. But John was already caught up in a round of practical activities; he was already looking for opportunities to be of service.

As for Sister Anna, I could not have imagined a less promising companion and confidante. I had watched her as I ate breakfast. Despite her diffidence, she affected to be jaunty. 'Carry on regardless! . . . Thanks be to God! . . . Mary keep us safe and sound!' she called out, rushing from one busy duty to the next. She had made huge efforts to appear starched, to keep everything swept and shipshape in a House that was under hourly threat from the encroaching, enveloping fertility of the jungle.

Between each chore she made visits to O'Rourke's private chapel. Then she would hurry down to the Arabelas' settlement where she was popular among the children. They would swarm around her skirts as she gave out sugar lumps or little bits of sweet biscuit. I watched her throughout the morning, bustling with that comic rhythm of her rump: bustle, bustle, bustle, bustle. She never relaxed;

she never sat down to talk. Everything she said and did in her relationships with us men seemed a prim, pietistic evasion.

By lunch-time I pleaded with John to walk with me for a while. We went a little way from the cabin. He was quiet now and thoughtful, smoking a cigarette. I asked him what he was thinking.

'I feel,' he said, 'like somebody who has been appointed first mate and contemplates mutiny.' I was aching to tell him about the true circumstances of the death of the missionaries, but I could not broach what O'Rourke had confessed.

John did not linger. His twenty years in Peru had given him a restless stamina for practical chores. He was off to inspect the sanitary arrangements in the encampment; and he left me alone with my anxieties.

As for O'Rourke, his day was regulated strictly according to a religious routine he called his 'life-support': Mass and thanksgiving, divine office, spiritual reading, study (the Zapara language under Luis), the Angelus, night prayers, meditation. O'Rourke was an unashamed traditionalist, a believer in asceticism over and above the natural privations of our circumstances. Our meals were grim and tasteless, taken in silence and to the accompaniment of readings; during lunch Sister Anna had been toiling through the *Ascent of Mount Carmel*, a book I had not laid eyes on in thirty years.

Afterwards O'Rourke spent an hour with the Arabela Indians instructing them in Christian doctrine. They were learning by heart a catechism in their own language and recited their responses mechanically. They looked bored and seemed to regard O'Rourke with a listless acquiescence.

Luis the interpreter, who was in attendance during these sessions, treated O'Rourke with a sullen obedience that bordered, I thought, on fear.

And in addition to the regular round of spiritual duties O'Rourke prayed in private in his little chapel. I could hear him sighing and twittering under his breath, moaning and calling on God.

During the long and terrible second night at Aranuba I tried to pray too. I tried to place myself in His presence, to find him somehow within, for I could not find Him outside myself. Could I encounter Him, I wondered, in the depths of my mind, my soul? This sense I had, of being a creature – finite, mortal, full of sinfulness and decay: could I not find His infinity, his abundant fullness and plenitude and goodness in the depths of my need?

As I searched for Him that night, across the inner landscapes of my soul, I began to recollect with a strange clarity those first impressions of the self-made God of my childhood.

Where did my soul have its being before my first memory? Was I anyone, was I anywhere, before this?

My father was carrying me cradled in his arms to a rising and falling chorus in the rooftops and the trees. We were on our way to the air-raid shelter buried in the back garden. But before going down into its dark safety he turned and held me up high. Then I saw it: flying high in the night sky, caught in the shimmering shafts of light, a momentary vision of a growling black cross shedding fountains of fire.

That was the *war*: a word that sounded like the flying thing in the sky. My father held me up, his arms at full stretch, as if making an offering of me. Then he took me down into the shelter buried in the damp sour-smelling clay where my mother knelt before an object lit by a candle. Lying on the top bunk wrapped in a grey blanket I contemplated her long pale face framed by dark spiky hair. She was kneeling, gazing at a naked creature pinned to a cross of wood, her lips moving constantly – mummummumm . . . I believed that through this object my mother could control the black cross in the sky and the wailing voices in the buildings and the trees.

There had always been the *war*, and the war would go

on for ever. At night dark growling shapes filled the sky. During the day the silvery balloons sailed high and away across the Wanstead Flats.

One morning I found a piece of metal gleaming in the wet street. A cock crew over the garden fence and the milkman cried out to his horse as it clopped from gate to gate. The oil that seeped from the tall old bus made rainbows in the puddles. The bus shuddered all the way to school; sitting by the window I scratched away the sticky tape with the piece of metal and peered out at rain-filled holes and blasted rooftops. I got off the bus on the edge of Epping Forest (the forest, my mother told me, where a boy might wander for ever lost), and ran all the way to school.

Sister Jude wore steel-rimmed spectacles that made her coal-black eyes flat and enormous. She put her putty-white freckly face close to mine and kissed me on the cheek. She pinned back her veil and turned the heavy leaves of the picture-roller until she came to Adam and Eve, pink and plump in the Garden of Eden. The snake coiled towards Eve along the bough of the apple tree. The apples were bright red. The snake, called Satan, had a forked black tongue.

Sister Jude said: 'Adam and Eve were happy in the beautiful Garden of Eden and would live for ever. But Eve ate the forbidden fruit, and she gave it to Adam; then their eyes were opened, and they knew that they were *naked*. So the angel with the sword banished them from the Garden; they had to work and to suffer pain, and God punished them with death. When you are dead, little children, you are buried in the earth.'

She turned the picture-roller and showed a scene of naked people standing in beds of fire. 'These are the souls of the dead who died in a mortal sin,' she said. Talk of sin made me think of dirty cinders in the grate; seven black cinders all in a row. 'They are burning there for ever.'

Then she showed a picture of the 'holy souls in purgatory', where people stood in a pit of grey ash. When Sister Jude said 'holy souls in purgatory', I heard 'sorry holes in the lavatory', and I could smell the sharp stink of the school playground latrines. 'Let *perpetual* light shine upon them, O Lord, and may they rest in peace, amen.' A strange thing to say, for I heard *'petrol'*, and I saw the petrol rainbows in the puddles.

One afternoon when the sirens wailed we lined up in the playground and marched into the brick shelter. We sat on benches in the musty darkness while Sister Jude led the singing of a hymn:

> We *will* be true to thee till *death*.
> We *will* be true to thee till *death*.

There was a distant explosion in the direction of Epping Forest, like the slam of a heavy door.

On the bus home I saw a hole at the edge of the forest; trees had collapsed in swaths around its rim; they were stripped of their bark and branches and lying together in clusters. A crowd stood looking up into a tree where a pram was stuck high in the branches.

In church on Sunday I noticed the peculiar stinks and columns of steam and barking noises from the scraping kneelers. It seemed strange that the people faced one way: rows and rows of backs and bowed heads. The man up at the front danced this way and that amidst clouds of smoke, and he could make himself shorter or taller at will like a concertina jack-in-the-box. As he sank into the ground or stretched himself up high, the people sighed and bowed and sang together. I did not know how they knew when to do that. When he raised his arms he made the bells ring.

The man turned to us holding up a clock, and when the people bowed their heads the clock ticked and the steam clouds billowed. The clock, Mother said, was 'God'. 'God' made people bow and sing and walk in circles.

From the pipes on the back wall came a groan like aeroplanes in the night sky. The double doors at the side of the church opened and in came a host of women and children and men in long dresses. There were girls in white frocks with baskets of rose petals, which they sprinkled on the floor of the church as they went. Some of the small girls were members of my class – Rosemary Duffy, Patricia Murphy, Helen Cooney, Ann Casey, jostling each other and looking wide-eyed around the church. Next came a party of women in blue dresses and white veils, and there among them was Mother, helping to carry a swaying statue on a stretcher. Mother's face was grey, and inward-looking. She moved around the church hunched and unsteady under the weight of the statue, while everybody sang: 'Hail, Queen of Heaven . . .'

There was a fat man bearing a banner with picture of the Holy Mother, and here came the man with the clock under a gold umbrella. Everybody bowed deeply and looked away in fear from the clock. Shutting my eyes tightly I felt a thrill of excitement as 'God' went by.

Mother stayed in church after the people had gone, kneeling before the statue of the Holy Mother where she had planted a lighted candle. Her shoulders heaved and she frequently held her handkerchief to her mouth and eyes, sighing and moaning softly.

Mother called my father Tom. Father was a squarish man with sleek dark hair, glittering steel blue eyes. When it rained he would take me on his knee and sing gently: 'You are my sunshine . . .' Father worked at night and slept all day.

When he got up in the afternoon he would stand before the mirror brushing his fine black hair with two shiny white-backed brushes. Sometimes he would gaze into the mirror and wave his arms to the music on the radio, his eyes smiling, his hair wild.

In Mother's bedroom there was a statue of the Holy Mother decked with beads, and a vase of paper flowers and a blue lamp which never went out. On the wall was the picture Mother called the 'Sacred Heart', the man with hungry eyes and blood on his hands. His hungry eyes followed as I moved about the room, and I knew that the picture had a life of its own. I offered a piece of bread to the 'Sacred Heart' man, holding it up to his bearded mouth. Observed by the all-seeing man of blood I put my mother's silk dress around my shoulders; I pretended that the little dressing-table clock was the clock-God in the church. Shaking with excitement I carried God around the room slowly.

CHAPTER 8

The day the waiting ended O'Rourke had celebrated Mass in Latin, weeping profusely, lingering over the *'Domine non sum dignus'*, beating his breast harshly and repeatedly, his tears mingling with drops of candle-wax from the altar flames. He was in such a state of ecstatic recollection that he failed to notice the crazy misshapen Indian who approached the altar and exposed his erect penis to the amusement of his fellows.

Then O'Rourke addressed us in his private chapel. He appeared so haggard and exhausted that I thought he might be close to a heart attack. 'Last night,' he said tremulously, 'I went to pray in the jungle, and as I prayed I had a vision. A girl of exquisite beauty appeared to me. She was seated on throne of ivory and bathed in beatific light. She beckoned and pointed to a clearing where stood a tall red cross, huge and tapering. I fell to my knees, and as I prayed it burst into flame until the whole structure was a fierce white torch. I raised my arms and out of the fire gushed springs of blood corresponding to the wounds of Jesus. And where the blood ran across the ground there sprung up carpets of orchids.'

He bowed his head as if to keep back the tears. 'My dear brothers and sister,' he said, 'I fear – yet it is a fear not unmixed with hope – that our project may have been granted the grace of the blood of martyrdom. Watch and pray for you know not the hour nor the day.'

Sister Anna was gazing at O'Rourke with rapt, almost horrified, attention. But John raised an eyebrow, acknowledging that I was not alone in wondering whether O'Rourke wasn't unhinged. At that very moment there was a volley of gunfire and we rushed out to see the Arabelas dashing about excitedly as two dugout canoes came into view on the river-bend. Then five more appeared, approaching the landing-stage slowly, cautiously, the Zapara Indians sitting very still with oars upraised.

These were the first Indians I had seen untainted by civilization. I should have been fascinated by everything about them; but they seemed to me dejected, in poor health, and exhausted by their journey. They wore their hair long, almost to the waist, and were dressed in little more than loincloths and jerkins. They carried on poles the items they intended trading at the station – crestfallen songbirds and terrified baby monkeys tied by the ankles.

After they had landed the Zaparas scowled and drew back as O'Rourke bore down on them, beaming with pious enthusiasm. They called out 'Catarrha?' (their word for influenza) which they feared above everything. After Luis had assured them that there was no 'catarrha' at the mission they accepted his proffered trinkets and beads and slunk off muttering among themselves. Then I tried to make friends with pieces of sugar-candy. They took my gift with poor grace, looking away as if in disgust. John murmured: 'It's booze they want, not candy.'

All afternoon O'Rourke, John, Luis, and I sat observing them from hailing distance. Sister Anna was inside the house, watching through the window. Then O'Rourke and Luis went slowly forward to the Zaparas' bivouac; there were some twenty of them lounging near their fire where they were cooking. With the aid of gifts O'Rourke started up a dialogue with one of the leaders who explained grudgingly that they had lost some men on the journey. They had come in contact with prospectors who were infiltrating their reservations. The headman made it clear that to take back a woman and us priests would slow down their passage and put them in further danger. As he returned to our house the anguish on O'Rourke's face was plain. Everything he had heard indicated that the mission would be frustrated for another year. Refusing supper he went into the chapel and began to pray out loud.

The night was purgatory. Hour after hour we listened in the darkness as O'Rourke lay prostrate before the statue of the Holy Mother, groaning and sighing and calling on God in his tremulous voice.

After morning Mass O'Rourke and Luis had been parlaying with the Zaparas. Then at ten o'clock there was a breakthrough. O'Rourke came striding back to the house calling for the rest of us. His face was triumphant. 'We're going, we're going,' he cried, 'get the baggage down to the canoes.'

Now the negotiations started in earnest. Hurrying back to the Zaparas O'Rourke began pleading for an arrangement that would include all four of us, together with Luis and our considerable baggage. But with only seven Zapara canoes he was being forced to revise his plans. The arguments went to and fro, along with a new round of gifts.

O'Rourke wanted to take two of our large timber boats with three Zapara guides in both vessels. By noon the Indians had agreed to transfer just three of their number, and for the next hour it seemed that this was the most we would achieve. But O'Rourke was obstinate. 'We must *all* go,' he insisted.

Then for no apparent reason another group came forward and offered to accompany the second boat. Seizing the moment, O'Rourke gave instructions for a new round of presents and supervised the distribution of the bulk of the baggage through all seven canoes and our two boats. There was fuel, clothes and blankets, hammocks; mosquito nets, hurricane lamps, tents, waterproof awnings, cooking utensils, tools for building and carpentry, bags of nails and screws, a radio-cassette and medicines; food stores, principally flour, meal, sugar, salt, yeast, and tinned foodstuffs; musical instruments, vestments and altar cloths, statues, relics, crucifixes, pictures of the saints and illustrations of

Christian doctrine; missals, breviaries, books of devotion, quantities of writing paper, pens, materials for painting; glass beads, knick-knacks, mirrors, brooches, hairpins, combs, pans, knives, and axes.

I stood watching these preparations with a mounting sense of unreality, as if I had been caught up in some historic theme-park charade. And yet, I was conscious that I was witnessing the prelude to a scene that had been played out countless times in the ancient saga of the Christian evangelization of the 'Children of Darkness'.

Meanwhile there was a confused argument going on about the quantity and distribution of the stores, with the Zaparas squealing among themselves. My sympathy was firmly with the Zaparas, for their canoes were cramped, finely balanced affairs, and the clumsy bulk of our stores made them look perilous. O'Rourke was close to tears; I suspected he was thinking how dependent we should be on these possessions, more than two hundred miles of hazardous river and impenetrable jungle from our last outpost in the region.

Then a row broke out among the Zaparas themselves about the recent distribution of gifts. They ran about gesticulating and weeping, throwing themselves on the ground in temper tantrums. O'Rourke watched this for a while, his mouth agape. Then striding some fifty paces distant from them he fell on his knees and raised his arms in supplication to the sky. It was such a bizarre sight that I had to turn away, stifling a laugh.

For more than half an hour he knelt transfixed like a figure in a stained-glass window, until the Zaparas fell silent and one by one squatted on the ground to watch the priest with bewildered fascination. O'Rourke later told me that in his prayers he made a special vow to Saint Ignatius Loyola.

When he rose all was peace and concord.

So it was agreed that Sister Anna and John would travel in one of our two timbered boats with three Zapara companions, and I would travel with O'Rourke in the other with two Zaparas and Luis and the most valuable items of luggage. Three dugouts would be assigned to accompany Sister Anna's and John's boat, and four to ours.

The earlier preparations had been drawn out over several hours with tedious discussions and arguments. Now the Zaparas wanted to be off without delay. We scarcely had time to step into the boats and start the outboard motors before they were paddling their dugouts into the strong currents of the river.

CHAPTER 9

There were no reliable maps to the Mekroti country. The route took us up a sinuous tributary of the Napo with scores of impetuous rapids until we reached a lake, beyond which only the local native travellers knew the way. According to the reconnaissance of the ill-fated mission seaplane we were to travel up to a maze of swamps where we would find a new river close to the borders with Ecuador. As O'Rourke frequently pointed out, an aeroplane would have been useful for reconnoitring our route and supplying us from the air. But 'Providence' was always on his lips.

Travelling more slowly, for Anna wasn't paddling, John's boat and dugout flotilla soon fell behind and eventually disappeared from view altogether. O'Rourke seemed unconcerned, invoking God's protection. But I was anxious; I saw that John was having difficulty with his crew, who were cursing him for his failure to paddle with sufficient strength and speed. Our own guides resented the weight of our baggage and were angry at our failure to keep steady stroke to add power to the outboard motor.

But the tedious hours of paddling were nothing to the difficulty of the rapids, when we had to leave the boat and guide it through by hand. Our ankles were bruised by rocks and jagged stones on the river bed; we were terrified of open cuts which could attract the piranhas. We could do little more than stagger through the currents which clutched and pulled at our knees and sometimes even our necks, filling me with panic. O'Rourke, despite his age, was impressive in these crises, attempting to take the weight of the whole boat on his huge shoulders. Sometimes we had to carry the boat and the baggage around high torrents, taking at least two journeys through a mile of jungle.

O'Rourke had insisted that we go 'Indian style', which meant working like our guides until we dropped at the end of the day and eating a little mandioca meal with fish before putting up our hammocks and mosquito nets.

On that first night I was wracked with pain. My hands and thumbs were raw with blisters, my legs and shoulders screaming with cramp. All day I had paddled, watching the long muscular back of Luis, the stroke of his powerful arms and shoulders ceaselessly plying the oar against the current.

O'Rourke was reading the Office from a waterproof-bound breviary which hung from his neck by a lanyard. He said we should take it in turns to keep watch by the light of our hurricane lamp. He believed the Zaparas would butcher us in order to steal our baggage and escape up-river without our burdensome weight.

After years of sedentary occupations I was surprised at my body's ability to react to the strain of the journey. I was feeling, despite pain, the return of muscle tone and vigour. I was taking a pride in the mere fact of physical survival. But my grim satisfaction was short-lived.

On the second day, as we worked our way up the narrows in the deep cathedral shadows of the forest we were attacked by swarms of 'piums', blood-sucking flies that settled on our exposed flesh and especially around our eyes. Their bites were more painful than a gnat or mosquito and blood welled out of the punctures. In the first hour of the attack I must have been bitten two hundred times; then the site of each bite began to throb and itch.

O'Rourke ignored them as if they did not exist, although he said without a trace of anxiety that certain people reacted badly to the poison. 'If your bites have blue edges to them by tomorrow you'll have to go back down.' As a nonchalant afterthought, he murmured: 'It's possible to die of these bites. Be sure to say your prayers tonight.'

91

I had a suspicion that he would have preferred to find me dead in the morning than to have taken me back down. I was lying hitched up in the hammock, writing up my notebook by the light of our hurricane lamp. With the descent of darkness the flies had vanished. The bites felt infected and I was frightened; but I could only wait till dawn to see if I was allergic. By the light of the moon I could see the river reflecting the forest wall and the sky, upside-down. Far away in the forest there was a rending and cracking, then a rush of foliage and a sound like a muffled explosion followed by a brief moment of silence. Close by I sensed the bats flitting between the river and the encampment. The frogs started up their foundry-hammer racket again; then the mournful screech and chatter of howler monkeys; close at hand a snapping high in the trees and a twittering. Was there a deadly poisonous jararáca snake coiling along the branches above?

Tense in the cradled sway of my hammock I looked up at the night sky. 'Journeying on from infancy,' Augustine had written, 'I passed into childhood. Or rather did childhood come into me. I was no longer an infant who could not speak, but a talking child ...' How was it that I still believed that the soul could be a free self, free of language, in exile in the world?

Looking up at the hard bright stars in the blackness I remembered that point of light hovering like a spark in the darkness, floating down from above – first to one eye, then to the other. 'Look at the light,' the man had said. 'That's right ... straight into the light.'

Now the blinds were pulled and in the brightness of the eye clinic I was fitted for spectacles. They were flattish and round like Sister Jude's, with brown plastic rims and wire sides.

'This boy,' said the man who had held the light, 'has bad sight in one eye, and needs help in the other.'

Emerging on to the street my eyes were opened. I looked

up at the sparkling vault of the sky and saw hard-edged birds wheeling and soaring to the trees. The trees swayed in the wind and I could see each and every one of a thousand fiery red-gold leaves. I looked into Mother's watery eyes and saw a delicate tracery of bright red hair-lines. I laughed with delight at my new world.

At school I looked on Patricia Murphy with my opened eyes as she danced a jig in front of the class to Sister Jude's hand claps. Her forehead was white as milk, her cheeks like pink blossom, her eyes as blue as the sky in spring. Pinned to her starchy blouse was a medallion of the Holy Mother attached to a silk ribbon. When she danced a jig on tiptoe she raised her knees so high that I glimpsed her brilliant white knickers. 'Patricia Murphy,' said Sister Jude with a thin little smile, 'will one day be Queen of the May.'

We went to church and gazing up through my new flashing spectacles I saw the altar with all its fine detail of flowers and statues, and I saw for the first time that the man was holding up a small circle of whiteness. The circle of whiteness was the secret of everything; it was for this that the people bowed and sighed.

Then I saw, for the first time, that the man on the altar was wearing a cloth-of-gold cloak. His ability to shrink and expand like a jack-in-the-box was no more than his going down upon his knees and his stretching upwards in the folds of his all-enveloping cloak. Now I saw that the clock-God was a glass case to hold that circle of whiteness, that the ticking and the billowing sweet smoke came from the bright metal can the boy swung on the end of a chain.

The man who wore the gold cloak on the altar came into school. Here was Father James with smiling bright round face and silver hair; he was dressed in black and carried a silver crucifix which flashed in the light of the sun.

'Who made you, little children?' he asked in a soft, oh-so-loving voice; and he beamed down on us with sparkling eyes.

All together, we chanted: '*God* made me.'

'*Why* did God make you?'

'God made me to *know* him, love him, and serve him, in this world, and to be *happy* with him for ever in the next.'

Father James moved gracefully and went on speaking in his soft lilting voice; Sister Jude brought him a cup of tea and a biscuit, which he left without touching.

A table was set out with gleaming implements and white linen, brilliant as Patricia Murphy's knickers. Father James was going to show us his secrets. We stood pressing together around the table gazing at his hands – scrubbed pink and sweet smelling. I loved the way he touched the silver cup and the pieces of spotless white linen as if they were alive. And there, barely visible until it was placed gently on the saucer of gold, was that circular wafer of bread.

Father James said the special words over this 'bread', which he called a 'host' (which made me think of a 'ghost'), and it became the body and blood of Our Lord and Saviour Jesus Christ, who is Almighty God. It gave me a strange feeling to think of the pure white host filled with blood.

Father James picked up the little red book of questions and answers, and waved it at us.

'*Why* is God called Almighty?' he asked with a smile.

'God is called Almighty,' we responded together, 'because he can do *all* things.'

'Does God know and *see* all things?'

'God knows and sees *all* things, *even our most secret thoughts.*'

In Mother's bedroom I made an altar of the chest of drawers. I placed the two dressing-table candlesticks on either side of a crucifix. Then draping my mother's dress around my shoulders and bowing down before a circle of white paper, I started genuflecting and gibbering like Father James. To be able to put God, who could see all things, even my most secret thoughts, into a piece of white paper! To be able to finger such a God, whisper to him, carry him.

Was God anyone and anywhere in the world? He was

squarish like my father; he wore a beard like the bleeding Sacred Heart man; he had protruding green eyes, and watched and watched. Now I knew he was sitting inside everything. He was in the curtains, in the drawer, in the light-bulb. And inside my head where I kept my most secret thoughts.

For how many hours did I bob up and down before the chest of drawers, mumming and whispering? Hearing a movement I looked towards the semi-darkness on the landing; peering towards the door. Through the crack of the open door I saw an eye watching me intently: was it the eye of the Holy Mother of God?

CHAPTER 10

I wasn't allergic to the piums; and they didn't return.
But in the morning I was feverish and covered in boils
from the waist down and all over my legs. That day we
carried the boats, struggling up to our knees in the slime of
water-logged undergrowth, hacking our way with machetes
through entanglements like coiled razor-wire to join a river
where the current was with us.

Rocketing along the tumultuous waters I was only dimly
aware of the lofty jungle canopies swinging by. Despite
pain and fatigue, I began to feel at one with the rhythm
and pulse of the water, its ever-changing glassy mass, the
eternal pattern of drumbeats, whorls, and spume. The smell
of the river filled my nostrils.

At length we entered a tranquil stretch where we slid
smoothly on a ribbon of black water and saw clouds of
wailing birds rising and falling out of prairies of reeds like
spring rice; the sky was mirrored in the water, a perfect
image. Expanses of swamp opened out to the distant horizon
where brooding jungle groves lent melancholy vastness to
the skies. We had entered a still and silent lake perplexed
with weeds which streamed from our paddles and snagged
the outboard motor. We seemed to be approaching the very
edge of the world. Our guides sang quietly, rocking gently.
The lake became a maze of creeks and stagnant ponds
hemmed in by a havoc of jungle roots. A nauseating
stench of corruption rose on the water as if we were
paddling through a vast sewer; unfamiliar birds cried out
and camouflaged creatures flopped in the slime.

After several hours we approached the margin of the

swamp and our guides steered us to a stream beneath a sombre bower; the stream became a river, which flowed slowly at first then faster. The boat slapped and skittered on the brown torrent and we paddled until our arms were paralysed.

Late in the afternoon we bivouacked in the water for fear of jaguars which were said to infest this part of the jungle. We tied our vessels to submerged stumps. There had been heavy storms since noon, and sheets of rain had kept us imprisoned under our canvas awnings. O'Rourke insisted we stay put for a day and one more night to wait for Sister Anna and John, for the Zaparas had indicated that we would soon arrive in the Mekroti country.

I had eaten little except dry biscuit rations and bananas, and I longed for a cooked meal and hot tea; the prospect of a prolonged fast filled me with dread. I was in a condition to eat almost anything, but I rejected the slimy lizard Luis managed to catch. He rocked to and fro and sang to himself before eating. When I asked him what he was doing, he said he was thanking the animal's spirit for letting itself be caught.

O'Rourke raised his eyes heavenwards at this evidence of pagan superstition and went back to reading the Divine Office aloud. I listened to the prayers, but the images of hospitable nature in the Psalms seemed utterly alien in that terrible place.

At sunset the clouds lifted; after a green flash across the vast sky, the tropical night descended with frightful suddenness and the stars rushed out to float like fireflies in the gaseous air.

As I sat and mused beneath the hurricane lamp, listening to the rhythm of O'Rourke's devotions, I felt saturated by the odour and the atmosphere of the jungle; I felt enveloped as if by music: I tried to place myself in the presence of God; but despite my longing for a sense of His presence in that wilderness, He remained absent.

However did I gain, I wondered, the idea that God and

all great things inhabit the wild places of the world? That civilization, houses, streets, cars and aeroplanes distanced human beings from their true, sublime source?

O'Rourke looked up and smiled. He seemed depleted, feverish. I asked him how he was and he bowed his head.

'I am suffering,' he said in a hoarse voice. 'We all have to begin by these sufferings to bear the cross that Our Lord gives us to redeem us from our sins . . . If I sleep, watch over me in the night, my dear fellow. I believe our guides are full of evil intent.'

The Zaparas cautioned us not to put even a finger into the water for fear of piranhas which attack their victims in shoals, their razor teeth, assisted by strong clenching muscles, severing sinew and bone at a bite. The Zaparas watched every floating log with apprehension; Luis said they were on the look out for caymans and anacondas.

In the late afternoon – rain! And despite our awnings everything got soaked. We sat in silence hour after hour amidst our drenched baggage. Twenty-four hours had passed and there was still no sign of John and Anna.

Before we prepared to leave we pulled into the shore a while and took turns to enter a short distance into the forest. I squatted alone in the undergrowth and looked up at the canopy, listening to the gibberish and sqawks and howls in the upper storeys. In my weeks at the university in Iquitos I had spent many hours poring over books Adolfo Pasco had given me on the flora and the fauna of the rain forests. Now I was summoning up images of the teeming denizens about me; the black spider monkeys that fly through the treetops, the shaggy red howlers with their fifth hands, the squirrel monkeys, tree porcupines, dwarf ant-eaters no bigger than rats, the sloths with their pincer-like claws; the macaws, parrots, popinjays, and multicoloured toucans; the giant green lizards, the iguanas that crash through the branches; the green tree snakes and giant tree frogs; the peccaries, armadillos, tapirs, agoutis, paccas, waterhogs, jaguars and pumas and panthers; the jungle deer and bush-hogs; the hundreds of varieties of butterflies; the morpho with a wing-span like a bird's, the bird-eating spiders, Goliath beetles, the thousands of species of ants and termites that swarm and thrive like plankton in the ocean of vegetation.

It struck me, squatting there, Nicholas Mullen SJ taking his morning shit amidst the riot of eerie greenery, that what is mysterious, ineffable, in human experience, is the carpet of sameness in all this prodigious variety. I had only stepped a few paces from the river to see a torrent of variegated greenery, pierced by several points of bright-blue light in the canopy and the sparkling cascades of sunlight diffused in the foliage of the upper storey. But as my eyes grew accustomed to the gloom I saw hundreds of species of trees on every side: trees that exuded milk, violets the size of apple trees, grass more than sixty feet high; the thrusting saplings of myriad kinds alongside groves of palm trees and the ancient giants, every one unique, thrusting upwards like mighty columns and steeples to their vanishing points in the softly undulating lake of vegetation.

In that strange twilight, in an atmosphere as mysterious and sacred as some vast vaulted minster, the stupendous life of the jungle pressed skywards in a chaos of growth, greedy for the light. Beneath the massive, gloomy folds of its outer mantle, the mass of tendrils, ropes, and cables, thick as a man's thigh, snaked and coiled and burrowed, sucking up the wetness in the humid air and the rank undergrowth. The seething unending struggle of growth and death overwhelmed my 'civilized' humanity, and I drew even further into the recesses of my inner world and my memories.

I was remembering that confessional box. It was like entering the wardrobe, dark and fusty; boxy echo; wood smelling of vinegar. Father James squatted sideways to me, his bowed shining white head framed in the darkness in which I sat. Mumblings and grumblings, then his sweet voice: 'Say, "Bless me Father for I have sinned" . . . When you offend God you make dirty marks on the beautiful white robe of your soul . . .'

The way Father James sat in the box reminded me of Father squatting on the toilet.

'To wash the dirty robe of your soul,' he said gently, 'you must be sorry for having offended him. Can you remember your sins?'

'No, Father.'

'What sins have you committed?'

'Seven Father.' I could see them in the little red book – seven black cinders all in a row.

'I'm not asking you count the seven deadly sins,' said Father James, looking through the grille at me with kind smiling eyes. 'Just tell me one of the sins you have committed.'

In the silence he rustled the leaves of the book that sat on his lap. Did he have my sins written down in his book?

'Have you been disobedient to your mother?'

'No, Father.'

'Weren't you naughty in class . . . disobedient to Sister Jude?'

'I didn't do it, Father.'

'Are you sorry for having offended God? Say after me: 'I am heartily sorry for having offended God . . .'

Father James forgave me the sins I could not remember. For my penance he asked me to say one Hail Mary for the holy souls in purgatory.

The next day dawned, overcast and threatening rain. Sister Jude would say: 'Rain is Our Lady's tears for sins. Blue sky is her cloak when she is pleased for our repentence.'

Mother scrubbed me hard in the bath. She dressed me in a white shirt so starched that I could hardly bend my arms. There was no breakfast that morning, not even a sip of water from the tap. She held me at arms' length and said: 'This is the most important day in your life.'

We travelled on the bus to school where the children were

gathered in the the assembly hall. Sister Jude, breathless and trembling, fussed over the girls white veils and adorned the boys with bright yellow sashes, crocheted insignias, and silvery medallions. As we walked in a crocodile to the Jesuit church the traffic slowed down on the main road and the women in the passing bus waved. Everyone and everything seemed to know that this was the most important day in my life; even the row of tall chestnut trees with their candles of dark pink and white blossom. In the churchyard there was a crowd of onlookers; I could see Mother gazing at me mournfully. The people stood nodding and calling out 'Good Luck!' and 'God bless', as if we were about to set off on a long journey.

In church the altar was a blaze of light and flowers. We were led to the front pews: the girls on the left, the boys on the right. At each place was a prayer book with shiny white binding like the back of my father's hair brush.

Then the church filled up behind us and Father James dressed in a sparkling gold robe came on to the altar.

We sang a hymn over and over again:

> Jesus Thou art coming,
> Holy as Thou art . . .

Slowly as thou art! The Mass progressed with its mumblings and toings and froings and I fidgeted on aching knees, until Sister Jude began to call out in a voice that echoed to the rafters:

> Lord, I am not worthy
> that Thou shouldst enter under my roof;
> Say but the word,
> And my soul shall be healed.

Father James was coming down to the altar rails. His eyes were twinkling behind those gold-rimmed spectacles. He was saying in his kindly voice, 'Little children, this is the day when Jesus, God himself the Almighty, the creator

101

of heaven and earth and all things, will for the first time come to dwell inside you . . .'

We approached the altar rails and held our hands under the white sheet as we had been taught. Flashes of white, silver, and gold, and the pleasant murmur of Father James's mumble-grumble . . . I put out my tongue and there it was – a piece of dry, slightly sour skin. So this was the taste of Almighty God. You must not bite him: that would hurt him. Would he not squirt blood? Let him rest on your tongue until you are ready to swallow him. Yes, there he goes, I can feel Him sliding down inside me, Jesus inside me, in under my roof. I was a little house and Jesus could sit inside me.

I had seen Tom Daley carrying a fledgeling bird across the playground in his cupped hands, his shoulders hunched, heeling and toeing a straight line; and this is how I saw him now, walking before me back to the pews. And that is how we were all walking on that morning, as if we carried in our mouths, fearfully and gently, a delicate little bird.

As I knelt, hunched, my hands joined in prayer, a ray of sun burst through the stained glass above the altar and I saw the figure of the child Jesus looking out at me from behind the crucifix. He had bright eyes and He gazed down sorrowfully on me. Was he angry?

After Mass the grown-ups milled around us in the churchyard, now drenched in sunlight and carpeted in pink blossom. The nuns handed us holy pictures and medals. But I longed to go home and to set about bringing God down on my own altar, to make him sit inside me again.

In the evening we returned to school.

A stage and lights had been erected in the assembly hall. The first communicants sat in the front rows and behind us were the nuns and Father James and our parents, but not my father.

The curtains were drawn to reveal a group of children in the top class dressed in costumes, their faces covered in greasepaint. Against a backcloth of gaily painted mountains and woodlands, and to the sound of tin drums, children in feathered head-dresses danced in circles and crawled about in the half-light on all fours eating with their hands from the earth.

Then the Head Prefect appeared dressed like Father James; he held up a crucifix and a prayer book and made signs of the cross. The savages were baptized, their confessions were heard, and they were given Communion. No longer did they crawl like wild people scavanging for food. They planted and harvested the fruits of the earth, and they learned to read and to write. They ceased their drum dances and walked in procession to an altar on a stage decorated with banners and lights. They knelt in adoration before the cross and a statue of the Holy Mother.

CHAPTER 11

We had paddled for several hours through a warm white fog. When it lifted we found ourselves in a complex network of tributaries, channels, and torrents, gushing across beds of scree and rocky ledges. As we fought our way ever upwards, against the current now, our boat was tossed and battered by the convergence of one river after another in a torrent of yellow mud, tumbling with the flotsam of the higher forests. The Mekroti country, we discovered, was virtually an island two thousand metres high in the foothills of the Selva Alta, formed by a maze of rivers and waterfalls.

It was late afternoon when our guides paddled up to a pebbly strand and dumped us along with our baggage among clouds of mosquitoes. Despite our pleas that they should accompany us all the way to the Mekroti, our Zaparas fled as if we were contagious. As they made off down-river O'Rourke sank to his knees, his arms extended to the sky. In a loud and tremulous voice he recited the *Te Deum*,

Hiding our baggage we set off, following a trail through the forest until we emerged in a clearing of some five acres with views of higher ground and wooded hilltops beyond. The scene before us was pitiful: what had been a series of gardens was a chaos of undergrowth, the rectangular houses burnt to the ground; only a few charred poles remained. Luis explained that the people were obliged to destroy their villages once the soil had become useless: we were witnessing the practice of slashing and burning in the higher forest regions. He told us that the people of the Selva Alta believed that the voices of their ancestors were to be heard crying out from the ruins.

O'Rourke greeted this information with a snort. He was impatient to be off, to find the living members of the tribe.

Then we discovered a new track and continued through the early evening twilight to the accompaniment of low gibberings and shrieks of the forest until we emerged in a clearing where across an open space we saw a party of about sixty Indians of all ages standing in silence before a semicircle of thatched huts. They were dressed according to the custom of higher forest people, in simple loose-weave clothing of unbleached calico, and wore their hair long and parted in the middle. They did not appear to me to be primitive, or neolithic, but they looked poor and undernourished. The men carried little bags across their shoulders from which protruded pipe-like sticks.

O'Rourke stood statuesque for several moments. Then he took from his pocket a silver crucifix and kissed it. His appearance in the twilight was startling. He stood towering on tiptoe, casting a long shadow in the rays of the setting sun, holding the crucifix aloft so that it flashed and sparkled. His finger pointed towards the sky and he raised his eyes so that the whites showed beneath.

The Mekroti stared at this vision for a few moments; then they started to howl, throwing themselves to the ground as if wishing for the earth to cover them.

PART THREE

Strange Gods

Partout où nous metions les pieds, ou la mort, ou la maladie nous suivoit. Nous verrons dans le ciel les secrets, mais toujours adorables jugemen, de Dieu là dessus.

Les Relations des Jesuites 1640

CHAPTER 12

Why did I feel such well-being, such exhilaration, in that strange country? Was it the purity, the sweetness of the air of the Selva Alta after the humidity of the low jungle? Or was it some primal sense of Eden that lurked in the recesses of my Christian memory? The rich clarity of the light, the dappled greenery, the fragrance of the blossoms, the remoteness from the world, gave the place an air of dreamlike holiness.

On that first evening I began to take notes with all the excitement of an amateur ethnologist or cartographer. I wrote down a record of my observations, and theirs of us, as if I would in due course report back to the outside world.

I noted that the land of the Mekroti could be crossed along forest tracks from one end to the other in about half a day; that the forest region was hospitable, although much of the game had been depleted; that floods had been increasing each year to the detriment of their primitive garden agriculture. Their favourite quarry, I gathered, was peccary, and they also fished and trapped tortoises. They were in the habit of clearing areas of the forest to establish gardens for the cultivation of mandioca, babatas, sweet potatoes, and sugar cane. They also grew cotton and other fibre-producing plants, and coca leaves, which explained the strange calico satchels carried by every mature male member of the community. The principal activity and ritual, the entire purpose of life itself, it seemed, was to chew coca quids mixed with a little lime powder to attenuate the bitterness of the leaf and provide a narcotic stimulus. The instrument-like sticks I had seen protruding from their satchels were attached to small gourds that every male received at puberty; this was the container for the lime, which was added to the coca quid in the mouth.

There was no sign in the village of modern technology or convenience, nor had they any form of written language or number; yet their clothing showed a mastery of simple weaving techniques; their pottery was well made, and they had metal tools, which indicated a history of contact, at least with their primitive neighbours. Their dress appeared typical of the poorest peons of Latin America, a simple shirt or smock worn outside a pair of loose-fitting trousers; the women wore skirts. Everybody went barefoot. They looked not so much like a 'lost tribe' as a reclusive community in hiding from the world, confirming a notion I had heard in Iquitos that the Mekroti were a people like the Kogi of Colombia and Rakas of Ecuador, who had fled many generations ago from the brutality of the colonizers.

When I suggested this to O'Rourke his eyes flashed with anger, his mouth became obstinate: 'I know that they are precontact,' he said in a low voice, 'because it has been revealed to me.'

The village was an assembly of some thirty huts of varying sizes, the smallest housing no more than an extended family of half a dozen people, the largest housing some twenty members of a clan. The entire tribe numbered no more than 350.

The grass-weave houses were situated three deep in a semicircle around a compound or piazza of raked sand. The men seemed permanently at leisure, lounging in groups, while the women came and went, carrying water from the nearby streams, or appeared, laden with produce, from their gardens. The children and dogs ran freely and noisily, with no apparent discipline.

In their loose grey-white calico garb, their long hair parted Christlike in the middle, the Mekroti looked like

110

the members of a religious sect. They were swarthy with hooded eyes and delicate chins; their noses were strong and hooked with deep and prominent bevels, which prompted O'Rourke to comment that they seemed Jewish. The men had hardly a trace of facial hair so that it was sometimes difficult to distinguish them from women in the middle-age group except for the women's skirts. The elderly were apparently healthy and said to live to a great age. The young women were attractive, with peerless olive skin, appealing eyes, and finely chiselled high cheek-bones.

The Mekroti treated us at first with a suspicion and a reserve bordering on hostility; the women seemed especially terrified and hissed, calling out a word we could not at first grasp. It gave me the uncomfortable impression that our arrival had been expected, and feared.

The headman, Anonha, was a small fellow, very thin, slow in movement and reverential, with many fine facial lines. He spoke with a sense of natural authority and there was even an air of dignity about the way he wore his clothes. O'Rourke immediately called him 'Joseph'. The name of the village was Ikana, and O'Rourke promptly renamed it Corpus Christi.

Anonha had invited us to live for the time being in his house. This dwelling, which housed several extended families, was a windowless tunnel with walls of neatly woven heavy grasses and a thatched roof on a strong frame of poles. There were holes in the roof for the emission of smoke; hammocks were hung from the supporting poles, and three cooking fires were positioned down the length of the hut, each one shared by several families. From the vaulted roof hung bags of provisions out of reach of predators.

I entered the hut gingerly, recoiling at the acrid stench. In the gloom I could see thirty or so people – shrivelled old women, arrogant-looking young men, mothers and children – all in various states of undress, some of them showing the full scope of their private parts.

111

O'Rourke, who seemed unaffected by the scene, was making theatrical gestures, rosary in one hand and a silver crucifix in the other; he was laughing uproariously, calling out greetings in Quechua and Zapara. As he strode about the hut the Mekroti shrunk from his path, many of them hissing and calling out that mysterious word.

Meanwhile our baggage had been brought up to the village and placed on the side of the compound, where our hosts arranged themselves in a kind of auditorium in preparation for a parlay.

As our first halting discussion got underway, I began to understand the effect of our arrival among them. When the Mekroti first saw us in the clearing they thought we were ghosts of the dead who sometimes came to visit the ruined villages at night and left them presents. If we were not ghosts, what were we? And where had we come from? And why? Anonha's most insistent question, which was posed in nervous and hushed tones, related, it seemed, to a tribal myth which told of a white visitor called 'Nakak', who would come from another world. The arrival of Nakak, which meant 'The Death Man', had been foretold by their great-grandparents. The Nakak, who was to be feared as Christians fear Satan, was half spirit and half human; he had a long beard and he was white. He carried a knife, and a rope for strangling and hanging his victims; he feasted on blood and flesh, and his son would take his place if he were killed. The Mekroti were asking among themselves whether O'Rourke was Nakak; and this was the word that was being hissed by the women. They thought that his rosary was a noose; that his crucifix was a dagger. O'Rourke laughed happily when all this was explained, and he attempted to reassure them that their myth about Nakak was nonsense. He, O'Rourke, had come not to harm them but to save them.

I watched them carefully as he tried to get this across. Some seemed relieved, but others were suspicious and muttered among themselves; they made gestures and pulled faces, indicating that they thought he was repulsive to look at. It seemed to them that with his baldness and huge beard, his face was upside-down; some of them even peered at him upside-down through their legs. They also found the blackness of his cassock repugnant because it reminded them of the feathers of a bird of prey in the region; which was ironic, for when he tried to teach them his name they pronounced it 'Rook'.

As for me, they were curious about my spectacles which they took to be a badge of office. Sitting there on my haunches listening to everything that was said, I felt a sudden exhilaration of unexpected insight. I saw Christian O'Rourke with new eyes – as if seeing him through *their* eyes. Looking at his silver crucifix and his ornate rock-crystal rosary, I saw them as death-bearing talismans shining and glittering in an unearthly light. And I had the unsettling feeling of being seen anew myself.

With the inhabitants of the entire village sitting before us in the compound, O'Rourke now rose, slowly, majestically, and retrieved from one of the bags our battery-operated radio cassette-player – a huge black and chrome ghetto-blaster.

As a large pale moon rose in the evening sky, he switched on a tape of the 'Gloria' from Bach's Mass in B Minor – silver trumpets, massed choirs, thundering organ and orchestra.

The Mekroti were entranced; they sat paralysed, all thoughts of Nakak and his sword and noose now forgotten. Some of them began to dance in silent appreciation of the music; they seemed to be telling Rook through their dancing that he had combined the sweetest notes of all creation. They looked on the flashy machine with wonder and now seemed convinced that we were endowed with wonderful powers.

When O'Rourke switched off the music he gestured that they should gather round. Then he embarked on a brief parlay about geography, and it became apparent that they believed they lived at the centre of the world with no idea of continents and oceans or the fact that the Earth was round. As I looked about me at the dusky people dressed in their simple loose overalls, ghostly in the light of the moon and the fires on the compound, it excited me to speculate how it must feel to think of this spot as the centre of the world. I had a sudden, aggressive urge to shut O'Rourke's mouth for him.

Meanwhile the Mekroti wanted to take things slowly, one step at a time. They were not sure what to call us. The word Mekroti meant human being; it also meant the People of the Tortoise. Their region was surrounded by flowing waters, and the shape of their country, with its gentle contours, reminded them of a tortoise, which was an essential feature of their creation myth. They were struggling in our palavers to understand how the white men fitted into their scheme of things. Various theories were circulating about our hairiness, including the idea that our first ancestor mated with a monkey.

But O'Rourke had no time or patience for *their* view of human nature and the world; he wanted to get across the purpose of our mission, plying Luis with questions and statements and announcements, and barely controlling his temper as the poor fellow struggled to keep up. Luis seemed to understand a great deal of what the Mekroti were saying, but his greatest difficulty was coping with O'Rourke's impatience to impart something of our Christian message.

From the very outset O'Rourke had attempted to talk about God. I was both irritated and fascinated by his determination to evangelize without delay. But it soon became obvious that the Mekroti were devoid of any notion of God as a creator outside, or above, or different from, the world. And they had no idea of the infinite, or the spiritual as separate from the physical, or any understanding as to how a being could exist without a body.

As these difficulties arose in our early conversations, I had a pleasurable sense that I was purging my mind of inessentials; as if I could relearn the truth of my Faith with a borrowed eye of innocence.

O'Rourke was trying to make them understand his idea of God by use of exaggerated mime, casting his huge body in outlandish postures and stretching his haggard face into animated contortions. He was trying to demonstrate the being he worshipped: falling to his knees he bowed until his forehead touched the ground, then he groaned in a tremulous voice. At last he indicated that the object of his worship was something high in the moonlit sky. This something in the sky, he was trying to say, was the owner of everything – plants, trees, animals, the Earth, and all the Mekroti. He made them say after him, with exaggerated gathering gestures, 'Papa-Belong-All', a Pidgin English formula he had used with success amongst the native peoples of Papua New Guinea. Some of the Mekroti thought that O'Rourke's antics were a kind of game or dance and they imitated him, laughing and giggling as they did so. I myself began to laugh, which caused him to cast a look of annoyance in my direction.

When things had settled down he tried again to put across the idea that Papa-Belong-All owned everything; but his crude gestures seemed to indicate that Papa-Belong-All was *harvesting* everything – the forest, the animals, and the Mekroti themselves. With this the laughter subsided; they fell silent, which only further hampered O'Rourke's attempts to extricate words for his use.

Then diving into our baggage he brought out a bell and rang it like a schoolmaster calling for attention. They were shutting their ears with their hands and screaming, and he was trying to tell them with elaborate gestures that the instrument, which they seemed to take for a gleaming magical pot, was the voice of Papa-Belong-All and that they should listen to it when he called.

Now he brought out some pictures of the Madonna and one of Christ, which he showed them by the light of the fires. The slick photographic precision of the illustrations impressed them and some reacted as if the pictures had a life of their own. After they had seen three different pictures of the Madonna, and O'Rourke had attempted to explain that she was the Mother of Papa-Belong-All, Anonha asked, quite sensibly I thought, whether this meant that Papa-Belong-All had three mothers. O'Rourke laughed pleasantly at this and I was pleased to see him relaxing a little into his task. Turning to me he said fondly, 'They are just little children.'

Next he showed how the images of the Mother and the other pictures had been placed in the baggage and brought across land and water to their country. He was trying to tell them that these were representations of the world, which enabled him to communicate with his relatives at a distance, and his dead ancestors, and even Papa-Belong-All. But only Anonha and one or two elders seemed to grasp the significance of this.

Eventually the meeting was called to an end by Anonha around midnight. The audience dispersed, still discussing the events of the day among themselves, while we went to our tents which Luis had erected on the edge of the compound close to a stream and the margin of the forest.

I felt pleasantly tired and relieved, settled in the hammock, writing up my notes by the light of a pencil torch. The Mekroti seemed to me a friendly people who would pose us no harm. I felt anxious for Father John and Sister Anna, but I was feeling more at peace with myself than I had done for years. The exercise and fresh air, the abstinence from alcohol and rich food, the need to concentrate on my very survival, had taken me out of myself. As a token of my burgeoning health I fell quickly into a deep and grateful sleep.

CHAPTER 13

I awoke refreshed to the sound of the dawn chorus and the running water of the stream. The tent flaps were up and I lay for a while looking out at the sunlight and gently stirring foliage. O'Rourke was already at prayer; I could hear him muttering and groaning and calling on God in his tent. I was inclined to slip back to sleep, but I was disturbed by some of our hosts who had wandered over to stare at me and at our stuff; then one of them began to explore the bags with nimble fingers and I knew it was time to get up. As I washed and shaved a crowd formed to watch in silence. For privacy O'Rourke and I took it in turns to go a little way into the forest.

After making his preparation for Mass, O'Rourke erected our collapsible table as an altar. By the time he had robed and laid out the vessels and candlesticks, the entire village had assembled to study the ritual we were about to perform, chatting among themselves and pointing and pressing ever closer to the table. They were curious about the black cross with its realistic figure of the crucified Christ painted in natural colours; they scrutinized this object, craning their necks to peer at it and touch it gingerly to see whether it was alive or dead. The appearance of the Eucharistic wafer and the red Communion wine provoked more noise and discussion; when O'Rourke finally consumed them at the Eucharist they crowded around jostling and bickering to such an extent that the table nearly went down.

Throughout Mass I had felt strangely detached, attempting to see the ceremony through their eyes rather than my own. When O'Rourke prayed for John and Anna at the bidding prayers he looked across at me sternly and had to repeat himself as I was standing in silence, gawping with open mouth like our hosts.

After O'Rourke had made his thanksgiving, which he did on his knees in his tent, he came out and asked for something to eat. We were immediately given a kind of bread made from maize, which we washed down with plain water. Despite our reserves of iron rations O'Rourke was determined that the Mekroti should feed us and serve our physical needs. He was already arranging for Luis to purchase stocks of food in exchange for our beads and baubles.

Everything had to be done through Anonha, the thin and wizened headman, who was watchful in all his dealings with us and who seemed determined to conduct the business of getting to know us with a sense of quiet discipline. He had large sensitive eyes that never missed a gesture; he seemed sensible to every shift of vocal inflexion and alteration of facial expression. He had a look that indicated it would not be easy to get anything past him. I noticed that he was very clean, both in his personal hygiene and clothing, which seemed to enhance the impression of his authority. When he spoke the people paid attention. He had ways – gestures and little strategems – that distinguished him from the rest of the villagers: he never engaged in hurried and excited speech or histrionic reactions; he was not among those who pressed forward, and he was courteous in everything he said and did.

By the light of day I began to notice Anonha's son, a young man of perhaps thirty years of age called Chieske, who in ludicrous contrast to his father seemed to be suffering a form of hyperactive disorder (the signs being glaringly obvious to *me*). Unlike most of the adult members of the tribe, who appeared unused to anything but a sedentary life, he was muscular and athletic and forever leaping and jumping about. His eyes were wild with a glint of madness in the prominent whites. The muscles stood out in his neck and even his cheeks; his low forehead looked solid as a rock. The Mass on that first morning seemed to have provoked him to hysteria pitch. Now he was screaming with laughter; next he was frowning fiercely; then he was leaping about and dancing, spewing out a torrent of speech.

We learned that Chieske was Anonha's second son; the first had died in an accident. Anonha's daughter-in-law, the dead son's widow, Mabla, was introduced; she was a good-looking woman, graceful in figure, with fine high-cheek bones and intelligent eyes. She had an equally attractive son called Bedla whom O'Rourke instantly took a shine to. Mabla, her mother, and the son, lived in privileged status in a separate house, which suggested that the boy, and not Chieske, was the favourite for the succession as headman.

After breakfast the semicircle formed once again in the compound and Anonha invited us to another parlay. He wanted to know about our morning ritual; the men were chewing rhythmically on their coca quids and gazing at us in anticipation. There was a curious impression, I thought, of anxiety and disillusionment at that first meeting of the new day.

Anonha explained through Luis that what the people had seen at our morning ritual had frightened them. Some believed we had a dried human foetus nailed to a piece of wood; they wanted to know whether it was true that O'Rourke had been feasting on human skin and blood. As they made these fears known I was so shocked that I gasped out loud. I clutched O'Rourke excitedly and said, 'This is terrible, Christian, we've got to allay their anxieties . . .' I was thinking of their gruesome Nakak myth, and how their misinterpretation of the Mass would only confirm their worst suspicions about us.

O'Rourke shook away my hand; he said, 'Their notion of what we were doing this morning is as accurate a version of the truth as we could wish. I'm not going to disabuse of them of the idea any more than Christ did when he was challenged by the Jews.' He added for good measure, and in Latin, the text about the 'hard saying' – 'Durus est hic sermo et quis eum audire' [This is a hard saying; who can listen to it].

He tried to get Luis to tell them that they 'saw what they saw'. Then, turning to his hosts, he put on an expression of mild disdain to make it clear that he had nothing further to say on the matter, which resulted in a confused babble of raised voices.

O'Rourke now embarked on a series of questions about their own beliefs with the aid of mime and the use of pencil and paper. Even when they understood his questions it seemed to me that they said less than they knew; but O'Rourke badgered them and tried to draw them beyond their limits. At one point, after O'Rourke had been repeating a question about the destination of the Mekroti tribe after death, Luis turned and said, 'They don't want to tell you because they don't want to give away their ancestors' secrets.'

We had passed about half an hour like this and seemed to be reaching an uncomfortable impasse when our hosts fell silent and looked expectantly towards the forest. A slight man of indeterminate age was approaching. He was dressed as the others but he was wearing a short cloak and a decorated headband, and there was something strangely elegant and ceremonial about his movements. When he arrived in front of us we found ourselves looking into a face of dramatic contradiction: one side of it had disastrously collapsed, eye, cheek, mouth and jaw, while the other remained taut, youthful, and lively. One side of his face contemplated us with a gleam of sly cruelty through a half-shut lid, the mouth curled down in a sardonic leer; while the other fixed us with a wide-open eye of innocence. It was a baffling, frightening spectacle. Anonha said that this was Ikana's shaman or priest, known as Takakhe, who had been away searching for herbs in the forest.

Takakhe immediately went into animated conference

with Anonha and various village elders while O'Rourke pleaded with Luis to translate, which he could only do in patches. What O'Rourke gathered from Luis he did not like. Takakhe was warning Anonha that Rook was indeed the Nakak as had been told in the legends and that he was bent on destroying the Mekroti people. As the arguments went to and fro it appeared that Anonha was not prepared to swallow this verdict without further evidence. Anonha was well-disposed towards us, and yet something alarming was happening before my eyes and I could see no way of preventing it. O'Rourke had taken against the shaman and was betraying his feelings in a most obvious way – making threatening clucking noises and shaking his finger. All this was noted and commented on by the Mekroti, not least by Takakhe himself, who seemed to be enjoying the situation.

Then Takakhe called for silence. When he had the attention of the whole village he summoned three youths to his side and whispered in their ears. At once they hared away across the compound and into the forest in the vicinity of our bivouac. Next he summoned a girl of about fourteen years of age and said something to her that made the assembly laugh; taking her by the shoulder he pushed her forward to stand in front of O'Rourke. She was shapely and pretty; she was smiling coquettishly. Wriggling her shapely rump, she approached O'Rourke, making little forays as if to tickle his genitals.

O'Rourke endured this for a few minutes then he rose angrily to his feet and pushed her towards the shaman, which resulted in a roar of ribald laughter from the crowd with much slapping of bellies and rolling about on the ground. But the uproar gave way to expectant silence when the young men appeared from their errand in the forest. As they approached, O'Rourke and I exchanged shocked glances. The leading youth was holding his arms forward carrying something gingerly in his hands as if it were a small animal hidden in his palm. He went straight to the shaman to show him what he had found; then he revealed it to the villagers. It was clear for all to see: the object was a piece of our excrement. Takakhe scrutinized it, prodding it carefully with his finger; first sniffing at it, then tasting it and smacking his lips, while O'Rourke gasped with exasperation.

Takakhe then summoned Luis and questioned him as well as he could, frequently pointing at our genitals and describing his meaning with his forefinger.

In faltering fashion Luis translated the shaman's enquiry. Our hosts, it seemed, had been convinced that we had no penises, a theory that Takakhe had intended to put to the test by getting the girl to feel O'Rourke's private parts. But when our excrement had been brought from the forest, looking and tasting like any other excrement, he had decided that we were men like any other men and that we probably had penises too. Perhaps, he suggested, our penises were wrapped around our waists. When Luis told them that our penises were quite normal, Takakhe smiled and nodded his head. He seemed glad to learn that we were capable of generating life, and that by the same token we were capable of losing it.

CHAPTER 14

Later that day I walked down the trail beneath the high trees to the river. I sat on a rock looking into the fast-running waters. I was in a dreamy mood, as though I had been drugged, and I was wondering whether I was headed for a relapse into hypermania. I had been experiencing moments of spiritual elation, as if my soul were floating in a pure, rarified stratosphere, interrupted by sudden lecherous fantasies.

The trees were etched a deep velvet black against a sapphire sky; my mind was strongly impressionable and I kept thinking of the young unmarried Mekroti girls who swung their hips and wriggled their shapely little rumps, and seemed by their very coyness to be flirting artfully with every male that came into view. I wanted to laugh and chase and fool around with them. I was feeling randy, shamefully randy, to the point of plotting how I could take a girl there and then into the secrecy of the forest.

I had asked about the girl who had been pushed towards O'Rourke. I learned that she was known as Sakel; when she was not draped over Chieske she seemed to be roaming the village with an air of unbridled lust. She was below average height and plump, with petulant lips and a coy expression that would break into a lecherous stare. Each time she passed me by her eyes were lowered, then she would look up at me, a look that seemed bewitched and dazed, stupefied with libidinous intent. I felt those eyes undressing me, watching me as I turned away in nervous retreat.

Sitting by the river, I imagined Sakel enveloping me with

her soft, tremulous flesh, sucking the lust out of me. I chucked a pebble in the river; I quenched the fantasy and thought about Jill.

I was remembering a day when we had fooled around and chased each other on the Sussex Downs. There had been something sad, and funny, about that; a Jesuit in his late forties, a believer in the split between body and soul, racing his mistress over the Downs. We had left my car on the roadside and leapt over a five-bar gate behind a farm, climbing a track that bordered a silent beach wood. The chalky ruts in the path were hard underfoot, harshly white in the afternoon sunshine. We walked with our arms around each other's waists, her hip pressing rhythmically, intimately, into mine. Dominic was toiling ahead, his little body agitated by the breeze. One more gate separated us from the open fields. Then we took off over carpets of sweet-smelling close-cropped turf, scattering the sheep and pelting each other with dry droppings, sprinting and dodging and calling out; climbing ever upwards; Jill trying to push me into the gorse bushes with their fierce prickles and bright-yellow star-shaped flowers.

At last we stood at the summit of a steep down. I could see the farmhouse far below to the left, and the roadway – a thin winding ribbon bordered by hedgerows. We were high as the sky, and the apron of the hillside fell sheer beneath us. Jill said: 'Race me to the bottom!'

I took off, Jill chasing me, screeching from behind. Down I went, and for three or four seconds I seemed to have wings; the sky and the hills were a blur of speed, then my feet gave way and I somersaulted out of control thumping the ground with my head and limbs until I landed painfully on my back.

I could hear Jill and Dominic laughing above me. My glasses had come off on the way down; I lay on the side of hill looking out towards the bright line of the distant sea. I could see the indistinct shape of an old droning biplane rising and falling like a dragonfly away in the blue haze. There was a wonderful sweetness in the air. Then Jill was leaning over me, her hair fanned out, her lips on mine. I shut my eyes and opened my bruised arms wide.

For a moment I felt part of the world, as if I had fallen out of the sky to land at last on the Earth's firm surface; but in an instant the impression had vanished.

Sitting by the river I felt wrung out with remorse; no, I did not want Sakel, the village prostitute; in the calm of the early evening I tried to think about female beauty as a symbol of beauty in nature; the former disciplines of my youth − sublimation, the tantalizing allure of intellectualizing one's baser thoughts: the pure, bracing mountain air of metaphysics! Scotus! Suarez! Loyola! I could be liberated from lechery by purer thoughts. My soul could transcend the body's fleshly appetites by the disciplines of Ignatian meditation. I started to think about Anonha's graceful daughter-in-law, Mabla; her beauty seemed ethereal, untouchable . . .

Then I remembered John and Anna.

I imagined them stranded somewhere down-river without boats or supplies. I was sitting there in the vague hope that they would come into view, and I offered a small, weak prayer for their deliverance.

Oh, the seductive power of prayer! Having walked back up along the trail to the village, I found Luis in our bivouac searching our bags for medicines; Father John and Sister Anna had been found wandering in the forest.

We ran together to Anonha's hut, and as I grew used to the smoky twilight I saw O'Rourke leaning over the figure of Sister Anna. She was looking up at him blank-eyed, her face a mass of cuts and bruises, her hair matted, her naked and filthy body covered with infected insect bites. Father John was sitting on the ground pale and bent and without his glasses. Next to him, lying on a mat, was a young Zapara shaking with fever.

Luis used the nearest hearth to heat water for washing

and to make a soup; while John told us in a low, exhausted voice the story of their journey.

Two days after they had started out one of their guides developed a viral fever and died the following night. When two more Zaparas came down with fever the guides got angry and blamed him and Anna, accusing them of spreading the 'catarrha'; they beat Sister Anna about the head and when John tried to defend her they ducked him in the river. Arriving in the Mekroti region they had dumped them and a sick young Zapara on-shore and made off with the missionary belongings, including the plank boat with its outboard motor. Anna and John, with the youth on his back, had been wandering for two days in the forest.

As John told his tale, Anna started to sob. 'On the slightest whim they ill-treated us,' she whispered. 'A hundred times I thought they were going to kill us.'

O'Rourke sent Luis for one of his shirts to clothe her and I treated her bites with antiseptic lotion. As she revived she started to look about her for the Zapara youth. 'That boy is ill and probably infectious,' she kept saying. 'He should be in isolation.'

Tents were erected and no sooner had Anna and the Zapara boy been settled than O'Rourke insisted that we kneel and sing a *Te Deum*. Afterwards we sat in a circle around our fire and Luis cooked a meal from our own rations. John, pale and blinking (his glasses were lost in the river), kept checking on the Zapara boy who was running a high temperature and suffering from congestion of the lungs.

After giving Anna a sedative for the night we built a fire; the villagers were standing a little distance from us, the male members chewing their coca-leaf cud.

As we discussed the hazards of our journeys up from Aranuba I was struck once again by the remoteness of our situation. With half our baggage lost, we were even more dependent on our own resources. I said this to O'Rourke, but he seemed unconcerned.

Before going to bed he insisted that we go down on our knees again and say a second *Te Deum*. Then he sat for a little while longer beaming at us, before launching into a speech.

'Now that we've arrived here safely we're going to build our own hut and chapel,' he said, his voice quavering with emotion, his huge lined face wreathed in smiles. 'I'm overjoyed that we have finally started our mission.' Then, lowering his voice and grinning in a peculiar self-regarding way, he whispered: 'It has been *revealed* to me that it is God's will that we bring the Gospel to these people. Just think: in this remote place we have the opportunity to build the New Jerusalem. And once we teach them about Christian baptism they'll long for it. Yet we'd better hold back a little longer until they're better instructed and have rejected the influence of Takakhe's supersitions.'

'Christian, I'm not happy with this,' said John.

Despite his ordeal John was managing to be polite, bringing a hint of a committee room to the remoteness of the high forest. 'Don't you think we should make an effort to understand their beliefs before we start undermining them?'

'Not happy with what?' asked O'Rourke with forced patience. 'Not happy with spreading the word of God!'

'Not happy with us behaving like Protestant evangelicals,' went on John. 'It's not our style, Christian, to wade in and trample on primitive social structures. We have to respect their own notions of equity and order, we must try to understand and respect their own belief systems . . .'

O'Rourke had spoken gently up to this point. He now snorted, and murmured under his breath, 'Belief *systems*!' Then he raised his voice again: 'Oh yes, I understand all about acculturation and inculturation and all that, Father John, but don't you feel inspired to look on these surroundings with the eye of Faith? We're completely cut off from the world; our situation is as simple as the stable at Bethlehem, and we have the opportunity to plant the word of God among these people in all its unsullied truth and directness. God has given us a special grace in transporting us here and placing us among these poor huts to renew the fullness of his message without compromise. And can't you see, my dears, this affords us the opportunity to renew our *own* spiritual lives. To prostrate ourselves before the Cross in the midst of this forest, to put on Christ in this desert – is it not to be in Paradise day and night?'

John now sat with his head bowed, refusing to look at O'Rourke and declining to argue further. O'Rourke seemed unaware of John's anger; he stood up, and raising himself to his full height he blessed us in Latin with a deep and wide sign of the cross; then he announced that he was retiring for the night.

After O'Rourke had gone into his tent, John and I sat talking a little longer, watched by Luis who seemed to be smiling enigmatically to himself.

'What are you thinking, John?' I asked.

'I'm thinking,' he said wearily, 'that Father Christian is barking mad. And I'll tell you another thing, they're no more pre-contact than any of the other tribes in this region; they may be remote, cut off, but you can see from their clothes and their gear and their tools that they've been in contact with their neighbours. Anyway the lime they're mixing with their coca comes from a coastal region; they're trading *somehow* and with *someone*.'

CHAPTER 15

Still weak and nervous from his ordeal on the river John was up ahead of us next morning, exploring the village and its surroundings with obsessive curiosity. I wondered what kept him going. He wasn't much interested in theology; he wasn't particularly ideological or political. He just wanted to help people; to make people's lives more comfortable. But what made *him* comfortable? Where did he get his strength?

We breakfasted briefly together and he talked about the need to come gently into the Mekroti lives, begging me to restrain O'Rourke's enthusiasm. I noticed that his hands were shaking badly; we had both run out of cigarettes now, and he told me laughingly that he was considering experimenting with coca chewing.

Then he went off to inspect the Mekroti gardens, eager to discover, eager to be of assistance.

As I breathed in the sweet early morning air, it struck me that I hadn't felt so well in years. The fresh air and exercise of the journey, the everyday crises, the enforced nicotine deprivation, seemed to have brought about a marked improvement in my health. Since we left Aranuba I had not taken Lithium and my thirsts were abating. And now that John and Anna had arrived my spirits had lightened considerably.

As for the state of my soul, I was beginning to live more entirely through my senses.

O'Rourke's first act of the day was to kneel in private prayer for an hour before taking the Eucharist to Anna in her tent and staying with her a while to pray. When he emerged he announced that he would say Mass at noon. Was I paranoid, I wondered, that I reckoned he wanted John out of the way before he planned his own morning itinerary? Summoning Luis, O'Rourke started work collecting vocabulary with the aid of a tape-recorder. I watched him as he interviewed a group of young villagers. His determination was impressive but the youngsters were playing games with their speech to confuse him. He would ask a word for an object and when he repeated it the onlookers burst out laughing. He seemed to take this with mild equanimity, wagging his finger and smiling wryly; but I could tell that he was angry. Eventually he summoned the villagers for a parlay by ringing the bell.

He had several items with him, including our hunting rifle, a firework, the radio-cassette, a model aeroplane, a clockwork model car, a magnifying glass, a magnet, metal plate, and nails, and large sheets of paper and coloured pencils.

His great rugged face was earnest; he said, 'There's something about these people . . . they're complacent, bovine, I don't know whether it's the effect of coca chewing or innate smugness, but I'm going to show them the gulf between our knowledge and theirs with the aid of some simple technology. While we do this it's important to put on a performance.' With this he donned his ragged old Jesuit gown, patched and green with age.

His appearance standing there with all these bits and pieces of Western junk seemed to me ludicrous. Father Christian O'Rourke SJ looked like a mixture of pantomime dame and ham magus. I had to stifle a temptation to cackle.

The people were gathering, and he began by trying to explain to the first curious knot of his audience, with the help of Luis and some drawings with coloured pencils on the large sheets of paper, that we had made a journey to their world across a vast river in a vessel that flew through the air.

They looked at him nonplussed; they hadn't understood a word of it. The men were chewing hard on their quids of coca; the women were frowning and chatting to each other. The children were restless.

Next he led them all to the edge of the forest and took aim with the rifle at a virtually tame songbird perched on a branch. With a single shot he brought it down, the report echoing through the trees. That had an effect, although not quite what he had intended. In the resulting pandemonium several women fell on the floor and went into convulsions.

At this point I was standing next to Luis and we exchanged looks. The ever-watchful Luis murmured an explanation: 'Their songbirds are sacred ... probably identified with dead ancestors.'

Again I had to stifle a tendency to giggle.

As the distraught audience reassembled John appeared hurriedly from the gardens, alerted by the sound of gunfire. He stood on the edge of the crowd, arms folded, his face a picture of alarm as he watched O'Rourke preparing the next demonstration: he was lighting a firework in the middle of the compound; as he withdrew it leapt into the air in a flurry of bangs and flashes, scattering the terrified villagers; in the meantime he was making theatrical gestures as if somehow *he* had been responsible for the prodigy he had set in motion.

Next he gathered the people around him and drew on sheets of paper a picture of a civilized town, showing how we lived in our world and explaining how the dwellings were skilfully made of bricks and wood and housed many families of people together and yet with sufficient space for single families to live separately. But his audience had clearly failed to understand a word of it. Some of them were laughing at him as if he were crazy.

He explained our different modes of transport – by land, sea, and air, and to illustrate the technology of locomotion he wound up the toy car on a flat piece of ground and set it off. That impressed them. They were delighted with the clockwork car; and he stood back, smiling complacently.

Then he revealed the mysteries of glass, explaining its varied uses in the construction of houses, the making of utensils, and as an adornment. He showed how glass could enlarge and multiply objects, and explained how my spectacles worked. Then he demonstrated the potential of the magnifying glass for generating fire.

He revealed the miracle of the magnet which he moved around beneath a plate of nails without attempting to explain how it worked. But the Mekroti, so it seemed to me, thought this was merely an interesting trick; they examined the plate closely to see if there were any glue attaching to it, much to O'Rourke's amusement.

Finally he demonstrated his radio-cassette again, playing a Beethoven violin sonata, which silenced and intrigued them, although without the same stunned admiration that had greeted the first demonstration.

All this time Anonha and his elders had been chewing their coca leaves rhythmically, frequently applying the sticks of lime to their mouths. I could sympathize with O'Rourke's comment about their 'bovine' appearance, and yet it struck me that much of what O'Rourke had told them was unintelligible, and we had made little effort to understand the habitual language of their faces and gestures. They seemed to me to be suffering from a sheer surfeit of unrelated information.

Eventually John came forward from where he had been watching everything and waved his hand as if to ask O'Rourke to desist. He leant over and switched off the cassette.

'For God's sake, Christian!' he said, exasperated.

The two priests confronted each other, O'Rourke looking absurd, as he was still wearing the Jesuit gown to enhance his 'magician' status; John, peeved and myopic, and evidently in poor health. I seemed to stand between the two of them, a perplexed bystander. In the background

I saw the shaman Takakhe lurking and sulking, squabbling with a group of elders who were chewing their coca and discussing the meaning of the morning's proceedings.

'What is upsetting you, John?' asked O'Rourke testily. 'Our simple displays of technology will serve to make them more docile, more ready to listen to us, when we introduce the mysteries of our faith. The belief and trust they acquire in our intelligence and capacities will help them consider the truths of Christianity more seriously.'

The pomposity with which O'Rourke delivered this statement almost made me laugh; I turned away from him towards Luis, asking him what he thought the villagers had made of the demonstration. Shrugging his shoulders, he said, 'They think you're strong in some things, but weak in others . . . Takakhe thinks O'Rourke is the Nakak, whom they call the *pistaco* in Quechua – the white cannibal witch . . .'

As he said this, I remembered the crazed old bag-woman in Iquitos, screaming and spitting, and kicking out at me: '*Hola gringo*! *Pistaco*!'

'This means they're frightened of you,' Luis continued. 'They believe that you've come to do them harm.' He added in a dispassionate voice, all the more chilling for its casual delivery: 'They look harmless, but they'll probably try to kill you.'

O'Rourke and John were still arguing in low voices about inculturation, when I intervened with a nervous insistence that shocked them into silence.

'Just *listen*,' I said, my voice hitting a manic high note. 'Luis is telling us . . . he's telling us that they believe we're cannibals. We *must* reassure them . . . It's no use impressing them with our superior technology, encouraging them to believe in everything we say, only to get our Christian message distorted in their minds.'

O'Rourke turned on me with a look of sorrowful reproof. 'Nicholas, my dear, we must remember the words of the Gospel. If they believe we are eating actual flesh and blood, it is no delusion. Remember the word used by Ignatius of Antioch, not *soma*, a symbolic body, but *sarx*, literal flesh and blood. Have you forgotten Christ's reaction to the Jews when they rejected his words? 'Unless you eat my flesh and drink my blood, you will not have life in you.' These people have grasped a sense of that truth, unpalatable as it seems to them now. Half the world struggles with our assertion about the body and blood of Christ. We've now got to inculcate an understanding of Christ's divinity, his Godhead, so that they know we consume both the body and the blood, the soul and the divinity, of God himself.'

No sooner had he finished this speech than he turned his back on us and went off to prepare for Mass, followed by the entire village – men, women, and children.

I stood for a moment outside my tent wondering whether to follow and vest with him, or whether to accompany John, who was setting off again to make a survey of the terrain beyond the village, stony-faced after his quarrel.

After any set-back O'Rourke forged ahead at once; he was always on the move, as if attempting to transform reality by sheer effort of will.

Why had I come all this way to the depths of the jungle if it was not in the hope of opening my eyes to the transformation offered by Christian truth? I decided to follow O'Rourke, to vest for Mass with him, to attempt to grasp once again what they saw when they looked on *our* mysteries. It was as if I was on the brink of seeing and understanding something profound in my life. Despite my rational assessment of him, despite my better judgement, I was fascinated by O'Rourke's uncompromising ministry. I wanted to witness its fruits to the the end.

O'Rourke began the Mass of the day with a loud, sonorous voice, his face suffused with piety and recollection. He had made a mark with a stick to indicate the 'sanctuary', showing them that they must not transgress the line. But as the Mass proceeded, the Mekroti came forward and began to press around the table, squabbling among themselves, pointing at the crucifix and the sacred vessels. O'Rourke seemed so lost in concentration that he appeared not to have noticed their incursion. By the time we reached the Offertory a youth had managed to steal one of the Communion wafers and hurried away to deliver it to Takakhe who was lurking on the other side of the compound as if by prior arrangement.

Immediately the crowd abandoned our makeshift altar and raced after the little shaman as he hobbled away to his hut.

By the time Mass was over, and O'Rourke was making his thanksgiving, I learnt through Luis that Takakhe had pronounced on the phenomenon of our Eucharistic rite. He had confirmed to the entire village that we were carrying a little boy in a box; from this little boy we sliced pieces of skin to eat, and drew off his blood to drink. They had also confused the status of the sick little Zapara boy with our practices; why else should Father John have been carrying him around on his back? Why else should the boy be hidden away in our tents, if it wasn't to eat his living flesh and drink his fresh blood? But Luis seemed to think there was sufficient disagreement over these theories for Anonha to be reserving judgement.

O'Rourke gave the Mekroti no time to mull over the implications of this new allegation; calling for Luis and bringing out his coloured pencils and paper, he rang the bell and announced another parlay in the compound outside Anonha's house.

This time Takakhe joined the elders, who were sitting in a little knot chewing their coca and watching us with cool eyes. I was so daunted by their gaze that I moved myself to one side so that I could see O'Rourke as they saw him: 'Rook' – the man with the 'upside-down' face. I was pent up with the atmosphere of suspense that pervaded the village population. John was still absent, going about his practical concerns.

After consulting with Luis, O'Rourke embarked on a repertoire of theatrical gestures, indicating that he wanted Anonha to answer a question. It took me some time to understand what he was getting at; when his meaning finally dawned I became as absorbed as they by the drama of the exchange that was about to take place.

'Who made the world?' he was asking. 'Who made you?'

Anonha stood up and called for silence. With a signal he sent a dozen or so men and women scampering for the huts and they reappeared within seconds bearing drums, simple finger-drums made of bark and skin.

Standing before O'Rourke he began to make graceful gestures, pausing for O'Rourke to confirm that he had understood before proceeding, and occasionally using Luis to interpret specific words that had eluded his mime. He was telling a story; and he told it several times over until he was sure that O'Rourke had understood. It was the fable of the origin of the world, and I found myself moved almost to tears by the skill with which he related it.

This was the Mekroti creation story, as far as I had understood it:

> The mother of the Mekroti, of the human race, was Iteka who lived in the sky where there were forests and rivers, and all the animals and birds that we know on the Earth. One day she was hunting a great tortoise which disappeared into a hole. Iteka followed the tortoise down the hole and fell through the ceiling of the sky, plunging through the air until she landed on the tortoise below in the underworld which is our Earth. Iteka now returned to her village in the sky and persuaded her people to come with her to the new world, and to bring all the animals and plants and the coca leaf. They returned by way of a rope made of vines, bringing all these things. Some people remained in the world above because they were afraid of the journey. Iteka herself returned to the upper world and drew up the rope behind her, cutting off the passage from the

world above from this Earth. But every so often Iteka returns from above to distribute the magical white substance 'lama' we chew with our coca. Coca and lama remind us of the happiness and peace of the upper world from whence we have come.

As soon as Anonha had finished telling his story there was a sound of a drum beat in the midst of the audience; then another and another. The women had bunched together and were clapping their hands and chanting, calling out and smiling.

The drumming started to speed up; the women's voices grew stronger, the rhythm more insistent and hypnotic. It was beautiful, thrilling, to hear such a sound in that remote clearing in the wilderness. I was becoming more excited by the moment, until, at last, I joined the chanting, clapping my hands and singing with the women. I looked around for O'Rourke. He was sitting hunched, his eyes shut, as if deep in private prayer.

Still the drumming and the singing went on, the sound building, the rhythm becoming more complex. Then the adult men leapt up and began to dance, forming a circle; they were feeding their coca quids with lime and chewing rhythmically to the stamp of their feet and the sound of the drum. There was nothing athletic about their movement, but it looked skilful and elegant.

After the men had been dancing several minutes O'Rourke got to his feet and came over to me. His face was flushed. 'How extraordinary, Nicholas,' he said. 'Did you understand?' he shouted above the drum-beats. 'Their fable contains distorted elements of Noah and the Diaspora. It also reveals the idolatrous significance of their coca-leaf addiction.'

Turning towards Anonha and his people, he rang the bell. The drums and the dance stopped. The Mekroti looked disgruntled; shrugging their shoulders and chewing their coca, they reluctantly gathered around O'Rourke again.

When he had got their attention O'Rourke launched once again into a charade. In an amazing exhibition of mime and odd words of Mekroti and Zapara he made it clear to them what he thought of their story of the origin of the world.

It was false, he told them; it was false and they must learn to reject it. He had shown them the superior knowledge of his white man's technology. Now, if they listened to him carefully, he would tell them a better story about the origin of the world. In fact, that was why he had come all this way to visit them: to tell them the true story of their origins.

I groaned as I began to understand his drift, for his mime suggested that he thought their creation myth not only untrue but silly. I could not believe that O'Rourke was capable of being intentionally contemptuous; and yet, in his determination to convince them of the Christian truths, that was the crude burden of his communication. As I grasped its meaning I became agitated; I leapt up and gesticulated; I was trying to tell the Mekroti that they should not listen to Rook. I confronted him, tears of anger in my eyes. 'What are you doing, Christian?' I shouted.

Turning on me, he said sternly in clipped Irish accents: 'Are you a Christian, Nicholas? Did Christ behave any differently than I? Did I come here to confirm them in their errors? By what right do you ask me to allow them to dwell in darkness? I came here for one reason: to spread the literal word of God Himself, His love and mercy, His goodness and His salvation. Would you have been among those who tried to stop Christ when He walked upon this Earth?'

Stepping away from me he rang the bell again and called for silence. They were watching him intently; they only had eyes for *him*. He was indicating to them in mime that he was about to tell them his own story of the creation of the world and of all peoples, including the Mekroti, and the plants and the animals, and the elements and the heavenly bodies.

With this Takakhe leapt to his feet shouting at O'Rourke and imitating his stumbling efforts to express Mekroti, to the astonished amusement of the audience. I was laughing with them, too, delighted that they were resisting him. He stood for a while gazing back at us, his haggard face sad and mournful.

He now pulled himself up to his full height, and we fell silent as if daunted by his stature and charisma. He began a new charade with mime and peculiar sounds, conjuring up odd words that he had learned in their language. His message was clear for all to understand.

'Yes. To you I appear no more than a child, and we all know that children make their parents laugh with their stammering. But in a short time, when I know how to speak your language, you will see that it is you who are children. It is you who live in darkness and ignorance.'

This communication seemed to stun them. It stunned me too, for I grasped for a fleeting moment through his outlandish gestures something of our predicament: I saw us as the Mekroti saw us, as incomplete human beings viewing their world the wrong way up; as only half-men, half-souls, signalling with grunts and bodily tremors a private inner life of figments and illusions.

He was telling them that we had come here, to this remote place, to this hidden people, to reveal the truth of the darkness in which they dwelt. And yet where did that darkness have its being – if not in the recesses of our own hearts and minds?

But he had caught their attention and they were fascinated by what he was about to do and say next. He was going to tell them, he said, his own story of the origin of the world and of the human race, and he would tell them too of their destiny beyond death in the next world.

I was sitting on the ground with the Mekroti all around me as O'Rourke, leaping and crying out, and shaking his limbs, uttering combinations of Mekroti and Aurac and Quechua, launched into his extraordinary story of

140

the Christian revelation. It was as if he were a frantic spirit trapped within a huge misshapen body, his face upside-down, his figure swathed in black, powerless to get outside; and he was shaking his limbs and varying his voice to impart signals, and shadowy impressions, of the wordless truths that plagued and harassed his inner being.

I sat with his audience trying to wipe my mind clean, to understand what our hosts made of his message.

He told them this:

> Papa-Belong-All created the world and all the creatures in it. He made the first ancestors of Rook out of the soil of the Earth. Then he made war on them and their descendents because they had eaten an apple. He set monsters on them, casting them into an underworld of fire and torture. The son of Papa-Belong-All had arrived in the world of Rook, just as Rook had arrived in the world of the Mekroti. He was gifted with magic powers and could heal the sick and perform other miracles. But the nation rose up and tortured and killed him by hanging him on two cross-branches of wood. This torture and his murder turned out to be good as it resulted in the release of all dead ancestors and future peoples from the underworld of fire.
>
> This happened many generations ago, but the shamans of Rook's nation had the power to resurrect the son of Papa-Belong-All, the Saviour, who appeared as a foetus and was tortured on the branches again. His flesh was eaten and his blood was drunk by Rook every day of his life. He ate the flesh and drunk the blood of the son of Papa-Belong-All, because only in this way could he avoid the place of fire and torture and go to the place of good things and pleasure in the sky.

O'Rourke's attempts to tell the Christian message had a dramatic effect on his audience: they had become visibly anguished and frantic; some were quarrelling bitterly among themselves over its precise meaning and interpretation. And it made a profound impression on me too. Listening to the story, as if for the first time, I was shocked by its complicated savagery, its violence and guilt, its sinister covenant of blood. As I stood there watching O'Rourke looking down upon the objects of his evangelism, it dawned on me, in a startling instant of recognition, that the scene was an emblem of my entire life. Had there ever been a time in my life when I had not seen myself as an alien in a strange country, as a trapped spirit, striving to communicate in this physical world by that barbarous medium – the incompetent gestures and antics of language?

The eight or nine elders who had been sitting with Anonha and the shaman were engaged in a noisy conference; Luis joined them for a while, shaking and nodding his head, and gesturing vigorously. At length he approached O'Rourke, and I joined them, eager to learn what had been said. Luis told us that once again the Mekroti had been dismayed by O'Rourke's admissions of cannibalism which, in the eyes of some of them, had now been confirmed beyond doubt; although Anonha, it seemed, was still reserving judgement. What was more, they found his story of the origin of the world, and the bloody myth of the son of Papa-Belong-All, so revolting that it made them want to throw up.

O'Rourke received this with a sharp intake of breath and a deep groan. His craggy features seemed to go through a gamut of emotions. One moment his face was suffused with compassion and tenderness, the next he frowned and his jaw hardened in stern fury. Now his eyes softened with sadness and affection; now they flashed with anger and consternation.

At length, in a low voice, a growl almost, he said, 'Surely, Nicholas, this is the work of the Devil!'

I looked at him horrified.

But almost in the same moment, his face softened again, and he said to me gently, 'We must win them with God's love, Nicholas. Love overcomes all.' With this he started to walk towards Anonha and his elders; he held his head up high now, striding with confidence and determination. Luis and I walked a little way behind.

To the amazement of everybody O'Rourke walked into the midst of the Mekroti elders and sat himself down, telling Luis to squat beside him. Once again he started to address them in an outlandish style of communication to this effect:

'My brothers, you have seen all those things I showed you today and which you admired. You were right to believe that we have great powers. Now: what is there so beautiful as the sky and the sun? What is there so wonderful as the trees and the animals of the forest? So why do you not join me in saying: "He, Papa-Belong-All, who made so many wonderful things, must surely love us very deeply"? Why do you not say: "He who gave so many wonderful things deserves our love and our gratitude in return"?'

When he finished, they seemed perplexed and argued among themselves for while.

Then Luis explained to O'Rourke that they were bewildered by what he had said, because the sky, the sun, the rain, the forest, the earth, and animals, were equally capable of sending harm and destruction and death as they were of bringing good.

Moreover they could not understand Papa-Belong-All as a being outside the world, or something different from the world. There seemed to be no distinction in their language between an idea and its use in the world. For all O'Rourke's passionate determination that they should understand our God, they could not fathom what he meant.

But O'Rourke was still on the move. He now asked Luis to fetch our school globe, which was in a box among our baggage. His looked tense, exhausted with his efforts to achieve some sort of breakthrough, however small.

When it arrived he immediately held it up in the air and spun it on its axis. Then he passed it around for all to see and to handle.

'This,' he announced, 'is the shape of the Earth . . . Now

143

you have told me that in your story of the beginning of your world that the Earth was shaped like a tortoise. How can this be when the Earth is shaped like this?'

The elders exchanged a few words among themselves, and sat glumly in silence looking at the ground. It seemed obvious to me that they disliked O'Rourke's hectoring approach as much as they disliked the content of his speech.

'You also say,' he went on, 'that your Iteka is immense and all powerful. Yet how can this be if she is a human being like you and me?'

Again they were silent.

'You say that Iteka came down from the other world in the sky with all its people and animals. And yet who made that other place and its inhabitants in the first place?'

No one gave an answer. So he asked the question again, and again.

At length one of the elders shrugged and said, 'We don't know anything.'

Then another, a bent old man with white hair, approached the globe slowly; he inspected it closely and pointed at it; he said, 'Rook, where did Papa-Belong-All live before he made this Earth you show us, and from which, if it were the case, we would all fall off?' He rested his finger on the globe then whipped it off as if to indicate an object falling into space.

The other elders began to cackle at this, and so did I, despite myself. I thought that O'Rourke would be furious; but this incredible man of paradoxes was gleeful. With a confusion of gestures and mime he tried to show them that Papa-Belong-All, being without a body and not in any particular place, had no need of a world to inhabit. But no one seemed to understand his answer.

Then he said, 'I want you to thank and worship Papa-Belong-All for the good things He has given you: the sun, the fish, the fruits of the earth. I want you also to praise Him for sending me here to announce our Good News.'

144

Anonha, whom I had begun to like and respect, listened to this patiently, for it took a long time to express (O'Rourke had called for various foodstuffs to illustrate his meaning). Anonha then said, 'We do not worship your Papa-Belong-All, Rook, because we do not know him. If we could see him we would thank him.'

O'Rourke seemed delighted with this reply because it gave him the opportunity, Jesuit that he was, to engage them in argument, however rudimentary.

'Children and animals,' he replied in mime, 'think that when they shut their eyes to another creature they cannot be seen. But you know that you can be seen even when you don't see in return. Papa-Belong-All sees everything without being seen; He sees even our most secret thoughts.'

'But *we* know who looks down on us from above,' said Anonha. 'We call on him each day and he does not hide from us. He is the presence of light in the sky.'

'And who is that?'

'Look up and see, Rook,' said Anonha. 'It is the light itself. Surely you can see that.'

O'Rourke shook his head and smiled wryly.

Anonha continued: 'And if we feel gratitude for anything, if we worship anything, it is the coca leaf and the lama which Iteka sends us from the upper world. Coca is the presence of Iteka on this Earth.'

With this pagan challenge to our Eucharistic belief, O'Rourke's face became dark. Rising from the ground he started another mime, and told them this: 'I came here to tell you of Papa-Belong-All so that you could live in happiness in a place of comfort and plenty, rather than burn in the place of fire and torture.'

As his meaning became plain I was aghast. I cried out, 'For God's *sake*, Christian! We don't teach our *own* children that any more!'

O'Rourke swung round on me. 'I *know* we don't teach our own children these truths, in these days of apostasy, and denial, and retreat, and secular humanism in our civilized world. But you know, and I know, that Christ's warnings of hell are explicit and insistent. Christ did not come to pander to our weaknesses and selfishness and complacency. He brought the fire and sword, and He promised that He would turn brother against sister, and parents against their children. I *know* it is a hard saying! But I am here to evangelize these people in our unadulterated Faith, and it's because I love them and hope for their salvation that I won't compromise one jot of Christian *truth*.'

I stood there speechless, guilt-ridden and horrified to hear the Christian message proclaimed in such a fundamentalist fashion. Meanwhile, Anonha had risen to his feet and came between us, attempting to assuage us both with graceful gestures.

Turning to O'Rourke he mimed the following: 'I beg of you, Rook, not to speak of those fires, it disgusts us. Speak just of the good things you came to bring us. Have you not brought us presents?'

To which O'Rourke replied: 'If I did not warn you of the fires after death, my dear Joseph, I would be guilty of allowing you to suffer them.'

Anonha said, 'If Papa-Belong-All is so good, if we should worship him and thank him, why does he burn people in those fires?'

'He is to be loved,' replied O'Rourke eagerly, 'because He is like *you*, he is like a headman who punishes men for doing wrong.'

'What kind of a headman is it,' indicated Anonha, 'that burns a woman to death for picking fruit off a tree!'

The next man to speak was the bent old fellow who had made the joke with the globe; he now looked severe as he mimed as follows: 'Rook, let me say something to you. There is not one person here who would not prefer to burn with our families and our ancestors for ever than live with white strangers with beards in your place of pleasure in the sky.'

But before O'Rourke could make an answer the shaman

Takakhe asked: 'How many arms has Papa-Belong-All? Will we have coca to chew in this white man's place in the sky? And will we have beards?'

The audience began to laugh. But as soon as O'Rourke regained their attention he formed an answer with a variety of complicated gestures. 'Beards and colour of skin are superficial as the clothes you wear, Takakhe. Papa-Belong-All tells us that those who obey and worship Him will be very beautiful and more shining than the sun.'

While this parlay had been going on the women had been preparing a meal under the supervision of Anonha's widowed daughter-in-law, Mabla, and we broke off to be served with roast peccary and yams and sweet potatoes in calabashes. John had now joined us, and we sat down with the elders who encouraged us to eat everything that was put before us. The food lacked elementary hygiene as well as salt, but we ate hungrily and complimented our hosts. Sitting there cross-legged and in silence O'Rourke looked frustrated, as if he could not wait for the meal to end so that he could get up and renew his attempts to teach the Christian gospel.

When we had finished the meal, he was already on his feet; but Anonha forestalled him. Calling for silence, he faced us three Jesuits as if to make a speech for our special benefit.

With Luis's help and signs and miming gestures, he began to speak, taking great pains to ensure that his message was understood.

'Rook, you have told us a lot of things today that we don't understand. What do you want of us? You want us after death to join your ancestors and to abandon our own. You tell us that your stories and knowledge and your way of life are better than our own. All this is very difficult and sudden for us. Some of what you say, about the eating of flesh and the drinking of blood, is frightening. But I have talked with my elders and we have come to a decision. Please stay and live with us like brothers for as long as you please; we shall

147

see how you live and behave towards each other and towards us, and how you practise your mysteries and worship your Papa-Belong-All. Then we shall learn more in one month than in twenty years of listening to your words.'

I was impressed and delighted with this speech, but O'Rourke seemed cast down. His eyes were filled with sorrow; he looked aged and exhausted, his shoulders drooping, his chin sunk in his huge chest. All eyes were on Rook; the elders who had resumed their coca chewing were watching him carefully. They gazed at him steadily as if weighing his every facial expression and gesture.

Before the meeting broke up Anonha signalled to his son Chieske and his daughter-in-law and they brought us gifts of food stocks; dried fish and meat, corn and fresh fruit. I rose to thank Anonha's graceful daughter-in-law for the food, and as I did so she smiled and touched my hand.

CHAPTER 16

As we came away from our parlay I want to see Anna. I stood outside her tent and called her name. Then I lifted the flap and peered inside. She was lying in her hammock clutching a rosary. Before she spoke she made the sign of the cross, signifying a break in her prayers. She looked ruffled by my intrusion, as if her status as a nun made her physically and psychologically out of bounds even in that wilderness, even in her illness and exhaustion. She answered my enquiries about her health curtly, turning my questions back on myself. When I said to her, 'How *are* you, Anna?' she replied with all the jauntiness she could muster: 'I'm fine, Father, and how are *you*?' And I was thinking how appealing she looked lying there in O'Rourke's oversized white shirt. She had washed her fair hair, which had grown to her shoulders since we left Aranuba. It took me a lot of effort not to reach out and stroke her cheek.

The cordon sanitaire she put around herself irritated me; I wanted to tease her and irritate her in return. I said, 'Come on now, Sister, *you're* the one that's poorly . . . Can I get you anything?' But she was avoiding eye contact, looking down at her rosary, *praying* for me, it seemed, to be gone. So after a moment or two of awkwardness I left, feeling abject.

Later, lying in my hammock at sunset, I could hear the sound of girls laughing and giggling outside my tent. After the excitement of the parlays I was feeling listless; I found myself entertaining a lecherous banal fantasy. I saw myself lying in the golden afternoon light beneath a palm tree on the edge of the forest.

I look up to see Sakel, the lubricious Mekroti girl,

staring at me; she is virtually naked except for a very short skirt of chamois, her hair is braided to accentuate her smooth forehead. She has delicate Asiatic features; she smiles sweetly showing her strong white teeth. I call out her name and she comes up to me and kisses my ear. Encouraged by the evident delight on my face she begins to caress me, murmuring gently, and looking into my eyes to judge my reaction.

Outside it began to rain and the children's voices were overtaken by the downpour on the tent. I was disgusted by my own day-dream; I even felt a tinge of guilt, as if I had committed an adulterous offence against Jill.

I tried to feel aloof, unaffected by the messy, lecherous, unwelcome condition of this physical body. Yet even as I contemplated the immense strength of will I must summon, a small voice scoffed at the the impossibility of attaining such independence of soul.

As darkness descended I began to think about Mabla, Anonha's widowed daughter-in-law; I could see her finely chiselled face, her noble Mayan-looking nose with its deep bevel, her dark intrigued eyes and prominent brows. I was remembering her affectionate touch, her reaching out when I had thanked her for the meal.

Something about her had reminded me of Jill. I was seized with a need to talk to her there and then, to make contact with her. I felt that I could not sleep unless I talked with her that evening.

I got up in a state of nervous agitation; delving in our baggage I brought out some pans and knives and a mirror. It occurred to me that an approach that evening might be interpreted as an act of courtesy: a gift in recompense for the afternoon meal.

It had stopped raining and the moon was out, but it was still early in the evening; Luis was sorting through our equipment by O'Rourke's tent. I asked him to come with me to see Mabla, and he complied without any obvious reaction.

As we approached her hut I began to feel nervous. What was it like to be a woman in the Mekroti community – sexist, primitive, superstition-bound, where the young women were allowed licence to run around and flirt, and the married women were kept hard at work? How did a woman relate to a man in such a society? What would she make of me, the shaman white man and my attempts 'to make friends'?

Luis had to take the lead; and now he was looking a trifle reluctant as he stood at the door calling her name. Inside there was a cooking fire and the usual smoke and stench. I could see the shadowy shape of her son, Bleda, who was lying on a pallet. In the background her mother was silhouetted against the light of the fire; the old woman looked up for a moment then turned her gaze back to the flames.

When Mabla came she seemed embarrassed; she kept lowering her eyes and looking about her. One of her neighbours, an elderly man, was lurking at the side of the hut; he was watching us curiously, coming and going, muttering to himself. She told him gently to go away, which only made him more curious.

Luis spoke to her and pointed to the gifts, which she took with slow hands. When I asked Luis to tell her that it was a present for the meal that afternoon, she smiled and seemed more warm and open. I was asking Luis to invite her to sit down and talk a while; I was feeling uneasy, desperate, my heart pounding, but I felt so obsessive about my need to make contact that I was determined to see this initial awkwardness through.

The three of us sat at the door of the hut. She was inspecting the gifts and looking up at me occasionally. I guessed she was in her late twenties, perhaps the same age as Jill when I had first met her. I asked Luis if he could persuade her to tell the story of her husband's death.

She looked back towards her mother and her son; then in a low voice and sign language, she explained through Luis

151

that five years earlier her husband Nanyutil had fallen from a high tree on to his back. She said that he was paralysed after his accident; he had painful sores and she had to feed him and serve his every need. Life had been difficult because she could not go to the garden and be with the other women.

Much of what she had said up to this point was easy to understand in mime without words. Then her eyes flashed and she spoke harshly and waved her hands about. Luis questioned her closely, then explained to me that Nanyutil, her husband, had become aggressive during his illness, screaming and abusing her in his helplessness; but she had stood by him.

Uncertain of the propriety of the action I reached out. Mabla had the hands of a manual worker, strong and calloused. She accepted my grasp with warmth and trust. I gently squeezed her hands for a few moments, trying to impart a feeling of affection and regard; then I released them, watching her reaction. Her face was mildly amused at first, then she covered her eyes with her hands as if to ward off my look.

I told Luis to ask her why she had stood by her husband throughout his illness. She looked at him as if surprised at the question, and she just repeated that he was her husband. We talked a little longer, while several more men started to hover in the background, whispering together. She sensed my frustration and smiled apologetically. I did not share a single word in common with Mabla, but something had happened.

Arriving in the village I had looked at the Mekroti, and I thought that they had looked at me, as if we were viewing each other through the plate glass of an aquarium; as beings who live in different worlds. Sitting in that remote place with a woman of an alien culture, who knew nothing of my beliefs, I wondered what it would be like to have landed on a planet where there were rational creatures, creatures with immortal souls who shared my ideas about God, but

152

who had no hands or faces, no common human reactions. How would I make contact? What would I look for to communicate, to understand what we felt and thought and shared in common? With Mabla I had only to search her face and eyes, and grasp her hand, to understand her joy, her fear, her pain; to experience a sense of spontaneous human agreement and sympathy.

At length she started to get up, slowly, looking around her at the knot of curious bystanders. I told Luis to ask her if we could talk again. Would she come and find me down by the river, out of earshot of her neighbours? She would not look at me, or make any response; but I knew by her embarrassment that I had got my message across.

Returning slowly to my tent I asked Luis whether he thought my conversation with Mabla would cause her trouble.

He said, 'These men are jealous and watchful of women once they have married; even widowed women. But she is the daughter-in-law of Anonha and has his protection. You should ask *him* before you talk to her again.'

CHAPTER 17

We had been making surveys of the largest houses in the village, examining their construction with a view to designing our own, when we came upon a strange sight. Entering Takakhe's hut, which was larger than all the rest, I glimpsed several bodies separating in the gloom. For a moment I thought I had seen young men and youths in the act of giving and receiving the Eucharist, the youths on their knees taking into their mouths a gift from the fingers of the young men.

O'Rourke uttered a prayer and hurried out of the hut, while John and I went forward gingerly until we grew accustomed to the twilight and understood what was happening. The youths were being initiated into receiving the caleador, the lime stick for the coca habit, into their mouths. As we stood there gazing at the strangeness of the scene, Takakhe emerged from the shadows and hurled a pot at us.

Retreating into the daylight we found O'Rourke standing outside in a state of agitation. He said to us solemnly, 'We must put our whole trust in God to put this enemy to flight . . .' Then, in Latin, as if the liturgical language had more power to exorcise the demon-infested air, he declaimed: '*Nisi Dominus custodierit civitatem, frustra vigilat qui custodit eam*' [Unless the Lord protects the city, the guards watch in vain].

John was staring at him bemused as O'Rourke continued to mutter scandalized utterances. 'Mere children,' he was saying, 'and they are encouraged by the Takakhe to engage in bestial acts of oral concupiscence!'

Suddenly John laughed. 'I thought that at first, Christian,' he said. 'It was quite innocent; it was a coca ceremony!'

As the true situation dawned on him Christian seemed momentarily disappointed. 'You're certain of that?' he said, and he was looking at me for confirmation. 'It makes no difference,' he said abruptly, 'we can make no progress here until we break that wretched addiction; it comes between them and their readiness to accept our God.' And he turned away and strode back towards his tent.

Putting his arm through mine, John asked me to accompany him down to the river where we sometimes went to talk in private. He was telling me that he had found the sites of the Mekroti coca production in the depths of the forest. 'There are about forty acres, far too much for the needs of these people. They're secretive about the details, but I believe they trade coca leaves for their lime powder. The trader comes every three to four months by boat, and sometimes there are nocturnal visits by helicopter which a small circle believes to be a visitation from Iteka, their goddess.'

Peruvian highland coca practice, John explained, went back four thousand years and seemed to connect the oral presence of a creation divinity not unlike our own Eucharistic rite. The Mekroti kept the leaves for their own use in a storage hut; the chewer rolled the leaf into a quid which was prayed over before insertion into the mouth.

'The quid is softened up with saliva,' John was saying as we walked slowly along the trail. 'Then the lama, or *Ishku*, as the the native Andean Peruvians call it, is added on the end of the stick.'

Coca, he told me, was a link between the Mekroti and their goddess; it was a medium for medicine, for pain, fatigue, hunger, cold; not that it was thought to be a cure in itself, but the chewing of the leaf accompanied the ceremonies of diagnosis and cure.

John was worried that O'Rourke would interfere with

their coca practices; he said ruefully, 'If he tries to undermine their belief in its efficacy we'll have a disaster on our hands.'

I wanted to talk with John about O'Rourke. Despite that confession on my first day at Aranuba, and despite his behaviour among the Mekroti, some deep-rooted sense of loyalty kept me in awe of him. I was still trying to reconcile his saintly reputation with his tyrannical manipulations; still attempting to understand how such brutal ruthlessness could coexist with his deep Christian piety, his life of prayer, his devout asceticism and courage.

John was adamant about his own verdict: he was convinced that a dark potential had lurked within Christian all the years he had known him.

We were sitting by the river; John was looking down bleakly at the rushing waters, throwing sticks into the torrent and watching them spin away. 'Christian believes he has visions, messages from God,' he murmured, 'and he believes that he is uniquely in receipt of a revelation not for himself but for all of us . . . If you want an uncharitable verdict, he's a vicious, egotistical fanatic; if you want a charitable one, he's a holy man who has gone stark raving mad. Either way, he's dangerous and I want this mission brought to an end. As soon as I feel better I'm going back down to Aranuba and I want you to help me bring him with us, forcibly if necessary . . .'

I knew that John was right; but still, in the inner recesses of my secret self, somewhere in the dark depths of my soul, an attachment to O'Rourke's vision of God and our human predicament persisted; a yearning to be inflicted with His wounds, and to inflict those wounds on others. It was as if I could not let go of the savage mystery that lurked at the heart of O'Rourke's revelation. Something in me wanted to reject the blandness of John's reasonable, relativistic, social-worker Christianity; my soul still longed for the dark splendour of an uncompromising and exclusive destiny towards *Him*.

156

CHAPTER 18

On the day we built our own House the entire population of the village turned out to advise, gawp, chew coca, and get involved. A few helped energetically as if to lay claim to an interest in the building; others were just after the presents we were dispensing.

John, muted in his enthusiasm, spent much of his time watching with folded arms; as a missionary he would rather have put up a building than make a convert; but the construction of this House was a symbol of the mission's permanence, which he was determined to scotch.

The wild-eyed athletic Chieske led the Mekroti work-parties, selecting materials, shinning up poles, using his brute strength to lift and carry and push; directing operations with shrill shouts and gesticulations; running to and fro, and generally whipping up crises and hysteria with everything he did. I watched with amazement as he ran along the cross-beams fifty feet up, carrying joists and huge bundles of palm leaves on his head, pulling faces and singing and shouting as he went.

Luis was a paragon of patience, solving muddles and misunderstandings with equanimity and diplomacy.

Mabla came along and took a detailed interest in every aspect of the design, addressing all her remarks and gestures to me. I took great pride in showing her the 'property'; I placed my arm gently around her shoulder, and she did nothing to discourage me. It must have been obvious to everybody, including O'Rourke, that I was growing attached to her in a proprietorial kind of way.

The over-all design of our hut was like a garden bower, except that in the place of vegetation and flowers the frame was covered in a weave of strong grasses and palm leaves. The structure, larger than average, was fifty-six feet long and about twenty feet wide, built on a frame of strong sapling poles bent into an arch, the entire 'tunnel' lashed firmly together with lianas and braced with cross-beams. From the outside ours was no different from the other large huts, but inside we made some innovations. Normally it would have been a single chamber; we divided ours into four sections with partitions. The first section served as an entrance hall, common room, kitchen, and a place of storage for provisions, which O'Rourke had been purchasing from our hosts in ever increasing quantities. The next two sections were our dormitory arrangements; Anna had her own room separate from the men with an adjacent sanatorium in which she installed the sick Zapara boy, who was still delirious. The fourth section was our private chapel, which we adorned with holy pictures and statues, including the Sacred Heart and the Holy Mother; a crucifix and candlesticks were placed on a crude altar where the Eucharist was preserved in a simple wooden tabernacle. On the roof O'Rourke had a cross erected, painted bright red.

Sister Anna showed a dramatic improvement in health as the House neared completion. She made the chapel her special preserve, popping in and out to make small improvements. We had lost a lot of essential medical supplies in the stolen baggage, which caused John anxiety; but the holy objects for the chapel had been carried up by O'Rourke in our boat.

On the day we entered our House it rained long and hard, and it was a pleasure to see how the structure withstood the downpour. Anna was radiant. She took possession of the chapel at last, lighting a votive lamp and kneeling before the statue of the Holy Mother. But her consolation was short-lived. The village children soon managed to find, or make, little holes in the wall so they could spy on the chapel's interior. The noise and the disturbance around the spy-holes was so great at sundown that Anna was in tears.

But the high emotions of that day had not come to an end. After supper, which we ate at our new communal table (with readings by Anna from *The Devout Life* of Saint Francis de Sales!), O'Rourke led us through to the chapel for sung Benediction by the light of our precious candles and dedicated the building to the Most Precious Blood of Jesus. Our hut, he announced, was to be called the 'Gesu' in remembrance of Ignatius Loyola's first Jesuit Mother House in Rome.

After the service he took me to one side of the makeshift sacristy and spoke in a low voice; his face looked purple and bruised and his breathing was so laboured that I wondered whether he was heading for a heart attack. At first his great head was bowed; then he raised it to look at me sorrowfully, directly, his lugubrious eyes filled with tears. 'I must talk to you, Nicholas,' he said, his voice hoarse with emotion. 'we must be careful not to ruin ourselves by too close proximity with these people. Their young women are sensual, lax in morals . . . this is why I am so happy to have built this humble dwelling, which gives us a monastic enclosure into which we can retreat . . .'

I guessed that he was referring to my fraternization with Mabla, which had become the talk of the village; I nodded sagely although I was thinking there was no way I was going to spend my days cooped up in that stifling hut.

But he had not done with me; he was whispering something to me now about 'evil spirits' and 'devils' and 'perversions'. I could smell the sweat coming off him; it was a heady stench of fever and lack of hygiene.

I was almost throwing up from his halitosis and body

odour; but I tried to humour him. I said, 'Father, you must calm yourself; you know that Ignatius Loyola, our founder, constantly warned of jumping to conclusions about evil spirits.'

His right eye was cocked at me, a hard, mad eye of paranoia. 'D'you think I don't have every last word of our holy founder's *Discernment of the Spirits* engraved on my heart!' he rasped.

'But Father,' I said softly, 'Ignatius gave little credence to evil spirits.'

'Poppycock!' he growled. 'I'm sick to death of you so-called Christians who would deny the very existence of the Devil! Every page of the Gospel is filled with reports of demons and Christ casting them out! Read Saint Paul to the Ephesians, Father: "Put God's armour on so as to be able to resist the Devil's tactics. For it is not against the human enemies that we have to struggle, but against the Sovereignties and Powers who originate in the darkness of this world, the spiritual army of evil ..." Read Saint Peter: "Be sober and watch, *quia adversarius tuus Diabolus circuit sicut leo rugiens quaerens quem devoret*" [for your adversary the Devil goes about like a roaring lion seeking whom he may devour].'

Every time he launched into Latin now I sensed a note of paranoia.

Putting his face close to mine, clutching me painfully by the wrist, he said conspiratorially: 'I want you to do something for me, Father.' The ambivalence I felt towards him was was unbearable. His strong brogue and his melo-dramatic expression made me want to giggle despite his terrible breath.

'Yes, Father; just tell me what it is!' I replied, my voice shaking and nearly out of control.

'Find out where they keep that lime! That lime they use with their coca leaves. Just do that for me.'

His intention was plain enough, and I nodded my head

acquiescently, making to be off. But he tightened his grip. He hadn't finished with me. 'And keep yourself pure, Father . . . How can the grace of God be visited upon this House and upon this mission if one of its members lacks purity of heart!'

With that he lurched away muttering under his breath in Latin, leaving me to stagger to my hammock doubled up with stifled laughter and in state of rocketing hypermania.

That night, as I lay sleepless, I seemed to hear O'Rourke's voice repeating over and over again: 'Pure, Father . . . purity of heart, Father!'

Lying in the darkness of the early hours, I thought of my vow of chastity, of celibacy, of *purity*. 'Pure, Father . . . purity of heart, Father!'

I saw her face in the darkness, across the span of the years; she was standing as I remembered her, frozen, high up in a rose bower on the sanctuary of the church of the Jesuits, her sweet lips slightly parted, her eyes gazing upwards and glistening in the lights of a hundred candles. Adorable Patricia Murphy.

She was dressed in a long gown of shimmering white and blue, her plaits combed out, her lovely long golden hair spilling over her shoulders. Behind her was a backcloth of clouds and sunbeams. She stood like the statue of the Holy Mother. Then Tom Daley appeared in a white satin suit as if by magic, above and behind her, a sparkling crown in his hands. Slowly he lowered the crown until it rested on her head.

That May time a picture of a new Saint of Holy Mother Church, Saint Maria Gorretti, was enshrined in our classroom, surrounded with flowers and votive lamps. Sister Jude had pointed to the picture of the girl-Saint; she said, 'This is the child who was stabbed because she would not submit to the youth who would take away her purity.'

I could see the girl Maria, her white dress soaked in blood, and it made me feel strange. But what did it mean: Maria Gorretti's *purity*? What was *submit*? The story filled me with a peculiar and pleasurable anxiety.

I shared a desk at the back of the class with Sean McMahon. McMahon with the harelip, who couldn't read or write, had hair like a dusty crow's feathers; his clothes smelled of stale pee. Beneath the desk he was busy with cigarette ends and marbles and bits of string, and his trouser buttons. He was fidgeting with concentration below the desk, eyes glazed, mouth wide open, when Sister Jude swooped: 'Look at this little savage! Look at this wicked sly-boots! What's he doing, in the name of the Holy Mother?' Stony knuckles rained down on my skull as McMahon slid below the level of the desk.

Failing to get a hold on the squirming McMahon, she pulled me instead right out of the desk and smacked my ears. 'This one's the provoker to be sure!' she cried. Twisting a burning ear she led me to the front of the class. Worse than hair-pull, wrist-slap, or being stood in the big square rubbish basket, she pushed me into a desk at the front to sit next to Patricia Murphy. Why were the the boys laughing and clapping and stomping their feet? And especially my friend Tom Daley? Sister Jude looked down on me with gloating eyes, arms folded.

Through scalding tears I stole a look at my companion. I took in her smooth knees, sugar-pink fingernails, glister of golden eyelashes, wispy little curls about her shiny white forehead. She was very still and poised, her neat exercise book before her, so spotless. I was cast down with love for Patricia Murphy. Her breath was like a fresh sweet apple, her hair like blossom after rain. Every time I looked at her, smelled her, brushed against her, I felt a thrill of painful pleasure. What was that painful pleasure?

*

162

The Sisters lived behind a high wall down Monkham's Lane, close to the edge of Epping Forest and the dark dell called Nightingale Wood.

That afternoon McMahon and I came up stealthily behind Patricia Murphy in the lane. There she was, on her way back to school after a taking a message to the convent: goody footsteps in the fallen blossom, milky-white neck bowed between stiff straight plaits thick and gleaming; bum like a neat apple wibble-wobbling under her tight gymslip. Was it Satan who whispered the suggestion in my ear?

I said to McMahon: 'Pull her knickers down and put your finger up the slit between her legs.'

McMahon came up behind her without a word; taking her by both arms he steered her into the wood by her elbows. Thinking it was a game she squealed with laughter; but when he dragged her through the bushes she pulled back, her eyes wild.

I was standing to one side, watching from a hidden place, as McMahon wrestled her to the ground and pressed a grubby knee between her legs. Patricia Murphy was looking up at him as if she could make him stop with nothing but her appealing eyes. But her expression turned to horror as she seemed to read in his face a look of open-mouthed emptiness.

I was peering from my hidden place, enthralled at the sight of McMahon trying to push his finger up between her legs. Then my heart leapt. There where his finger was lodged, in the pursed little lips of her slit, oozed a trickle of bright blood spilling slowly down her thighs and over those white knickers. Patricia Murphy was screaming up to the trees; she was rolling in the damp leaves and the soil, her knees now drawn up to her stomach, yelling at the sky.

McMahon was already heading for Monkham's Lane, but I continued to watch from my hidden place, my heart filling with such peculiar, unfamiliar feelings, shocked by the power of my secret thought to invade the world. I wanted to come out from my hiding place; I wanted to to reach out for her golden hair; but I crouched out of sight, breathless and shaking. Then she leapt up; she was running, her legs streaked with blood, away from Nightingale Wood and along the lane towards school.

McMahon entered the classroom, mouth open, eyes vacant, and Sister Jude came out from behind the door.

'Filthy dirty little savage!' she cried.

Grabbing him by the hair she drove him with a flurry of punches and slaps to the square rubbish basket. The class was paralysed, expectant. Then our eyes were drawn to the corridor where bearing down, all sails flying, came the tall black figure of Mother Martha. As she entered the room, we stood. In the pause we could hear the sound of traffic far away on the high road.

She contemplated McMahon for a few moments, fingering her black and silver crucifix. I had never seen her face so sad, so grave. Turning to the picture of Maria Gorretti on the wall, she made the sign of the cross and spoke in her special praying voice: 'Sweet Saint Maria Gorretti,' she intoned, 'thou who offered the gift of thy life in defending thy chastity, may thy prayers keep us faithful to God's *purity*. Amen.'

Then she turned to McMahon and said in a quite different voice, an Irish breathy voice with shrill high notes and strange sounding *t*'s, 'Here is a boy,' she cried, 'who has made his First Communion and his Confirmation and yet has already besmirched his baptismal garment. Pity the mother that gave birth to such a dirty beast. Here is a boy who has befouled the body of a sweet and innocent girl who was this very year the Queen of the May. The body as I have so often told you is mere husk, but it is the sanctuary of your immortal soul and the temple of the Holy Ghost; thus the act of this filthy fellow McMahon is in truth an act of *sacrilege*!'

With this she brought out a cane from the folds of her skirts, grabbed him by the hair, and began whipping him rhythmically across the backside and the tops of his legs, chanting as she did so: 'Filthy! Dirty! Little! *Beast!* Filthy! Dirty! Little! *Beast!*'

Now she had his head in a vice under her elbow and McMahon was looking back at the class, his face crimson, his eyes swollen and uncomprehending; he was looking straight at *me*, the cause of his pain and shame and misery.

When the beating ended Sean McMahon was taken away. And for the rest of the day the nuns spoke in hushed voices.

Dawdling home after school I paused at the gate of the Jesuit church; the building looked tranquil in the peace of the late afternoon. I entered its cool, incense-laden interior. In seclusion, unseen and unheard, I knelt before the statue of the Holy Mother. She looked down on me in her unhappiness. I prayed up to her, I *begged* her, in a harsh whisper, that I should not be found out.

That night I dreamed about Patricia Murphy. In the speckled darkness I saw her approaching, emerging from the gloom, naked, pale, and shadowy; she was looking for me in the forest.

Now I was peering directly into her face; I was lying on my back, shaking and trembling in the leaves. She lay on top of me and pressed me down into the soil. I could see nothing; I was trembling like the wing of a trapped bird, and I felt the rhythmic pressure of her hips, thrilling me through and through till my bowels hardened.

I woke up still straining against her soft weight and with a thrill of unfamiliar pleasure, I throbbed with gorgeous relief.

For an age I lay breathless and awake, exhausted with dark excitement. In the silence and loneliness of the night I began to feel afraid. Here was a sin more grievous, more

165

wicked, more pleasurable than anything I had imagined possible.

Why was this secret sin so pleasurable? So wicked? Was it because I had no words to describe it? Was it because God, who knew my innermost secret thoughts, had alone seen it and recorded it in the book of my life?

CHAPTER 19

What a strange and transforming courtship was my approach to Mabla! And it seemed to keep pace with our relations with the Mekroti community as whole. We had settled down, built our House, established friendships, learned a little of the language, defined our relationship as missionaries. Now we began to emerge as individuals.

At first we had seen them as children; then, as we struggled to learn their language and customs, we had seen ourselves as children. Yet the latter parallel had always been false. The relationship between us had been one of power over the powerless. At first this had not worried me.

I had not succeeded in persuading Mabla to come down to the river, although at the outset I sat there for several evenings at an appointed time conveyed through messages via Luis. So I continued visiting her hut, and eventually contrived for a degree of greater intimacy to move right inside. Yet what a paradox this lesson in intimacy. When she offered me beer, I could not drink it, suspecting that it was made with the saliva of the Mekroti women. Then there was the intimacy of family contact. Mabla's hut was often filled with people; a screaming baby; Bedla and a friend, quarrelling at the tops of their voices; her mother and her cronies lounging by the fire. And poor Luis, my translation machine, hating every minute of it.

One calm evening, as her mother and her son slept, we were left alone free of the prying eyes of neighbours, Mabla and I and Luis sitting in her doorway. She looked so beautiful, her large dark eyes glistening in the light of a full moon. She had told me that she did not like the way

I 'looked' at her; she said this shyly, covering her face with one hand. Was that a gesture, I wondered, of flirtatiousness, of skittish provocation? I was thinking about my struggle to master lewd fantasies; about the predatory way I sometimes 'looked' at women; quite different from 'seeing' them. I was thinking too of the priestly imperative to maintain what we called, in our early celibate formation, 'custody of the eyes'. *Control* of the intentions. Was she referring to the same thing? Or was I projecting my own thoughts on to hers?

I said, 'Are men allowed to *look* at women, Mabla? And are women allowed to *look* at men?'

'Men mustn't look at married women, they mustn't look strongly, *stare*,' she replied through Luis. 'And nor should married women stare at men.'

'But why not? Is it because it is a bad thing to do, Mabla?' I was thinking *conscience*, I was thinking *innermost secret thoughts*! I was thinking secret intentions known only to me and my God.

'If a man stares at me,' she said, 'the other men will see it and think that he wants to steal me, to own me. When he knows that he has been seen by the others he will feel shame. After manhood it is forbidden to look at a married woman like that, even if her husband is dead; the other men will see it and come and sting him with nettles.'

What was it that I wanted of Mabla? My interest in her as a sublimated fantasy of untouchable beauty, a literary fantasy of the female 'noble savage', was developing into a tumescent, predatory infatuation: I had begun to see her, in my urge for a sexual adventure, as an erotic stopgap for my frustrated physical longing for Jill. And as I became more sexually interested in her I began to realize how difficult it would be to have an 'affair', a 'secret sexual liaison', with any member of the tribe, let alone the beautiful widowed daughter-in-law of Anonha. I suspected that all I should ever achieve was a frustrated non-sexual gesture of human contact. Holding hands!

As our intimacy developed, I allowed her to make the

pace; and she continued, as she had started, with wholly *outward* talk: how to garden, how to cook, how to bring up children, how to make clothes; how to deal with men; how to cope with her mother, her kinsmen and friends; how to manage a sick husband; how to live as a widow; how to interpret the weather, how to understand the plants and insects and birds and animals of the forest. This was how I was getting to know her. But where was the inner meaning? What did this tell me of her inner motivations, her conscience, her moral sensibilities, her self-deceptions, her innermost secret thoughts? Her soul?

It was clear from the outset that she had never heard of such things.

She was curious about my questions, but she had never heard stories of such inner landscapes about herself, nor about others; her culture had no such ideas, no such images or metaphors. Yet I sensed that I was getting closer to her. As our meetings continued, I was equally amazed at the skill with which she grasped my own interior intimations and sketched out suggestions and answers that began to resemble a comparable interiority.

Had I penetrated the landscape of Mabla's soul? Or had I merely distorted what Luis was telling me to create confirmation of such a spiritual territory through confusions of understanding? Was I guilty of the same brutal clumsiness as O'Rourke?

At times I felt that our conversations put me in the role of confessor; the priest in his dark box, the *camera obscura*, probing, suggesting, leading the penitent on, until those wordless intimations were laid bare. But how much had I really understood? How much of Mabla's 'confession' was merely a consequence of letting in the light on my own distorted retina? Could I ever escape my own personality, my own *subject*, my behaviour, my language, the blind-spot focus of my own cultural prejudice? Could I be anything other than a confessor? And could I fully understand the distortions that arose through Luis as I attempted to converse with Mabla in private?

Could we, it struck me, be anything but superior towards the Mekroti? Examining what they did and thought, and knew? Becoming the final arbiter of their reality? And were we not structuring even our own identity in their eyes by our actions? Where, and how, we had built our House. What rules we established about their entry. How we acquired our food. How long we worked. What we kept secret from them. Why we spent more time with one member of the village rather than another.

My fascination with the Mekroti's interior lives increased as I penetrated more deeply into Mabla's soul. Yet I suspected that the more I probed, the more I created a selfhood in the image of my own likeness.

CHAPTER 20

O'Rourke was hard at work in the common room on a simple Mekroti Catechism of Christian Doctrine. With the House now built, he had been wrestling with the Mekroti language to form words and metaphors to express our Western and Christian notions of free will, conscience, sin, God, heaven and hell, guilt and deserving. And the more he toiled the more he feared that he would be at a loss to bridge the gap between their understanding of the world and the truths of salvation he had brought them.

That morning he was sitting at our table with Luis, attempting to teach Chieske and Mabla's son Bedla. Chieske had taken to Christianity with a lunatic enthusiasm; he accepted anything and everything with impatient alacrity. 'Where is God?' catechized O'Rourke. 'Wherever you say!' shouted Chieske promptly.

Bedla, the beautiful boy whose name I had discovered meant 'Evening', had an astonishing ability to parrot everything he was taught. He watched O'Rourke and Anna carefully, and mimicked whole prayers in English and bits of Latin by heart.

As I brewed a pot of tea from our precious store of tea bags I witnessed a typical and instructive difficulty. Such was the capricious nature of the Mekroti langauge, the words *father* and *son*, *mother* and *daughter*, always required a possessive pronoun. Thus they could not say simply 'father' as a metaphor of the masculine God of all Creation; they had to say '*my* father', '*your* Father', and so on, for they could not grasp the concept of such a relationship divorced from the reality of living kinship. Moreover, it was a great insult to speak of the father or mother of those who had been bereaved of a parent. Hence it was inconceivable that the bereaved should utter the first words of the prayer 'Our Father'. But O'Rourke was pressing on, insisting that the solution was for them to adopt the following formula: 'In the name of *their* Father, and of *his* son, and of the love that exists between the two.' Which was clearly nonsense to them, but which they parroted with alacrity.

By the time I had finished breakfast a highly emotional unscheduled meeting was taking shape. Anonha and several village elders now joined the table, with O'Rourke presiding and Anna and Luis in attendance. John also slipped into the room and stood in the background; he had taken now to supervising everything that O'Rourke did and said, observing without intervention or interruption.

O'Rourke was attempting to translate our notion of the soul into a single Mekroti term. When he tried to put across the idea of their souls as 'indivisible', they shrugged; the idea of an indivisible person was as foreign to them as the idea of an indivisible body. They had a word which meant 'presence', but when O'Rourke attempted to apply it to our Western idea of 'soul' they pointed out that every part of the body, the different limbs and organs, had separate presences; so had the forest, and an individual tree, a branch, a leaf, and a flower.

He fared little better when he tried to explore the idea of personal survival after death. They had told him that the 'ghosts' of dead children, a word that also meant 'shadows', were said to inhabit the abandoned villages; that they could be heard at night chasing birds in the deserted plantations and gardens. The children did not have the strength to travel like more robust 'ghosts' to their proper place in the west. Moreover, the dead did not form one single society; those who had died as result of violence, or from suicide, formed separate bands. As Anonha proceeded to explain their myths of the afterlife it became apparent that

172

they could not conceive of such a 'life' without physical bodies.

Anonha had been telling stories about the special hazards that attend 'ghosts' beyond the grave, and had said that there was a special monster that sucked the brains out of the dead.

O'Rourke, who had been getting impatient, suddenly interrupted. 'How do you know that?'

'This does happen, Rook,' said Anonha gently.

'All the work of the Devil!' he murmured, and I could hear John giving a quiet whistle.

Anonha went on to explain that in the afterlife there was hunting and fishing and feasting, and coca chewing, and indeed sexual intercourse. The only difference was that the 'ghosts' of the dead spent much of their time complaining.

With this O'Rourke pounded the table with his fist. 'God of truth,' he muttered. 'You'll be doing more than complaining in the real afterlife!' Then he called up to the rafters in Latin: '*Domine! Illuminare his qui in tenebris et in umbra sendent!* [O Lord, enlighten these who sit in darkness and in the shadows].'

As the tortuous palaver unfolded O'Rourke was becoming more unhappy and impatient: now he would interrupt their discourse to launch into a baffling description of the mystery of the Trinity; then he would grow impatient when they failed to answer his close questions about their own mysteries.

After his reaction to their creation fable it had proved difficult to persuade them to talk of their beliefs; yet no sooner had they opened their mouths than O'Rourke heckled them, as if wishing their minds already wiped clean to receive the truths of his doctrines.

After an hour or so of exchanges in an atmosphere of mounting tension, O'Rourke once again raised the subject of hell.

With Anonha and the elders leaning forward intently, he

embarked on this harangue with the usual combination of sign language, mime, charades, and odds and ends of Mekroti:

'After this life each of you, whatever you now believe or desire, will go to one of two places for ever. You will either go to the place we call heaven, or the place we call hell. Heaven is a place abounding in good things and free from all pain and want. Hell is a great fire where people are burned for ever. You must decide now which of these two places you prefer to go to after death.'

Even as he was expressing all this, his voice stern, his great forehead corrugated with deep lines, John was looking at me, signalling that we should bring the meeting to an end. But before he could make his move, Anonha stood up and made an assuaging little speech, to the effect that he and the elders naturally wanted to avoid burning in a fire, but they preferred Rook to stop talking about it. One by one the elders chimed in, saying that they wished to see taken away the various rocks, trees, thickets, and other obstacles that were in the way of their understanding. But they would like to change the subject.

This barely pacified O'Rourke, who had tears of frustration in his eyes.

Turning to me, he said: 'Nicholas, make no mistake. We think of them as children; but look at them! They're obstinate old men deeply attached their evil customs.'

Then the old man, who had angered O'Rourke at the demonstration of the globe (whom O'Rourke called 'Michael'), stood up to say his piece. He said that as far as he was concerned he could see nothing particularly bad about burning after death.

I had an inkling that he had said it to provoke; and he achieved the desired effect.

As the meaning was translated to him, O'Rourke erupted. Bellowing at the old man, he accused him of playing games and wasting his time. He was still ranting as the elders made their hasty departure.

Sitting down at the table next to O'Rourke, John looked at him earnestly and put a hand on his arm. He said, 'Father, the Mekroti will never accept the idea of being separated from their ancestors after death; to persuade them otherwise would destroy their precarious community.'

John's approach was both tender and firm, and I was moved by the sense of family loyalty that can exist between us Jesuits however distant our ideas and goals. But as his meaning became plain O'Rourke snatched away his arm. Thrusting his face straight into John's, he exploded, 'Yes, I've heard of this new diabolical *heresy* of our age, which preaches that one religion is as good as another. But that was not *Christ's* way. And let there be no doubt that Christ did not scruple to employ fear to encourage the Faith among people who were smug and settled in their ways!' Then turning to Anna, he said in his rapid nasal voice: 'I wonder, Sister, would you ever help me depict a more realistic and horrifying picture of hell for these people?'

Anna had been painting holy subjects during her convalescence and had evidently impressed O'Rourke with her talent.

He went over to our store of books and snatched up the collection of illustrations he used for instruction. Pulling out an illustration of hell, he said, 'Our picture is too vague for teaching the truths of the punishments of the damned. The devils are so mingled with the men that nothing can be identified.'

Holding it up to the light, his hand shaking with anger, he went on: 'If you depict for us, Sister, three, four, or five devils tormenting one soul with different kinds of tortures, one applying to it the torch, another holding it bound with chains, it would have a salutory effect, especially if everything were very distinct, and if rage and sadness appeared plainly in the face of the lost soul – and if we could associate these tortures with their coca chewing all the better!'

Almost as soon as he had said this he reached for a chair.

He seemed to crumple physically, then he burst into tears, his huge torso wracked with sobs, the tears coursing down his ravaged cheeks.

At length he said with a groan: 'Forgive me, my dears.' Then he thumped his breast with a force sufficent to crack a few ribs and said over and over again: *'Mea culpa! Mea culpa!'*

John put his arm around his shoulder and made some soothing remarks while Sister Anna bustled around to prepare a pot of tea.

When he had calmed down, he said to us quietly, his eyes raised to the roof, in that special Celtic tone of voice he reserved for what I was beginning to identify as his more mawkish blarney: 'You know, my dears, among the jewels with which the labourer in a mission should shine, control of anger must hold the first rank, and never will this soil yield fruit except through mildness of temper. I know that all of you strive in this virtue. I alone am feeble in it, to my great disadvantage.'

It was at this moment that John, who I knew had been seeking an opportunity to broach the closure of the mission, seized his opportunity.

Sitting down with him, his hand once again placed on O'Rourke's arm, he said, 'Listen, Christian, I've been meaning to talk to you ... I know how much you've worked and prayed for this mission. But there have been too many set-backs: the loss of the boats and supplies, the sick Zapara boy in there, who's had a relapse and who could put these people in danger ... We're none of us in good health. I want to put it to you that we should bring the mission to an end and attempt to go back down before the rains begin and before our own essential supplies run out ...'

Sister Anna had put a mug of tea at his elbow and John was leaning forward, warming to his theme, when O'Rourke rose from the table shaking with wrath. Knocking the mug to the floor, he shouted, 'Over my dead body! And over yours too! . . . Get behind me, Satan!' And he stormed out of the common room on his way to the chapel.

That night, lying sleepless in my hammock, I heard the sound of a strange creature, roaring and trumpeting in the darkness; and I felt a terrible premonition of death. The early days of the mission had filled me with a sense of well-being and new hope; the land of the Mekroti had seemed hospitable and dreamlike; now, in the depths of that night I had intimations of disaster and despair.

I tried to compose my soul; I tried to pray to God, out of my helplessness and fear, in the words of the Psalm: *I rise before dawn and cry for help, I hope in your word. My eyes watch through the night to ponder your promise. In your love hear my voice, O Lord.*

In those lonely hours before dawn I could find no consolation, no relief and no hope. God was absent. After the animal fell silent, the silence of the forest, the silence of all creation, and of Heaven itself, pressed on my eardrums like the numbing silence of the tomb.

CHAPTER 21

On the day following O'Rourke's outburst the atmosphere in the mission House was more tense than at any time since our arrival. O'Rourke and Anna had formed an alliance; refusing to acknowledge or to talk to John; treating me curtly, as if I had yet to prove my good standing and loyalty.

Anna spent much of her time nursing the Zapara boy, who was dangerously ill again and still more or less in quarantine; but for two hours or so in the middle of the morning she hurried about the village. She would poke her head into each hut in turn, making funny faces at the children who came out and flocked around her begging for sweets.

Anna claimed that screaming infants were calmed when she made the sign of the cross over them; encouraged by O'Rourke, she had taken to teaching the children the first line of the 'Hail Mary' in English.

O'Rourke said an outdoor Mass for the children, then Anna led them in a procession carrying a statue of the Holy Mother on a litter of saplings. In the afternoon O'Rourke held 'catechism' class for the children while Anna taught them to make signs of the cross. In the afternoon I saw Bedla and his friends walking in a troop to greet O'Rourke where he was pacing up and down in the open air saying his Office. Pausing in his devotions O'Rourke distributed Miraculous Medals of the Immaculate Conception and rosaries, and scapulas which they placed in festoons about their necks.

O'Rourke was capricious about the Mekroti children, who were generally indulged by their parents. When an unruly child threatened to disrupt his discourse, he would rail at the mothers for failing to discipline their young. But when he had succeeded in teaching the children a prayer, or had seen them on their knees singing '*Ave*' and looking the picture of innocence, he beamed down on them and shook his head fondly. After one children's service he was so softened that he turned to me, having ignored me for a whole day. When you consider, Father,' he said, 'their parents plunged in concupiscence, coca addiction, culpable ignorance, and smugness . . . it explains why God has rejected them until now. Little wonder Our Lord selected them to be the last people on Earth to be evangelized. But as for these children, the Lord holds out His arms to them and draws them to Himself. What a consolation it is, to hear this place echoing with the name of Jesus, where the name of Satan has been adored and recognized as God throughout so many ages.'

At supper, he said: 'Imagine, Nicholas, the flocks of guardian angels of these abandoned people continually striving and labouring to save us from danger and making this opportunity for the salvation of their charges more fruitful.'

I noticed that while he had taken measures to pile up foods stocks in our missionary storeroom by trading our trinkets, he ate little more than bread and water himself.

That night I heard him praying until the small hours in the chapel; then, just before dawn, I recognized the hideous swish of a rod, and the haunting sound from my early Jesuit years of a discipline striking bare flesh.

His joyless religiosity was encroaching on everything he said and did, even in his relationship with Anna. When she had talked that evening of the joy she experienced working with the children, he said, 'Sister Anna, have you never heard of the text *fortis ut mors delectio* – love as strong as death?'

She looked at him mystified. 'Detachment, Sister, detachment! The love of God should be as strong as death in its power to detach us from creatures and from ourselves. There may be sometimes a little self-love and regard for ourselves if we merely look at the selfish satisfaction of putting souls into heaven.'

She fell silent, unhappy and rebuked, while he continued to stare us down with stern reproof. His eyes were hard. He had developed deep-set lines of anger and disappointment about his mouth and cheeks. His face was a leathery mask.

And I found myself thinking for the first time: He is going to kill us all!

CHAPTER 22

The mission was now split in two. John and I met frequently, usually down by the river, to make practical plans for our departure back to Aranuba. In the meantime O'Rourke's mind dwelt increasingly on dark and painful things; incapable of enjoying a single untrammelled moment of happiness. No sooner had he overcome one obstacle than he was inviting new challenges and sufferings. Above all, he was obsessed with the Mekroti coca practice, which he termed 'the idolatry'.

He continually pressed the elders on the significance of coca chewing; he wanted to know how they employed it in the interpretation of dreams, their healing rites, the choice of marriage partners, gardening, hunting, and fishing, and as an aid to predicting future events. He saw their coca chewing as the single most important stumbling block to their acceptance of Christianity; he said: 'The coca leaf does everything: it is their God.'

And he saw the shaman Takakhe as his principal enemy.

From his first day in the village John had tried to make friends with Takakhe, attempting to understand and record his practices. John said that he believed his lopsided face was the result of a condition known as Bell's palsy (which had no appeal for O'Rourke, who preferred to believe the disfigurement was diabolical).

Takakhe was in his early forties. He was shy, a misfit, and we discovered that he had been married twice unsuccessfully. He spent much of his time hanging around out of sight with the young boys who were preparing to be coca initiates. In gesture and posture he appeared a typical homosexual according to our Western stereotype; there was something delicate and ceremonious about the way he moved. I noticed that when he lifted his coca stick he used his third and fourth finger in a strangely mannered fashion.

His half-collapsed face suggested that he was at war with himself, as if a youth lived on trapped in the body of an ageing bachelor. John learnt through his careful enquiries around the village that Takakhe was a social oddity, that his father was unknown and that his mother was an outcast given to beating him. His two marriages had failed, John was told, because they were childless. And he now had a penchant for small boys; there was a suspicion, but no definite evidence, that he indulged in paedophilia. Takakhe was to all intents and purposes the village priest.

He was also the village diagnostician and healer, the doctor, a function which earned him gifts of coca and lime.

His practice was attended by some harmless trickery that duped nobody. We had seen him playing with fire and performing optical tricks. I saw him make a woman vomit up a piece of stone as large as my fist after taking a 'medicine' of rainwater. I saw sand coming out of the ear of another patient after Takakhe had shaken her head.

But whenever we were about to persuade him to teach us something of his healing arts O'Rourke would appear, especially when there was an audience of elders.

Takakhe was not accustomed to being hectored, and it was clear from his irked expression that he would have loved to shut O'Rourke's mouth for him. On one occasion Takakhe was attempting to treat a woman with stomach-ache when O'Rourke came up and started to badger him. Takakhe stepped aside from the patient and indicated with mime: 'All right, *you* know everything. *You* cure the patient.'

I thought this very funny and I burst out laughing, but O'Rourke took him at his word. Turning to Anna, he started to lecture her on the importance of using every opportunity to impress the Mekroti with the superiority of our medical knowledge. He said, 'This lady probably has indigestion, can't you give her something?' His diagnosis proved correct. After Anna had given the woman an antacid mixture (which relieved her symptoms within minutes), O'Rourke harangued the onlookers about the emptiness of Takakhe's powers.

I looked on as John tried to dissuade O'Rourke from this kind of intervention; John was concerned that Takakhe would blame us for the decline of his powers, which might prove ominous when our own feeble antidotes failed to deal with serious illness. But O'Rourke was determined to have a showdown between himself and the little shaman.

Things came to a head when Chieske came rushing into our common room to announce that Takakhe was going to perform a demonstration of his mysteries before the village. O'Rourke leapt up, muttering that this was would be an opportunity to expose the little deceiver.

We went out of our hut to find an excited crowd. Takakhe had erected a hutch or tent made of thatch; he was announcing that he was going to move the tent by magic. 'I'm going to lie down flat on the floor of my tent,' he was saying, 'and I'll stretch my arms and legs outside and you'll see it shake violently without me touching it.'

To my amazement O'Rourke signified through Luis that he would give a present to each member of the village if Takakhe achieved his boast. When this promise had been understood, the villagers began to dance around laughing and yelling. But before Takakhe got his show underway O'Rourke confronted him and embarked on a complicated harangue with the help of Luis, the gist of which was this: 'Be careful, Takakhe, because if you are the one moving the tent I shall raise it in the middle of your demonstration and show that you're an impostor. But if it is Satan, the unseen enemy of Papa-Belong-All and the human race, I shall make him confess that he is deceiving the Mekroti. When he sees himself ridiculed he will fly into a rage and kill you; he will also beat the people in the village.'

Takahe listened to this attentively, and even while O'Rourke was attempting to express himself I could see that the little shaman was suddenly afraid that he was taking on more dangerous powers than his own. I was unsure whether Takakhe understood the entire speech, but he had gathered that O'Rourke was predicting his violent death if the show succeeded.

Playing for time he changed tack. 'Will you give the people the same presents,' he said, 'if I perform another piece of magic? I can put a stick into your hand and make it disappear.'

'Yes,' said O'Rourke, when he had understood the proposition. 'I accept. But I am very clever, Takakhe, and I will see how you perform the trick and expose you. But if it is Satan I will expose him too and he will give you a good thrashing.'

The pathetic little fellow once again understood enough of O'Rourke's promise to realize that if he succeeded in his boast he would get hurt, and if he failed he would incur the anger of the villagers who would be deprived of the presents. Trapped between the alternatives he shrugged his shoulders and said that he would postpone the demonstration until later.

But O'Rourke would not let it go. Turning to the audience he said: 'See how he deludes you. Make him perform his powers, come on. I'm longing for you to see how he tricks you.'

With this Takakhe announced that he was busy and had to go off on a pressing engagement.

'I'll be ready for you at any time you care to name,' indicated O'Rourke, 'and there will be plenty of witnesses.'

Later Takakhe came around to the Gesu and tried to persuade O'Rourke not to make a public contest of their rival powers. O'Rourke was exultant; but I gathered through Luis that Takakhe had now been put in an invidious position, for the village shaman relied for his coca and lama supply, and his very sustenance, on the credence of the people. To lose face was to lose his precarious livelihood.

While Takakhe was talking at the door of the Gesu several villagers came up and O'Rourke appealed to them. 'Look who's here,' he called out. 'Aren't you going to keep him to his bet?'

Poor Takakhe pulled on the sleeve of O'Rourke's Jesuit gown (which he had taken to wearing at all times now), begging him in a whisper to drop the subject.

Before dismissing him, O'Rourke put both hands on Takakhe's shoulders and looked him directly in the face.

'Do not consult with the Father of Lies,' he said in English, as if by some charism of the Holy Spirit he could convey his meaning without translation. 'Satan will tell you that he is the spirit that makes the light, but it is Papa-Belong-All that makes the light by having created the sun. The spirit will entice you to do much harm to others and he will in the end kill you and drag you into the flames.'

All of which which was so much gobbledegook to the unfortunate man.

I walked a little way with Takakhe across the compound as if to express some fellow feeling; but he stopped and looked accusingly at me, turning away as if I were tainted with O'Rourke's antagonism. As I continued on by myself towards the trail, I felt ashamed.

CHAPTER 23

One evening Luis and I were alone again with Mabla. The ever amenable Luis had begun to amaze me with his ability to negotiate an intimate communication between the three of us, and I was wondering whether I was on the brink of some kind of breakthrough.

'I want to ask you something, Mabla,' I was saying. 'Let me try to explain by telling you something else. John and I sometimes tell each other things – secrets. He has to keep quiet and he listens as I tell him a story that I have had in my head, a story that I have never told another human being. Sometimes it is a story that happened; sometimes it is a story I made up to enjoy by myself. My story becomes his story, just for the two of us. That is the meaning of telling a secret. Do you understand? I sometimes have an image, a story, a daydream, just in my head, not a story that happened. It's about a woman. In that story I have stared at a woman in a way that would bring me shame, were others to see me, and then gone on to do things to her . . . Do you understand? Is it all right if we talk about this?'

Mabla laughed as my meaning gradually dawned. She seemed excited at the idea of playing at telling secret thoughts. She seemed eager to please.

'Do you ever see a story in your head about a man who looks strongly at you as you say?'

She laughed again, putting her hand up to her face.

Then to my astonishment she began to cotton on to what I wanted.

'Is this just a story for you?'

'Yes, just for me.'

'I see it like this,' she said. 'In my story there is just me and a boy that I knew. We are young, maybe twelve years of age. And we are together.'

'What do you see first in your story,' I asked her, 'is it his face, or a tree, or the river, or the garden?'

I was breathless with excitement.

'It's on the edge of the forest; not far from the huts . . . We are playing there among the flowers and the grass. We're playing at collecting sticks for the fire.'

'Is it morning or night?'

'Afternoon.'

'And are there others there too, or is it just you?'

'There are some boys there, and we're all fetching firewood; and he takes me off a little way. Just the two off us to hide in the long grass.'

'Who goes first, is it you or the boy?'

'He pushes me; he takes me.'

'Is he looking strongly at you? Is he staring?'

'Yes.'

She laughed as she admitted it. I was laughing too.

'And what do you feel when he stares at you?'

'I am thinking, "He wants to ask me to do what I've heard my mother and father do at night."'

'And what happens next?'

'I hide my eyes and I smile at him.'

'What happens then?'

'He asks me to look at his penis.'

'Are you happy that he asks that?'

'Yes, I'm happy.'

'What happens next? Does he remove your clothes? Is he forceful?'

'Yes, he's forceful, he lies on top of me, and he comes into me just a short way; it is the first time . . .'

'When do you have this story, this daydream?'

She covered her face again and started to laugh.

All this had been translated to and fro by Luis with extraordinary finesse.

187

'What is she thinking?' I asked him. 'Is she upset at your being here?'

Luis, inscrutable as to his own feelings, as ever, was looking at her. 'She is happy talking to you,' he said. 'She is shy and excited. I don't think she thinks about me. She has pleasure just with you, talking with you. She wants to *please* you.'

I broke off my conversation with her and just held out my hands, which she took in hers. I was thinking how *feminine* she was; not just beautiful and youthful; not just her figure. She was *so* feminine. But what did that mean? Was it a betrayal of her erotic desire for me? Or was it my projection on to her of my erotic desire for *her*? She reminded me of Jill's femininity, although not as provocative as I first remembered her. But where had I got that idea 'provocative'? Wasn't it my own projection of an imagined intention, an imagined secret thought?

Mabla, I thought, would have been outstandingly feminine in any culture, in any part of the world. She was especially feminine even among the Mekroti.

What qualities, I wondered, make a woman femininely beautiful? Was it what she did with her hands? Those small expressive gestures rarely used by men? Her subtle facial expressions? The softness of her voice? The gentleness in her eyes? The smoothness of her skin? What were those secrets of Mabla's feminine eroticism? Were they an objective fact in the world? Or were they in my mind alone – a token of my rampantly obsessive sexist eroticism? Or were they in hers?

I wanted to sleep with Mabla, I wanted to make love to Mabla; I had to *have* her. She seemed to me completely ripe and receptive now. Would she come with me if I looked at her strongly, if I asked her to walk a little way into the long grass at the border of the forest?

As if awaking from a dream, I was shaken by the enormity of what I was doing.

Holding hands with her in that primitive hut, lost in the remote high forest, the Selva Alta, the Eyebrow of the Jungle, with its mists and strange echoes, I saw the image of another deed, another self, in another place, in the dark recessess of my childhood memory. I was looking at the powerful male wrists extended towards her. I saw myself – the powerful Western man with his accomplice, manipulating a woman-child. I saw myself now, with my wealth, my technology, my white Reebok trainers, my denim trousers, my Rolex watch, my prismatic-lensed spectacles, my ability to come and go, my two thousand years (plus fifty) of mental dualism. I saw myself, the self-serving, intrusive, disrupting controller; the soul-man, the video-game button pusher, the space invader, the virtual-reality manipulator, inside the dark box of my mind.

What did I think I was? What did I think I was doing? Posing all these questions, assessing all the answers; concealing myself in my *camera obscura*, while disarming and dominating, stealing the soul of the other? Had I cared whether Mabla had been afraid of being used and manipulated and harmed by me? Had I made known the true extent of my sexual interest in her? Had I taken my private, inward interpretation of her *femininity* as a signal of her interest in *me*?

And here I was, sowing the seeds of desires and thoughts that this woman had never imagined. What did I know, what did I care, for the effects, both powerful and subtle, on this unsophisticated woman! What did I know of the death-dealing contagion of the mind, of the soul, which O'Rourke and I had brought into the land of the Mekroti, and to which Mabla, in her poverty, in her awe and admiration, and envy, and perhaps in her genuine trust and affection, might have no resistance.

I let go her hands; I said farewell to her, and immediately left the hut with Luis at my side.

*

That night I lay awake, and afraid, on my hammock in the darkness; I could hear O'Rourke in the chapel, fidgeting and sighing and muttering his private prayers, his unmediated orisons, funnelled straight up to our God on high. I sensed John, restless and anxious, tossing and turning in the small hours, and Anna praying her rosary to herself as she watched over the delirious Zapara boy, who had succumbed to a second bout of the virus.

Why was I afraid? Why was I so afraid of death that night, unresting death, the dread of dying, and of being dead?

I was pondering, there in the darkness, the mystery of the billions of human dead. Were the dead anywhere, were they any *thing*, in the world before the moment of their resurrection? As a Christian I believed that this soul, this self, from the moment of death, would continue its existence in isolation from the rest of creation. Incommunicado, solitary! And yet not entirely forsaken. For in that disembodied, timeless moment, I would still be grounded in Him – He who is closer to me than my innermost secret thoughts. Dying in God's love, repenting my sins I would not be separated from Him. I would see Him face to face! But, should I die turning away from Him, saying *no* to Him like a clenched fist, my estrangement would make the darkness of death all the more appalling, and my remorseful self-possession in death, that weeping and gnashing of teeth in the outer darkness, that terrible knowledge that I might have done things differently, better – all the more terrible.

Did I believe all that? Did I *really* believe all that? Lying there that night in the high forest of Peru, I believed only in death's finality, and in consequence I had no language to shape the fear of my annihilation. I was thinking of those death-verses of Larkin's: the reality of death, not merely its possibility, but its numb, shattering, final truth: '. . . nothing more terrible, nothing more true', '. . . a special way of being afraid', '. . . the sure extinction that we travel to and shall be lost in always'.

What was wrong with me?

190

Why was I being tempted this night, after my strange conversation with Mabla, after the long journey with O'Rourke to the Mekroti, after the long, long journey of my life, to accept at last the real truth of my death? Why was I, in that remote forest fastness, ready at last to turn from my longings for infinity, that straining in every nerve to believe in the boundlessness of an infinite bodiless existence, for better or for worse, in everlasting happiness, or everlasting misery!

In the chill early hours of morning, looking back over my life and recollecting the years of strain in every nerve to rise up, *transcend*, I knew that it was not going to be easy to think mortal. But, at last, at long last, I had come to taste humiliation, not because of this wayward body, but because of the chimera of this *soul*, this inflated spirit, in its fragile, empty tube.

How and when had I conjured up this shadowy spirit, stranger to my body and to the world?

I thought of the war, of being cradled in my father's arms as he hurried me to the shelter buried in the sour-smelling clay of the garden; I thought of my father's grave, of unresting death that makes all thought impossible except how and where and when I shall myself die. Cradled in my hammock in the Gesu of the Selva Alta, the Eyebrow of the Jungle, I saw my mother dressed in black, as I had seen her on that day, standing on the station platform.

She was standing alone, pale and stooped, wearing the coat she had worn at my father's funeral. The billowing white steam clouds, the echoing pulpit voice, the pillars, the solemn light shafts from the vaults above, reminded me of church. The train pulled away from the platform and I leaned out of the window and watched until her figure disappeared from view.

The train picked up speed, gliding across high curving viaducts: I sat hunched forward gazing through the smutty window, astounded at the immensity of the aged and filthy city.

Sometimes at a crossing, or down there in the rows of streets, people would stop to look up as we sped by. A little boy standing with his mother waved up at the train; the little boy waved up at *me*. Then they vanished as in a dream. Were they still there when I saw them no longer? Could I make time stop by holding them for ever in my mind's eye? I thought that I would never forget the little boy standing with his mother at the railway crossing.

The houses thinned out and there were trees and parks, a cemetery with tombstones like rotten teeth, and the soft green expanse of a golf course with pennants stiff in the breeze; then, in glimpses between tunnels and high embankments, and finally in a startling, slow-moving panorama – the countryside opening out, vast to the horizon. We were rattling along a high embankment; below were neat fruit trees like green umbrellas all planted in a row; beyond was a friendly white farmhouse with red roofs and brick chimney-stacks; and rising, in fold after fold, wooded hills, dark green and mysterious, stretching to the edge of a huge sky with streamers of white cloud. Gazing through the window at the rapidly passing telegraph poles I felt a sense of sadness and longing, for the wires were rising, rising, rising, then suddenly snapping down; only to rise, rise, rise: long whips striking again and again, as the train carried me away from Mother, from home, from London; and from my father who now lay for ever in the clay of the Catholic cemetery in Leyton.

Uncle Eddie and Aunt Doris met me at Margate station. He was wearing a light-grey suit and his hair was sleek with sweet-smelling oil. Aunt was dressed in a flowery summer frock. Uncle's face was smooth. When he smiled his eyes narrowed until they almost disappeared. Aunt gave me a peck on the cheek with her orange-red lips. Her straw-coloured hair was kept in place with a white elasticated band. Close by was my cousin Rosie, a year or so older than me, her mouth sullen. Rosie wore a white blouse and light-blue skirt and she was suntanned like her mother and father. She was thin, almost scrawny, and she had very brown bare legs with a faint down of golden hairs.

Uncle and Aunt lived in a tall grey-brick house with a yellow door in a quiet street near the esplanade. Aunt took me upstairs and showed me my room, a narrow boxroom with a bar across the window. The wallpaper was decorated with a pattern of orange pineapples and the sheets were crisp and freshly laundered. There was a small white statue of the Holy Mother on the chest of drawers.

When I came downstairs I found them in the kitchen eating a sponge cake and drinking tea. Uncle was wearing a blue sleeveless vest. His skin was glowing and he smelt strongly of peppery scent. Something about his look, the way he stared at me, made me feel frightened.

I went for a walk. At the end of the street there were park benches and wind shelters and flower-beds with geraniums in neat rows like the cemetery garden in Leyton. The esplanade ran along the summit of the cliffs and I could see a wide expanse of the ocean to my left. Elderly holidaymakers were strolling along, occasionally looking out to sea as if something beckoned there.

A white-stuccoed Catholic church rose above the bungalows backing on to the golf course. The door was open and I went in to find an airy bright interior with white walls and clear glass windows. It was deserted and I knelt at the back. I was conscious of the sea and the great spaces beyond the cliff-top. The church was flooded with a special light. I felt safe in the church. I feared my uncle's strength and the way he looked at me.

Afterwards I walked back along the cliff-top. To the east,

beyond Margate, the sea was a band of brassy light against a dark orange sky. The strange light filled me with fear and sadness.

I rose early the next morning and went again to the church. I attended Mass and took Holy Communion, but I still felt frightened so I stayed a long time. Then I decided to walk along the cliff-top. The path was paved and there were railings to prevent people falling down the cliff. All the way there were couples ambling slowly along, looking out to sea.

I went back to the house for lunch, my face bright red with the sun. I had a headache and I found it difficult to see properly. Uncle Eddie eyed me with a comic look. 'Atta boy!' he said. 'Put some colour in those cheeks.' Then he said, 'When are you going to wear long trousers, Nick? Eh?' He was smiling at me gleefully. 'D'you know why lads start to wear long trousers?'

I did not understand.

After lunch Rosie and I walked along the beach. I had forgotten my headache. We climbed across the low rocks looking for mussels. I kept slipping on the seaweed and falling down, which made Rosie laugh. She was wearing a swimming costume made of towelling and her skin was covered with goosepimples. She was standing in a rock pool, the tips of her fingers as white as my dead father's face. I wanted to take her hands in mine and rub them back to life. She hunched her shoulders and wrung her hands together making gurgling sounds in her throat. I wanted to kiss her on the cheek; but I was frightened that she would laugh at me.

Looking out to sea I thought of the litany to the Holy Mother: 'Star of the Sea ... Pray for me ...' It seemed an odd thing to say of the Holy Mother. That day the sea seemed an appalling place – a cold, cruel waste of water.

We went to the foot of the cliffs and lay in the dry sand to get warm. Rosie turned over on her stomach and said: 'Why do you wear those goggles?'

I hated her question. 'I've got bad eyes,' I said.

'Take them off and let's see.'

She turned over on to her back and looked through them at the people on the beach. 'I can't see a thing,' she squealed, screwing up her eyes. It gave me a shock to see how my spectacles altered her appearance. I felt a flush of shame and anger at the disfigurement they caused me.

When we got back to the house Uncle was standing in the hallway; he said to Aunt, 'Let's all go up to the bedroom for a game.'

I looked at Rosie. She was leaning against the banisters looking towards the kitchen. Her face was sullen.

I said that I wanted to go to church, but Uncle took me by the arm and steered me up the stairs. We went into the large bedroom at the front of the house. It smelt of Uncle Eddie's peppery scent; there was a bay window hung with net curtains and heavy drapes. The double bed had a stained wood headboard with fretwork. There was a sombre-looking wardrobe and a dressing-table covered with little jars of ointments and powders and a set of glass candlesticks like my mother's. On the wall was a picture I recognized. It was of the Holy Mother in rich brocades, as though she were an Indian; the picture was called 'Our Lady of Perpetual Succour': Our Lady who always helps. I looked at the picture and it made me feel better for a moment; as if the picture made me safe.

Aunt and Uncle sat on the bed, side by side. Uncle had taken off his shirt and trousers and put on a bright red silk dressing-gown that made him look like a Chinaman. It had large loose sleeves and I could see his strong wrists. I felt a pang of fear at the strength of his wrists.

Aunt said: 'Let's give you a kiss and a cuddle, Nick.' I

drew back. But she said: 'Come on, sweetheart, I'm not going to hurt you.'

As I came and stood in front of her she took me gently in her arms and started to fondle and pet me, making purring noises in my ear. She smelt of cigarette smoke and sweet scent. One hand was going further and further down my stomach until she was stroking the front of my trousers and the insides of my legs. For a moment I felt a soft and pleasurable sense of excitement; then I caught a glimpse of Uncle Eddie and Rosie next to me. She was bending over his lap and he was stroking her, his large strong hands inside her knickers. He was making soft moaning noises over her head.

Terrified and excited, my heart pounding, my bowels hardening, I let Aunt undress me and stroke me and coax me, and guide me towards Rosie. How darkly pleasurable it felt to be forced; to be forced into that deed of secrecy and the night for which I had no word; to be forced into that deed in the light of day, in the presence of my aunt and my uncle, and on the thin brown body of my cousin Rosie.

How much of that deed was mine?

Even as I throbbed with dark sweet relief, I knew that God had been watching and weighing every last drop of my shame and terrified pleasure.

'Tch, tch, tch . . .' said Aunt Doris, and she laughed at me strangely. Uncle Eddie was laughing too.

I looked around the room, taking in the dressing-table with its powders and ointments, its candlesticks and sweet smells, its reminders of my priest games in childhood. I looked at the ugliness of the curtains, the silent street outside. I looked at the still and silent image of Our Lady of Perpetual Succour. I looked at this man and this woman, and at Rosie – her eyes glittering and swollen, her mouth set in a haggish little grin – and I felt that my eyes had at last been opened. I felt that I was squeezing tears of blood from my eyes and from my mouth; and I knew at last what I had always known, that this 'I', this *soul* – that Father James had told me was made in the image and likeness of God – was a stranger in the world; a stranger to this body.

PART FOUR

The Sacrilege

For he that eateth and drinketh
unworthily, eateth and drinketh
to his own damnation, not
discerning the Body of the Lord.

Paul [*1 Corinthians XI 29*]

CHAPTER 24

Chieske had pursued the young women of the village with a comical and beastly vigour that was obvious for all to see. While being aware of Chieske's appetites O'Rourke had been prepared to bide his time for a suitable moment to issue an ultimatum, and a bribe. The ultimatum, when it came, had been a lurid and particular instruction on the fires of hell especially prepared for the sexually incontinent, followed by the promise of certain articles of clothing and religious impedimenta, such as crucifixes and rosary beads, and the invitation to take a prominent role in liturgical ceremonies. The deal struck, Chieske and several of his followers had been baptized in secret in the chapel.

Now he went around the village wearing odd items of O'Rourke's vestments, including a biretta and a surplice, his neck festooned with beads and crucifixes, and looking more crazed and sad than I had ever seen him since our arrival. His lust for women had altered to loathing and contempt, and he would gesticulate and bark at them in a surly voice to be gone out of his sight – which they did with shrieks and giggles.

Chieske had never lacked an audience; and now these same hangers-on, who admired his brute strength and extravagant tomfoolery and lechery, began to emulate his sanctimonious posturing and eventually his exhibitions of public compunction, until they resembled a sect of flagellants.

The more his bond strengthened with O'Rourke, the more I struggled to talk with Chieske through Luis and to understand his mentality and motives. Only then did

I discover that Luis hated and feared Chieske and that he had been systematically mistranslating his dialogues with O'Rourke: he had been telling O'Rourke only what he wanted to hear.

In most of our dealings Luis had been nameless, serviceable; but the experience of coping with Chieske's craziness had been so frustrating and exhausting that he had balked. The polite and trustworthy Luis had been deliberately mistranslating the headman's mad son and so compounding the lunacy of his grotesque relationship with O'Rourke. Mercifully, Luis had been honest with me. Ten minutes work with Chieske, Luis confided, was like six hours with any other member of the tribe. Turning to me during one of these sessions, he put his head in his hands and said: 'This man is tearing at my whole life!'

Chieske had been sitting with us at the door of his hut; not for a moment could he keep his head or his hands still. Now he was looking back into the hut, now across the compound, now at Luis, now at the ground; and all the while he was drumming his fingers and fluttering them around his body and head, then fingering and scratching his genitals. His forehead was creased deeply in a frown of anxiety; his eyes were swivelling insanely.

Luis moaned with exasperation.

'What is it, Luis?' I asked.

'This man doesn't want to answer your questions . . . He's not a man at all.'

We had been engaged in a weird conversation about coca when Luis explained to me that Chieske had begun to speak in an uninhibited and obnoxious way about his sexual fantasies. I found it unnerving to be physically so close to him, looking into his lined face and his flitting eyes, mad yet intensely sad; his body never at ease.

I could see that it was undermining Luis's own sense of inner security to translate to me accurately the unrepressed meanderings of Chieske's mind; his ability as an interpreter, as well as his willingness, was breaking down under the strain. His voice was becoming tired, even as Chieske's was becoming more harsh and energetic. I guessed that Luis was using euphemisms to express Chieske's unbridled outpourings.

'When the stick goes in my mouth,' he was saying, describing the addition of lime to the coca quid, 'my skin down here gets hard . . . When the lama goes into the coca it's like the fluid shooting into my mouth . . . like I did it to the girls when the hair grew under my arms and the hair down here began to grow . . . I'd like to do it with Rook . . . he is my man, he is our visitor, a nice man . . . he brings gifts . . . he gave me all the lama . . . I'm going to make Rook's skin hard and let his fluid shoot into my mouth and make me strong . . . Where's *your* present? What are you going to give me? If you're a good man, give me things . . . If you want to ask more questions, give me a present . . . I'm strong, I'm strong and hungry enough to rip off your balls and eat them . . .' Then he began to cackle.

Looking at Chieske, listening to him, I was terrified. Despite his manic energy, and his cackling, he had the saddest eyes I had ever seen in my life – save for glimpsed memories of my own. That look was full of pain, a pain that was confused with anger and withdrawal; with demands for help that offered resistance in the same instant. The more I looked into his eyes, the more I saw his despair; the more I saw his need to test the commitment of everybody and anybody, a commitment that no one could ever fulfil. Where had I met that secret demand, that need, that longing for an affectionate, understanding person, Earthly or Heavenly, who would end the pain? That lurking potential to manipulate and control through fear of imagined or actual violence? In Chieske I thought I saw the face of a confirmed masochist, and I was afraid.

After that session Luis shocked me by saying that he believed that Chieske wanted to be like O'Rourke because he wanted to be Nakak; Luis said that Chieske believed that

O'Rourke was a fellator of little white boys and a cannibal. He wanted to be like O'Rourke so that he could chew the skin and drink the blood of the white boy he kept in his box. It would give him strength; it would help him avoid the everlasting fires after death. And what could be better than to nail a son of Papa-Belong-All to a cross to send him to heaven and to save all the people? He, Chieske, would like nothing better than to nail a son of Papa-Belong-All to a cross and eat his flesh and drink his blood!

Weeping profusely, Luis also confessed to me that he had, nevertheless, told O'Rourke only of Chieske's love of the white man's Papa-Belong-All, his desire for baptism, his longing for the Eucharist. He did this, he told me, not because he wanted to lie or to cause trouble, but because he had to end the tortuous interpreting sessions that were driving him mad.

After Luis's admissions I staggered off to find John, my head throbbing with anxiety and foreboding. As we walked together down to the river I described the new situation: if Luis had been systematically mistranslating the leading actors, I told him, we were in even bigger trouble than we had ever imagined. It was, I said, as if Luis, the only sane man amongst us, our translator and interpreter and mediator amidst the babble, had lost his nerve and fumbled all the scripts.

As John listened to me in silence, I began to laugh, a high-pitched giggle at the tragi-comic lunacy of it all.

What should I do? Should I attempt to resolve the misunderstandings? On our way back to the village John urged me to broach the matter with O'Rourke immediately. So I went straight on to the Gesu, determined to straighten him out about Chieske's true state of mind.

To no avail. Several times that afternoon I tried to approach him in confidence, but he brushed me aside with stern looks.

O'Rourke had more crucial goals to achieve – the conversion of the sexual morals of the entire village. He had broadened his tactics against Chieske's 'impurities' to include a sermon to the tribe on the subject of chastity, lambasting their loose morals before marriage and their practice of birth control, which took a variety of forms including fellatio, sodomy, and coitus interruptus.

I stood to one side, witnessing the debate between O'Rourke and Anonha and his elders, with the unhappy Luis in between. In the background was the lunatic Chieske leaping around and sucking on a crucifix he held in his hand.

Anonha was explaining that their birth-control practices enabled them to limit the population to numbers appropriate for the food supply in the forest, while O'Rourke was lecturing him on the importance of an option that he assumed they had not contemplated, namely, self-denial, even within marriage.

This led to a question about O'Rourke's sexual habits. The discussion seemed to put the elders on their metal. Seated in a semi-circle in their off-white calico smocks, they looked like a conclave of religious.

'What is the advantage,' Anonha wished to know, 'of sexual abstinence among you white men?'

O'Rourke replied that Papa-Belong-All recommended total chastity. 'We have bound ourselves by a vow to remain free of acts of sex until death.'

Anonha was astonished at this, which prompted O'Rourke to talk in complacent, incomprehensible, terms (or so it must have sounded to them), about the advantages of celibacy. One of the elders, though, seemed to have understood the harangue well enough to heckle with this question. 'If you haven't experienced sex, how do you know what you are missing?'

O'Rourke's face had become angry during these exchanges, his eyes curiously lustreless, as if he were blind. After the elders had gone, leaving only Chieske and few of his cronies, who hung on every unintelligible word that fell from his lips, O'Rourke said to me in a dull voice: 'We're going to teach them at every opportunity the meaning of the text *Quoniam qui talis agunt regnum Dei non possidebunt* [Those who behave thus will not possess the kingdom of God]. No doubt they will be shocked by the proposition, and will find it all but impossible to comply. But who are we to question the power of God's grace! Once they are filled with the Holy Spirit, He will impress on them in all places and at all times the respect they owe to His divine presence and they will be glad to be pure in order to be Christians.' He added, as if speaking to himself, 'I imagine that it was for this that I was inspired by God to put them under the special protection of Saint Joseph, the patron of chastity.'

Before departing for his night devotions O'Rourke whispered to me melodramatically, 'With Chieske's help I have got hold of a large part of their store of lime – I have it under guard in our chapel . . . and now we can make some progress.'

John was at my side and I confronted O'Rourke. I stood before him, almost as tall as he, and now as determined. I broached the matter of Luis and his mistranslations of Chieske's obscene and violent sentiments about Christianity.

Explaining the matter in blunt terms, I looked straight into his face and quailed; his eyes were as dead as stones, the lines about his mouth chiselled in granite.

I told him again, thinking that he had not understood.

Then he put one hand on my shoulder; it was like a steel clamp; he said: 'Oh, Nicholas! O ye of little Faith!'

After he had left us to repair to the chapel, John and I went down to the river to talk. As we sat together in the darkness he smoked greedily on a tobacco cheroot he had been given by the Mekroti.

'I'm going to bring it to an end,' John declared at last, his hands shaking, his eyes screwed up with myopia. 'I'm going to try to persuade Christian to come with us tomorrow. Failing that, we should go down with Luis and Anna on our own.'

He squatted on his haunches looking at me intently, drawing deeply on the little cigar and sharing it with me occasionally. He looked tired and defeated, far from ready for the arduous journey that lay ahead. We had reached a fatal crossroads and I began to feel nervous about the night and the day ahead. I had an intuition as we sat there savouring the peace of the evening that something awful and unexpected was afoot.

John groaned; he was exhausted. I knew his kindness, his generosity, his dedication. But his disillusionment on that evening seemed profound.

'We come with good intentions, Nicholas,' he said, 'but we're the ones who need the mercy.'

He seemed to guess that I was going to say something about O'Rourke. 'No, it's not just O'Rourke,' he went on. 'O'Rourke shows the symptoms, the grotesque and exaggerated symptoms, of the disease that lurks in our best intentions. I came here to this continent to fight poverty and injustice, but I'm carrying the disease too. Do you know the meaning of the word *demon*, Nicholas? It means the accuser of one's brothers and sisters. A demon denigrates other existences . . . We don't have to do it by tub thumping, or threatening hell fire, or by exploitation. We stand in their eyes for something even more powerfully insidious; we awaken guilt in our brothers and sisters, then we absolve it when we have extorted sufficient gestures of submission. And that's the image we make of our God: an idol, a totem, of our own accusing, self-seeking existence.' He paused a moment and gave a short laugh, a wry chuckle apt for a paradox. John had not spoken so much since he arrived at the mission.

He threw the cheroot into the current and watched it dancing away. 'If there's a grace in this mission,' he murmured, 'it's to discover our need to be pardoned, by the Mekroti, by the Peruvians; by the whole of fucking Latin America; for making it a *favella*, a slum, of the mind and the heart.'

As we walked slowly back together up to the village we heard the sound of rain in the trees; it had been raining on and off all day. I thought of the Psalms and hymns we had sung at compline in the seminary to ward off those demons of the day and especially the night, '*A saggita volante in die, a negotio perambulante in tenebris: ab incursu, et demonio meridiano* [The arrow that flies in the day, the pestilence walking in the darkness, the destruction that wreaks havoc at noonday]'.

Together we began to sing, echoing to the treetops and the nearby hills the haunting plainchant of the '*Salve Regina*'. And as we sang I thought of Jill, and of my dark remote childhood; and I thought of the healing I longed for, to cure the self-devouring despair which projects its own evil upon another as a demand and as an accusation.

That night, in my hammock, I knew there was worse to come. The real trial of this journey still lay in wait, like a terrifying animal of prey, circling and advancing slowly in the forest. I tried to pray, but all I could do was raise my empty hands in the darkness as if some sacred vessel had slipped from my grasp and lay shattered on the ground.

CHAPTER 25

From the very first day of the mission we should all have been better prepared for the 'pestilence walking in the darkness'. On the following morning at dawn the Gesu was awoken by screams.

Anna had risen with a fever in the early hours and gone to fetch some water from the kitchen. When she returned she found the Zapara boy dead. No sooner had John, O'Rourke, and I appeared on the scene than Anna collapsed, shaking and vomiting, and had to be carried to her hammock, where her condition worsened throughout the morning.

By breakfast time four mothers had come through the rain to the door of the Gesu with feverish and coughing children; they were suffering from the same viral infection, it seemed, as that which had killed the Zapara boy. It was now clear to us that Anna had been spreading the virus unwittingly for several days; yet she herself seemed to be stricken by something more critical.

O'Rourke, calm in the face of crisis, cited God's will. John was beside himself with grief and anger. Stamping about our kitchen and pounding the table with his fist, he shouted, 'For Christ's sake! Bringing infection into a place like this! Why didn't she keep that boy properly quarantined? Why did she go spreading the bloody thing all around the village? She's a trained *nurse*, for God's sake!'

His anger, I suspected, was as much directed against himself and his own failure to insist on proper discipline; but he was furious, I suspected, because it would now be impossible to persuade O'Rourke to abandon the mission.

After he had calmed down he supervised with Luis the

instruction of the mothers of the new victims, handing out asprin and advising them to keep their children segregated. But we had little hope of the effectiveness of quarantine now that the disease had spread.

Then we discovered that our woes had only just begun. By early afternoon we all, including Luis, were running high temperatures and vomiting. The Gesu was in the hands of Chieske, who leapt about cackling and shouting and laughing, and occasionally brought us water.

In the late afternoon O'Rourke managed to get off his hammock and with Chieske's help took the Zapara boy's body out through sheets of rain to perform a Christian burial in a plot of land close to our hut. I followed, shaking with fever, watching from a distance so as to avoid contact with the villagers. Chieske, dressed in his assortment of ragged missionary vestments, was leaping about and spewing out crazy word-salads under the cloudbursts, mimicking every detail of O'Rourke's ceremonial. It was dark, with low scudding clouds carrying squall after squall.

Afterwards O'Rourke, his face grey with exhaustion and illness, sat shivering in his hammock reading the Office for the Dead. Occasionally we dragged ourselves out of our hammocks to see Anna whose condition was worsening. She looked cadaverous, her face putty-white. Her symptoms had started with pains in the head; now she shook alternately with chills and with heat; she stretched and moaned and retched; and in addition to her fever she was tormented by anxiety and delirium: the moment she shut her eyes and dozed she would wake suddenly with hideous screams. I stayed with her a while holding her hand and cooling her forehead with a damp flannel. In an interval of her delirium she said to me, weeping: 'My dreams are the torments of hell.'

By evening she was quieter, but she was developing a livid rash which gradually covered her face and neck and then began to spread to her arms and breasts, her back and stomach, and finally her legs. The spots were at first flat, but after several hours became raised and enlarged like blisters. With a sorrowful shake of the head, O'Rourke pronounced that she was suffering a form of 'jungle fever' he had seen in other parts of the Amazon, and which he assumed she had picked up on her journey; it was a tropical disease, he warned, with a slow and insidious gestation period, that attacked only those who were not denizens of the region; he suspected that the virus we were suffering had made her more susceptible.

During the night the pustules became so numerous and so large on Anna's body that her skin was a single vermilion mass as if someone had thrown a basin of scalding water at her. Lying on her hammock, her mouth open in a silent cry of agony, we saw in her mouth and throat the identical lumps and ulcers of the disease that was ravaging her exterior.

At two in the morning, to the sound of rain hammering on the thatched roof and frequent blasts of thunder, O'Rourke administered the sacrament of Extreme Unction. He conducted the ritual with devout gestures, his voice gentle and mournful. Then he prayed for a while and delivered a short homily on the sufferings of Christ and His great love. But she turned her face to the wall.

After he had gone she began to sob; she gripped my hand and looked at me with terrified eyes: 'I want to see His face ... but I see only a huge black mountain that rises up to the stars and blots out heaven.'

She died an hour later and John insisted that we bury her at once to reduce the possibility of contagion.

Once again we made the journey through ankle-deep mud and driving rain to our Christian burial plot. Drenched and shivering we stood in the darkness attended by Chieske as O'Rourke led us in the recitation of the 'De Profundis'.

The following day my own nightmares were mixed with the daylight realities of illness and ceaseless rain. I had an impression of Takakhe turning up for a parlay with

O'Rourke. The shaman suspected that we were all about to die and thought there might be a dividend in it for him. He indicated that he had remedies for every kind of illness and on receipt of a gift he would set us all on our feet.

'What sort of present do you want?' asked O'Rourke from his hammock.

'A portion of lime for my coca.'

'I'll make sure you get the lot,' I told him, 'if you can give us an instant cure.'

O'Rourke was not amused. 'We can't accept his healing rites,' he said, 'they're nothing but a compact with Satan.'

'Never mind the lime,' indicated Takake, gathering O'Rourke's gist, 'I'll do it for nothing. I've got some of my own left and I'll chew my coca and sing an incantation and you'll get better.'

That evening we began to perspire and by morning we were over the worst of it, although still weak. Takakhe's healing rite was soon forgotten and was not to be mentioned by any of us again.

We rose from our sickbeds to discover that the virus was spreading ferociously through the village. Takakhe's coca chewing and incantations were proving of little avail to his own people.

During the night we heard the sound of women wailing above the drum beats of the rain: the first of the sick children had died. Sitting at our kitchen table drinking hot tea O'Rourke said quietly that our own illness was an act of divine Providence. 'I've seen this in New Guinea and in the Philippines, and in Africa. We might have been charged with witchcraft had we not suffered the same illness ourselves and had Anna not died: *periaramus nisi perissemus!* [we should perish had we not perished].'

John looked up and murmured hoarsely: 'You do talk such rubbish, Christian!'

O'Rourke said nothing further; eventually he got up and left the hut with Chieske at his side.

The village was now in the grip of the sickness, and there

was little we could do except dispense asprin; but O'Rourke had other ideas, which Luis reported back to us later the next day.

Carrying a stoup of water and hurricane lamps, O'Rourke had been out in the rain visiting the huts with Chieske and baptizing by stealth those infants who seemed destined to die. Chieske had been standing as godfather; at least, that was O'Rourke's impression of the situation, and each baptism had been recorded in a little black book that he kept for the purpose.

When he returned wet through at midnight, John and I were waiting for him.

His voice trembling, John said, 'You've been baptizing by deception, Christian . . . you know that is wrong . . .'

O'Rourke swung away from him with an imperious flourish of his ancient Jesuit gown. He turned on me, fixing me with a hard angry eye. 'Father, I wish to talk to you in private in the chapel.'

I glanced at John – a look of ironic complicity – then I followed O'Rourke through the length of the hut.

When he reached the sanctuary of the chapel he faced me. The young Mekroti who had been deputed to guard the lime store was squatting by the wall, watching us with avid curiosity.

'I want to confide in you, Father,' he said, 'and I want to do it under the seal of confession.'

I signalled with a nod that I had agreed.

'Today,' he whispered, 'during my examen of conscience I had a vision. I can't say whether it was real or imagined. I thought I saw a face peering at me from the corner of this chapel; it was the face of Father John, and it was wearing a grimace of pure wickedness: I realized that I was looking at the face of a devil.'

'So what did you do, Father?'

'I dispatched him by forcing my attention on prayer.'

I was finding it difficult to look O'Rourke in the eyes; his gaze was demented, as if his eyes were no longer his own. I was trying to think of something to say, to calm him and to steer him away from such notions; I asked him, 'Did you think the vision could harm you?'

'I knew that he couldn't harm me,' he rasped. 'Satan can't harm a hair on my head without God's assent.'

'Listen to me, Father, John is a good and loyal priest; you mustn't associate him with evil visions. I believe that what you saw was a hallucination brought on by the fever. You should rest and get some sleep.'

O'Rourke was not looking at me; he was gazing down the chapel into the gloomy shadows. He said in his Irish manner, as if I were no longer there: 'Indeed! Do you say so! Do you say so!'

I had gone straight to my hammock, still exhausted from the illness. I had tried to sleep, but for several hours I lay awake listening to O'Rourke stirring around, and crying out in the chapel. Sitting up and straining to hear, I realized that he was reciting the ritual of Exorcism. O'Rourke was declaiming the Latin in a frenzied high-pitched voice; calling out for Satan to be gone – every inflection parodied by Chieske.

Despite O'Rourke's request that our conversation remain under the seal of confession, I decided to wake John and confide in him. Never had I broken a law of the Church with a happier conscience.

He listened to the ghastly racket for a while, then together we went through the hut until we stood in the chapel entrance. O'Rourke was vested in surplice and stole, and Chieske was dressed in a ragged black cope; O'Rourke was reading the office of Exorcism by the light of a candle and casting holy water into the shadows; gesture for gesture, Chieske was imitating him.

Taking me by the arm, John hurried me back to our dormitory; he had decided to set off for Aranuba before dawn.

Accompanied by Luis, we went to Anonha's hut, waking him from his sleep. But after a difficult interview Anonha

214

refused to let us have the two young men we requested to accompany John down to Aranuba. The fruits of our presence among them, said Anonha, were now clearly to be seen, and while he remained sympathetic to me and John he wanted no further part in our doings.

For the rest of the night we worked with Luis transporting supplies through the heavy rains down to the river, where we kept the remaining plank boat. We made six journeys in all, and several times I thought I was in danger of sinking up to the waist in mud. The last burden we carried was the outboard motor and our remaining supply of precious fuel. We were spent as we stood at last on the riverbank in the grey light of dawn, the rain still falling unrelentingly from a low pall of cloud.

Standing there, my hand in his, I knew that John could not have chosen a worse juncture to make the journey. The rainy season had started in earnest and he had no skills as an explorer. There were a hundred perils on the way, not least the chance that he might get lost in the maze of tributaries to the Napo; I had little hope that I would ever see him again.

As Luis and I watched his departure in the twilight, O'Rourke appeared on the trail with Chieske and his group of followers. They watched in silence until the boat had disappeared on the bend.

CHAPTER 26

With John's departure O'Rourke's spirits seemed to lift. Later that morning he came into the kitchen as I was standing with Luis drinking coffee. Making no mention of John or what had passed during the night, he started to chat in an animated fashion with an Irish trip of the tongue. 'I do just wish, Nicholas,' he said, 'that the people here would bring forward more objections so that I could be given more of an opportunity to explain the holy mysteries of the Faith.'

Donning his Jesuit gown, he said jauntily: 'Would you ever accompany me, Nicholas, across the way to see a poor old fellow who's dying.'

We went together through the mire and the rain to a hut close by where the elder he had named 'Michael' was propped up on a bed of filthy skins surrounded by his family.

The old man was suffering from old age as much as the sickness; the bones were coming through his flesh and he was shivering with fever. Through Luis he managed to ask a question. 'Rook,' he said, 'do you think you are going to conquer this village?'

O'Rourke took this to mean the conversion of the Mekroti.

'We are not so presumptuous,' he replied. 'But what seems impossible to man is not only possible but easy to Papa-Belong-All.'

The old man, despite his awkward questions, had been one of O'Rourke's best allies, and had joined with Anonha in curbing Takakhe's attempts to condemn him as the Nakak. He was the first of the elders to make the sign of the cross

216

and had struggled to understand the Christian message. He had even tried to persuade O'Rourke from time to time that perhaps the Mekroti and Christian beliefs could be practised side by side. His chief objection to O'Rourke's evangelizing had been the desire to go to his own ancestors after death, even at the risk of joining them in the fires of hell.

O'Rourke's riposte had never varied. 'Let him have his ancestors. I can't countenance a situation in which we allow our Faith to be infected by heresy and paganism.'

Realizing that he was dying, the old man had ordered a feast for his family; they now sat around him chanting lugubriously in between bouts of coca chewing. O'Rourke brusquely declined an invitation to join in the chant and to chew some coca.

The old boy was a sorry sight, groaning and breathing harshly, propped up on his heap of verminous skins, miserably attempting to eat a piece of scorched peccary meat. Looking balefully at O'Rourke he said that when he returned after his death he would go into the mission hut and upset all his belongings. It was said in jest but when it was translated back to him O'Rourke flashed an angry look, commenting that it was further evidence of the old man's attachment to his superstitious ways.

Just as we were about to depart, the old fellow began to call out again. He was pleading with O'Rourke for our healing rite. 'Come on,' he cried, 'give me your special magic, I can't go to that place of fire.'

O'Rourke seemed undecided; here was a request for baptism, albeit from a half-demented dying old man.

'Surely he's not dying yet,' O'Rourke said to me. 'If there's still time left I'd rather wait until I'm satisfied that he fully intends the sacrament and has abandoned his superstitions.'

With this he left the hut and we followed him miserably through the rain and the mire.

Back in the Gesu, O'Rourke was still shaking the rain from his gown when a member of 'Michael's' family came in to say that the old man had passed away.

O'Rourke was unmoved. Turning to me, he said, 'God would not permit that what he had scorned during his life should be granted in death. *Judicia Dei abyssus multa.* We make no compromises; we start now as we intend to continue.'

In the days that followed John's departure, days of ceaseless heavy rains and floods, O'Rourke was out visiting the huts day and night, seeking suitable candidates for baptism among the sick and the dying. There were shortages of food among many families and I saw that he carried provisions on his frequent rounds of the village.

I was still weak from ravages of the virus; I felt at the end of my resources, capable of little else than dozing in my hammock and occasionally dragging myself to the latrine. O'Rourke, by contrast, never slept; he went on through the day and the night, working and praying and haranguing. He told me in the form of a brief homily as I lay on my hammock in the middle of the night that these baptisms were a holy strategy. 'Just think, Father Nicholas,' he said in lofty tones, 'if we can get a few of them into heaven from the very outset, then these new saints will bring in the rest after them.'

He stood in silence above me for a few moments, his clenched hands pressing against his mouth; then he said, 'Ah, but Satan has so many allies in this region that Heaven is labouring under a handicap . . . How pleased I am, Nicholas, that John has fled from this place! But we must still be on our guard . . .'

Then he disappeared into the darkness towards the chapel.

The following morning Anonha came into the Gesu through the rain to report that sickness was claiming deaths in every family in the village. He said that some people were falling victim not once but twice; the second time invariably proved fatal. He told us that the unprecedented heaviness of the rains had caused flooding from the hills above and that their plantations had been washed out. The village was facing serious food shortage.

Curious rumours abounded. After a circuit of the village, Luis returned to report that a story was going around that O'Rourke's cassock was poisoned; another had it that the food he dispensed was cursed.

One morning a man marched into our kitchen while O'Rourke and Luis were standing there. Throwing down a huge dried fish on the table, he signalled the following: 'This is how people should make a gift. You, Rook, are mean. When *you* give of the things you have already received from our hands, there is so little that we can hardly taste it.' Without waiting for a reaction or an answer the man walked out, his head high with indignation.

Although he felt the taunt keenly, O'Rourke was determined not to alter a policy he had practised on missions throughout his long ministry. He declared that he had been protecting the store of provisions in order to dispense them back when the need arose. He then delivered a lecture on the principles of conservation, husbandry, and providence, an essential feature, he maintained, of Christian and Western civilization. He also intimated that our ability to save the Mekroti from starvation *in extremis* might eventually prove an invaluable tool of evangelism.

After musing for a while, he said, 'I suppose these blows to our pride are sent from Heaven to try us.'

But the lessons taught us by the Mekroti during those days of death and ceaseless rain did not stop at charity. The following day at noon O'Rourke invited Anonha and the elders into the Gesu to talk about methods of combating the epidemic.

He greeted the old men warmly, then he gave each of them a piece of fish. While they were eating, he prompted Luis to ask them this question: 'Who shapes the body of the child in its mother's womb?'

They were sitting there looking up at him, sodden with the rain and hungry, some of them still miserably chewing their quids of coca although they lacked the lime essential for its efficacy.

'Who makes the heart,' O'Rourke went on, 'the liver, the lungs and the other organs and members of the body, all well proportioned and joined one to another? Is it the father? No, it cannot be the father, for these wonders take place in his absence and sometimes after his death. Is it the mother? No, for the mother continues to work and to sleep and carry out her duties in the hut unaware of what is happening inside her body. So how can the creation of a child be the work of the parents? Parents have not even the power to decide on the sex of the child. They have no power over the size, the beauty, or the intelligence of their children.'

The old men just sat there, eating the fish and now looking up at him pathetically as he asked this complicated question with vigorous gestures and help from Luis.

'So. Who makes the child?' he demanded. 'Come on! Who makes the child?'

Still the old men continued to sit in silence.

'Papa-Belong-All makes the child!' he thundered. 'Papa-Belong-All who is the father of all and whom I worship!'

O'Rourke repeated this 'lesson' many times over without eliciting a word from them. At length he bowed his head and seemed to be lost in prayer for a several minutes, his audience gazing up at him expectantly. Then he pointed to an elder, asking him through Luis what he had thought of his speech.

The old man pondered the question for a few moments. 'What do I think of your speech?' he indicated. 'Your speech is better than ours,' he said. 'We speak like a man wandering about on a journey and not knowing where we are going. You always speak as if you are following a straight path.'

'But do you believe what I tell you,' asked O'Rourke with ill-concealed exasperation. 'Is it true?'

After it had been translated for him, the old man said: 'We have no experience of such things in our lives here.'

'But are you willing to reject your own beliefs and follow ours?'

'Our beliefs are all that we have,' he said. 'Your beliefs are *your* beliefs, and it puzzles us why you should want to give them away.'

Then Anonha stood up and said, 'Rook, why have you taken our lama? The village is suffering from shortage of food and only coca with lama can relieve the pangs of hunger.'

O'Rourke seemed delighted at this question; his face was wreathed in smiles. He sat down among them, wringing his hands, as if in supplication. Instructing Luis to be especially careful with the translation, he said, 'Joseph, I have not stolen your lama, as you call it. I have merely confiscated it as befits our superior knowledge of its danger to your health. But I am prepared to distribute it in careful rations provided you renounce your belief in its magical powers.'

When the meaning of this had been conveyed the elders began to quarrel among themselves, gesticulating and rolling their eyes with consternation. I was wondering whether to intervene to plead on their behalf, but I knew that it would be fruitless. I was pinning all my hope now on John's eventual return from the outside world.

When Anonha had succeeded in pacifying his companions, he turned to O'Rourke and made a measured and dignified announcement. 'Rook,' he said, 'this is not something we can decide here in this room. We are going to go away and discuss it among ourselves, which is our tradition. In the meantime we should be grateful if you would give us some of our lama to help with our deliberations.'

When this was translated O'Rourke considered the proposition for a few moments; then he told Luis to tell them that he could not comply. 'When I have seen clearer signs of your readiness to accept the message I bring about Papa-Belong-All I shall be prepared to distribute a ration of lama. But I am not convinced that you have any such intention at present.'

As the meaning of this sunk in Anonha rose with dignity and shepherded his elders from the room. They were perplexed and suffering; they were, after all, confirmed coca addicts and their need for the leaf was even greater now to cope with the catastrophe of illness and hunger.

As he was going through the door Anonha turned slowly and faced O'Rourke. His face was stern and he asked this question with signs and gestures. 'Rook, can you tell me why it is that you white men have all survived in good health while our people in every household in the village are dying?'

'Joseph,' said O'Rourke, 'you may judge for yourself; it may be that Papa-Belong-All is angry with the Mekroti for their failure to listen to the message I have brought. You can discuss this with your elders when you decide whether to accept our beliefs.'

As he made his meaning plain I uttered a groan of dismay; turning on me now, O'Rourke declared, 'God will grant them if it shall please him the grace to recognize that we have not been afflicted because we have believed in his mercy.'

Detecting the bewildered expression on my face, he said: 'I'm not surprised, Nicholas, at the gossip, for most of them show that in their hearts they have no other god than their mouths and their bellies and their organs of generation.'

CHAPTER 27

After his noonday Mass O'Rourke had asked Anonha and the elders to parlay with him in the Gesu. They arrived looking dispirited, the withdrawal symptoms of their coca chewing clearly evident in their faces and postures.

As he opened the meeting O'Rourke pointed out that Chieske, who was in attendance dressed in motley liturgical cast-offs, had converted to Christianity along with a number of his young friends. Did this not encourage them to begin to make a move themselves in the direction of abandoning their beliefs in Iteka and trusting in Papa-Belong-All?

'Tell me, Anonha,' O'Rourke said at last, 'what is the result of your deliberation with the elders.'

Anonha stood up; he had a bad cough and was showing symptoms of the viral infection.

'We have talked matters through carefully,' he said. 'Chieske speaks for himself and his friends. Rook, you will never succeed in controlling him.'

As this was said Chieske started to cackle and slap his thighs; but Anonha went on: 'We have our own way of doing things, and you have yours. Your ancestors must have assembled in olden times and held a council to decide about your Papa-Belong-All. As for us, we have decided against him.'

As this was translated O'Rourke began to breath heavily, pacing up and down the room punching his huge right fist into the palm of his left hand.

Interrupting Anonha's flow, he insisted that he make an immediate observation. 'Christians,' he said, 'do not choose their beliefs or their customs by the agreement of an assembly, for Papa-Belong-All has *revealed* the truth about himself and how he wishes human beings to behave.'

He went on to say that it was true that between the different nations there were different customs – languages, clothes, modes of building – but as to what concerned Papa-Belong-All all nations ought to be in agreement. 'The truth of Papa-Belong-All is so clear,' he cried, 'that it is necessary only to open one's eyes to see it written in large characters on the face of the whole of nature.'

Much of this was lost on his audience, except the point he had made about Papa-Belong-All 'revealing' everything and thus precluding all discussion or agreement. O'Rourke had expressed this idea by saying that the son of Papa-Belong-All had appeared in our world to tell the people about His truth; to which Anonha replied that this son had not come to the Mekroti.

O'Rourke now began to smile and nod vigorously, impatient for Anonha to finish. 'Aha!' he shouted, beating his breast several times over. 'But *I* am sent by the son of Papa-Belong-All. *I* am his true messenger and representative!'

This statement pleased Chieske, who began to leap about and harangue his father, gesticulating and laughing and spewing out a torrent of verbiage.

Anonha, clearly sick and weak with the virus, was in no mood for further parlaying. He addressed his elders and they rose to file out of the room; but just as Anonha was about to go through the door himself, O'Rourke grasped him by the arm. 'You are sick, you are suffering from the *catarrha*, we must nurse you and say our prayers over you.'

'Thank you,' replied Anonha, 'but Takakhe is going to make a sweat and we will use the last of our lama and chew the coca leaf.'

As the little fellow went out into the rain, O'Rourke turned to me and said: 'You see, they are still steeped in their worship of the Devil.'

*

That evening we heard that Mabla's son, Bedla, was seriously ill with the virus and in danger of dying. O'Rourke was particularly agitated by this news and immediately made ready to visit the hut. He had grown fond of the boy for his expressions of piety, and what O'Rourke identified as his look of natural innocence and gravity. He was castigating himself now for having failed to baptize the youth earlier. 'I held off, Nicholas,' he said with a troubled voice,' because I thought that his Faith might crumble under the overwhelming influence of the pagans about him, which would have been a sorrier blow to our cause than if he had never been baptized. Oh, how much I have to learn about trusting in God!'

As we walked through the village together with Luis in tow, he told me that on hearing the recitation of the ten commandments in English the boy had said (according to Luis): 'That is a truly beautiful discourse.'

I cast a look in Luis's direction, but he turned away embarrassed.

When we reached the hut and called out, Mabla came at once and barred our entrance holding on to the door jambs. She was excitable and determined; she did not want Rook inside her house.

Ignoring her pleas O'Rourke simply removed her wrist with his huge grip.

I stood by the door as O'Rourke approached the fire. Bedla was behind a partition, we could just see him in the shadows sweating and coughing and breathing with difficulty; the grandmother had interposed herself between the boy and O'Rourke.

O'Rourke called out to him softly, while Mabla continued to plead with us to go away.

I looked at Mabla. Her grace and beauty were ravaged with hunger and anxiety and she avoided my eyes. I turned to O'Rourke and said firmly that we should leave, but he was not to be easily shifted; he lingered, trying to reason with Mabla and producing presents of food and knives from the capacious pockets of his cassock. And all the time he was conducting through Luis an incomprehensible lecture on the doctrine of baptism of desire.

At one point he called out to the boy, 'You can request baptism as a direct gift from Heaven, Bedla. Do you not wish to go to the place of all good things after death? Do you not believe all that I have told you?'

When the boy eventually replied in a weak voice it was to say, 'What do I know!'

I was agitated to the point of violence, when the grandmother solved everything by picking up a burning brand as if to thrust it in his face.

We left in the certain knowledge that the boy would die that night. As we walked to the Gesu O'Rourke said sadly: 'It was indeed the evening of life for him.'

Within minutes of reaching our house, Chieske came running up to say that another promising convert, the mother of Sekel, was dying and calling for Rook.

The woman was a widow who had been receiving titbits of meat and bowls of broth from O'Rourke for two days or so while keeping him on tenterhooks over her decision to receive baptism.

On our way through the mud O'Rourke told me that he feared she might be one of those people who had courted conversion for a time in order to enjoy the delicacies he brought, only to refuse baptism at the last moment.

As it turned out, Sekel's grandmother had a genuine religious difficulty that she could not resolve even on her death bed. As we entered the hut, Sekel, looking sullen and defiant, shouted something at Chieske, who immediately slapped her around the face. I shouted at Chieske to stop, expecting O'Rourke to back me up; but he merely said in a cold voice: 'That girl is just a prostitute.'

After O'Rourke had given the woman some aspirin and sweetened water, a short conversation took place mediated by Luis. O'Rourke wanted her to confess her sins before he would baptize her. She, on the other hand, was attempting to explain that she could not ask God's pardon for her sins because she was puzzled by what was expected of her.

'I do not know what sin is,' she moaned.

Over a number of days, it was apparent that, with the aid of similes and allegories, O'Rourke had been trying to impress upon her the need to seek pardon of Papa-Belong-All for having offended him. She did not understand.

I thought that O'Rourke would eventually reassure her and baptize her without further ado, but he seemed to regard the old woman as a personal challenge. The conversation was turning into a contest of wills, with the woman pleading innocence and O'Rourke insisting that while she refused to acknowledge her sinfulness he could not baptize her.

Watching the scene, incapable of intervening for fear of inciting Chieske and distressing the woman further, I began to weep at the pathos of the situation. Here we were, huddled under a meagre dripping shelter in the vast wilderness of the high forest; a European Jesuit steeped in scholastic dialectics in a combat of wills with a filthy dying old woman who would not tell a lie to herself, and was prepared to risk the eternal fires of hell rather than submit.

At length I said gently: 'Please, Father, for the love of God, leave her be . . .'

But O'Rourke flashed a quelling look of anger at me and returned to the old woman.

'Just tell me that you have committed sin and that you are sorry, and Rook will give you our water healing rite,' he was saying.

The contest went on for a further fifteen mintues or so, the woman gasping for breath and from time to time pleading with him: 'Give me the water healing, Papa Rook!' O'Rourke shaking his head and insisting: 'Admit you have sinned!'

Eventually the woman seemed to take a turn for the worse: fearing that he would lose her entirely, he redoubled his efforts by describing hell and all its frightfulness, assuring her that the place was filled with people who thought that they had never committed a sin.

At last she succumbed and admitted that she had indeed sinned. She was already dying, and she was ready to say anything to be left in peace.

Outside the hut I hung behind as O'Rourke and the others walked ahead of me to the Gesu. I went a little way into the forest, weeping with sorrow and pity for the dead woman.

I stood for a time with my head pressed against a dripping tree, and the memory came back to me of the cold brick wall of the church on Eastern Avenue, the night I pondered the multitude of my failings. How could it be, I thought, that these people, who had never known our Christianity and our God, were so secure in their sense of innocence; and that *we*, who were *saved* and *redeemed* and *transformed*, were so hounded and cast down by the sure conviction of our guilt!

CHAPTER 28

The next morning O'Rourke came and stood over me in a state of nervous excitment. I must rise at once, he insisted, and come with him to witness 'an historic event'.

No sooner had I got into my trousers and trainers than he hustled me to the door and out into the rain. On our way through the village he explained that Chieske had taken over an empty hut which had now been converted into a public church for the Mekroti converts. We were going to perform, he said, a public baptism.

The hut was medium sized, its former inhabitants having died or moved out. Chieske and his friends had decorated the interior in imitation of our own chapel in the Gesu; its crude approximations to our own altar and tabernacle, the rudimentary crosses and statues, reminded me of cargo-cult artefacts; but O'Rourke seemed unconcerned at the distortions. He looked delighted; beaming about him and pointing out various features that he thought noteworthy. And all the while Chieske was prancing about his 'church' festooned with rosaries and crucifixes and shaking a Bible in his fist.

There were some fifty or so villagers in the hut calling out in dreary sing-song voices for our 'water rite', although it seemed inconceivable to me that they did not regard it as merely a healing art for the virus.

O'Rourke said, 'I am convinced, Nicholas, that these people have been infused spontaneously by the Holy Spirit.' Then turning to Luis, he said, 'You must tell Chieske to make sure they understand that they now believe in Papa-Belong-All; that their marriages should be binding;

229

that they should no longer believe in the magical powers of the coca leaf.'

As Luis attempted to parlay with Chieske, who was ringing the bell (over which he now had exclusive control), O'Rourke shouted excitedly to me, 'Is it not a consolation to see God publicly glorified through the mouth of a primitive native and a former tool of Satan!'

Forming the Mekroti into queues he now set to, sprinkling water over the heads of each of them in turn and gabbling the words of the baptismal rite in Latin. Chieske stood godfather for each and gave presents of aspirin, sugared water, and the precious lama for their coca quids.

Even as O'Rourke poured the water over their heads, some cried out that they had been cured of the fever; and some declared that they had been cured of other ailments, such as lameness and headaches.

No sooner had the service ended than Chieske led them in a procession around the 'church' with unintelligible chants and peculiar posturing in imitation of our liturgy; but the restless O'Rourke was already moving on. Clutching me and Luis in each hand he said that we must now go to see 'Joseph' and the trickster Takakhe, who were dying.

It was a short walk to Anonha's hut; even as we approached we heard the rhythm of finger-drums and chants that made a strange counterpoint to Chieske's singing.

As we entered and grew accustomed to the gloom, we saw a huddle of bodies covered in skins and blankets around a mound of red-hot stones. Led by Takakhe, a group of elders, Anonha among them, were performing a ritualistic sweat while chewing the coca leaf and chanting lugubriously. O'Rourke stood over them, assuming a commanding posture and making disdainful grimaces.

Pointing to Anonha, O'Rourke called out: 'You are wrong to be doing that. Takakhe has not the power you think; it is only Papa-Belong-All who is the lord of our lives.'

But they ignored him and went on singing and chewing

alternately. They no longer had any interest in O'Rourke's harangues.

I went over to Takakhe and tried to offer him some encouragement and comfort. Luis had told me that the shaman had slipped in the mud and fractured his thigh. He lay close to the hot stones, evidently in pain, but uncomplaining, unabashed and apparently secure in his beliefs to the end.

I stretched out my hand to Anonha. He looked up and gave a faint smile with his eyes. He asked Luis to come over so that he could interpret for him. He wanted to pass on a message to the white visitors.

Faltering and gasping for breath, he said, 'Brothers, your eyes deceive you when you look at us. You think you see living men, but we are nothing but the ghosts of the dead. This world we tread is not solid; it will open very soon to swallow us and put us all among the dead.'

O'Rourke had already gone.

Later, in the afternoon, when I had returned to the Gesu, a messenger came to tell us that Takakhe was dead.

In the early evening a cry went up throughout the whole village, and it was announced that Anonha had also died. I lay on my hammock too fatigued to move.

Anonha's passing filled me with sorrow. We had never exchanged a word in a common language and yet I seemed to have understood his every look and gesture. His eyes were gentle and observant; his look was authoritative but sensitive. He seemed to react to every small shift in a person's feelings and moods. His eyes reflected everything they saw. He could be happy, sad, cold, open, and shut-up. Sometimes he seemed to be wary as if waiting for the slightest indication of one's mood. When he laughed he made everyone laugh with him. He knew secrets. He had a strange reverential way of moving his whole body when he turned. I said a prayer in thanksgiving for his life.

*

In the middle of the night I heard harsh cries outside the Gesu and a sound of hissing. The fabric of the building shuddered several times as if somebody was throwing rocks at the walls and the roof.

As I lay in my hammock weak and exhausted, my thoughts tended towards home. I had little hope that I should return to my own world: but I was tormented by the thought that the Mekroti tragedy might go unrecorded, forgotten, and without witness; that it should have been entirely in vain.

Then it struck me, a reflection that shocked me, even as I formulated it: that I wished Christian O'Rourke dead.

CHAPTER 29

I had awoken the next day to the news that there were running fights between supporters of the dead Anonha and Chieske's gang of converts; even as I put my legs over the side of my hammock, Luis came in to tell me that a confrontation was taking place at the door of the Gesu.

Dressing hurriedly I staggered outside to find most of the able-bodied villagers facing each other in two bands. The leader of Anonha's faction was a tall young man called Pedra, who showed no fear of Chieske and looked ready to take him on in any kind of physical combat; he was joined by a determined group of young men who were tensing their muscles and attempting to look menacing.

It had stopped raining and the worst of the flooding had abated; there was even a hint of the sun between the great boiling early morning clouds.

Pedra was pointing up at the red-painted cross above the Gesu; it appeared that he and his followers were claiming that the cross was to blame for the epidemic and the ceaseless rains. O'Rourke and Chieske stood before them, arms folded, daring the first to make a move against the emblem. Already, Luis told me, one of Pedra's group had tried to climb up the outside of the building to dismantle the cross, but Chieske had chased up after him, climbing the building like a monkey and pulling him down.

As I arrived on the scene the two sides were exchanging ugly looks, with Chieske in his manic element – pulling faces and making rude gestures with his genitals. The contest of postures went on for some fifteen minutes or so until a youth appeared with a handful of rocks and started hurling them up at the offending image, to the glee of his companions. Not one of the missiles hit the spindly target, but O'Rourke affected to be outraged at what he called 'the heinous blasphemy': stamping about and looking up to the heavens he took up a portion of his gown and rent it in hieratic gesture of holy anger.

This seemed to break the tension; in any case the young man had run out of rocks. In the uneasy lull that followed, O'Rourke instructed Chieske to ring the mission bell to call for silence.

With flowing gestures and an amazing series of facial expressions he succeeded in gathering both factions around him. He stood more than head and shoulders above them, and he looked strong enough to fell anyone who might challenge him physically. But he was now all gentleness, all smiles, all encouragement, beckoning them with graceful motions of his hands and fingers.

When they stood facing him in a semicircle, he asked Luis to come forward to translate, then he started to mime and speak, conveying as best he could the following speech.

'Neither we nor any man,' he cried, 'could bring or prevent sickness or the rains: Papa-Belong-All is alone the master of these things and distributes his benefits according to his pleasure. The cross up there was not the cause of the sickness and the rains and the floods; but perhaps, rather, Papa-Belong-All is angry because you have listened to the Takakhe and believed in the power of the coca leaf instead of regarding it as a herb, dangerous in excess.'

O'Rourke went on to say that they should take note that following the death of Takakhe the heavy rains had stopped, that the weather was now returning to its normal pattern for the rainy season; that the fever, which had claimed many lives in the village, now seemed to be at an end. He had nothing bad to say about Anonha; no. Anonha was a good headman and he lamented his passing; but they should now acknowledge the wickedness of their shaman.

He reiterated his argument in different ways, using all

the natural eloquence of his gestures and sign language until he was certain that he had carried them with him. Then, in a final peroration, he suggested that if they would acknowledge, all of them, the reverence that was due to the cross in memory of the son of Papa-Belong-All, he would make a special distribution of food and also of 'lama'.

I had been watching the faces of the young men, who had been gradually joined now by the women and children of the village, all staring with fascination and submission at the huge Rook. When the promise of the 'lama' was understood their faces lit up with smiles and they began to talk quietly among themselves in hushed voices.

In a brief interlude, during which O'Rourke sent Chieske and some of his followers into the Gesu on an errand, the young man who had led the anti-cross faction came up to O'Rourke and apologised for offering insult to our emblem.

O'Rourke was beside himself with complacency; but I saw in the young man's expression a sense of fatalism, and I was convinced that all would not end well.

Turning to me, O'Rourke said, 'You see, Nicholas, they are very docile and influenced by temporal considerations; they can be bent as one pleases, which is not a very happy state of affairs, is it now?'

As he said this I felt the angry blood pumping through my head; my fists were so itchy to belt him one that I had to remove myself several yards to get out of earshot.

Even as I did this Chieske had appeared with the large, realistic image of the crucified Christ from our chapel. O'Rourke took it in his hands and raised it above the heads of the people. Chieske's followers were also emerging from the Gesu with sacks of provisions and calabashes of lime.

With Luis's help he now launched energetically into a new harangue. He started to instruct them on the mystery of the cross, telling them of the great honour it was accorded everywhere in the white man's world. He told them how it

235

was to be seen on many of the houses and buildings in our world, and as he talked the eyes of the Mekroti were raised to the image he held aloft.

In a final burst of enthusiasm O'Rourke announced that they should form a procession to adore the cross so as to make recompense for the dishonour that had been done to it. He would then distribute food and lama to each person who was prepared to kneel and kiss the image.

Before he could complete the announcement the Mekroti were hurrying across the compound to their huts.

O'Rourke was as perplexed as I was by this behaviour until we saw them emerging moments later carrying bowls and receptacles. Within a few minutes he was surrounded by a jostling crowd, pushing and squabbling to be first to be served. Among them I saw Mabla and her mother, and Sakel, their faces intent on the promised food ration.

The crucifix was propped up by a length of wood so that it stood at a forty-five degree angle to the ground of the compound. Taking off his shoes O'Rourke genuflected and bowed three times before going down on his knees before the image and kissing its feet. Raising his head he cried out. 'We adore Three, O Christ, and we bless Thee, because by Thy Holy Cross Thou hast redeemed the world'.

One by one the Mekroti, both baptized and unbelievers alike, came forward and awkwardly imitated the act of worship, each receiving from Luis a small ration of food, the adult males receiving, in addition, a portion of lime. Meanwhile O'Rourke broke into song, intoning in a cracked and quavering voice the words of the hymn, 'Crux Fidelis':

> Faithful Cross, of all trees
> The most noble.
> There is no forest that boasts a tree with
> Branches and flowers as yours.
> Sweet the wood and sweet the nails,
> Sweet the load you bear.

When all the food had been distributed and the people had returned to their huts, I followed O'Rourke into the Gesu. He was standing in our kitchen, his face suffused with a strange look of joy and compassion; behind him Luis was reckoning up the remains of our food stocks, which looked to have been halved by the distribution.

O'Rourke was saying to me, 'Oh, Nicholas, their hearts have become tractable, and God has seen fit to bring forth from their deepest misfortunes their spiritual well-being.'

I was shaking with fury, my heart thumping with aggression.

'What rot!' I shouted. 'All you've done is given back the food you took from them in the first place!'

He inclined his head and smiled to himself. 'Have you not heard, Nicholas, of the text *unde exeunt flumina revertuntur* – the rivers flow back whence they came? It was for them, as for ourselves, that God provided in due season this manna from heaven . . .'

I was yelling at him, demanding that he acknowledge that the stores we had appropriated would soon be gone, that their plantations were devastated, that the people were going to starve. O'Rourke was talking over me, babbling texts and homiletic phrases in English and Latin, 'Nature contents herself with little; whenever self-gratification is banished, worldly anxieties and base passions are also excluded . . . And remember the words of the prayer *tu das illis escam tempore opportuno. Aperis tu manus et imples omne animal bendictione tua* – you give them sustenance in due season. O open your hands and fill all creatures with your blessing.'

CHAPTER 30

There was a light rain, and it looked as if the weather might come fine. I was standing at noon by the door of the Gesu ruminating on a list of options, wondering whether I could get down to Aranuba with Luis by dugout canoe, cursing myself for being such a hopeless, physically awkward, impractical kind of man, when my heart leapt. Just emerging from the trail, ambling slowly towards the compound, his hands behind his back as if he were out on a constitutional stroll, came the unmistakable, friendly figure of Father John. And with him, just a little way behind, a group of well-fed-looking people in Western clothes, laden with bulging knapsacks and other impedimenta.

As I yelled out and leapt with joy, an absurdly literary notion flashed across my mind; it was as if the jumble of scripts that had steered the mission through its tragi-comic nightmare of culture collision, mistranslation, and misfortune was about to make sense: as if the macabre theatrical were about to resolve itself in a finale worthy of *Henderson the Rain King*, or, better still, the *The Lord of the Flies*; that I was about to fall in tears at the feet of the saviour – the man of confident power in his crisply laundered uniform; indeed I could already see his trim cruiser lying at anchor on the horizon of my mind, ready to carry us back to security and to home.

As I raced up to John, my arms outstretched, I was at first curious, then perplexed; then I stopped in my tracks. As he continued to approach me I saw that his face was a swollen mass of livid bruises and lacerations; his hands were tied behind his back, and his eyes looked blank with despair.

The man who dogged his footsteps, a native Peruvian like the rest, was pointing an automatic weapon at his back and a woman's voice was calling out to me from the midst of this strange, heavily armed group. She separated herself from the others; coming forward, she shouted '*Hola*! Jesuit *gringo*!'

It was Augusta.

The members of the party, dressed in a variety of military cast-offs, had come to a standstill. There were about ten of them, all men, their dark bronze Amerindian faces hidden by eye shades. We stood frozen as we were, while the Mekroti came slowly, uncertainly, from the huts, gathering in the compound in a semicircle to face their new visitors.

At length Luis appeared; he said just one chilling word: '*Senderistas*!' Then came Chieske, wary and subdued, and finally O'Rourke, a dramatic constrast to the visitors – a towering scarecrow of rags and tatters, still wearing his filthy shredded Jesuit gown, his great grizzled head held high, his beard a matted, grizzled fan; fearless, indignant, but statuesque and silent like all the rest.

When the entire population of the village had assembled Augusta walked up to Father John; yanking him by the hair, she forced him to kneel on the ground; then, whipping a revolver from her belt, she shot him through the head.

Paralysed with shock, I was staring at the collapsing body of John as O'Rourke leapt forward in two or three swift bounds; he was kneeling over John's body, his arm raised in benediction to give him absolution.

As he made the sign of the cross Augusta screamed out an order through clenched teeth and two of the guerrillas seized O'Rourke in arm-locks.

O'Rourke shot up from the ground with a roar of fury and strength, coming straight up with a ramrod back like a missile from a silo, stirring up the sand of the compound, his neck rigid, his mighty battering-ram of a head bent forward; then he sent first one then the other flying off their feet in opposite directions. Weapon safety catches were snapping, orders were being yelled, the men were piling in on him, hitting him with their weapon butts, kicking him with their combat boots.

It took six of them two or three minutes to subdue him and tie his arms and hobble his ankles; when they pulled him to his feet by his beard, his face was covered in blood; but he was still reciting the *'De Profundis'*, still calling on God for the soul of his dead companion priest.

Together O'Rourke and I were frogmarched into the Gesu.

We were kicked and punched, poked and hammered with the rifle butts and forced to sit on the floor of the kitchen with our backs to the wall. Then they ripped away our upper garments and tied our wrists in front of us.

In the depths of our building we could hear the chapel being desecrated. Outside the Mekroti wailed and screamed as their huts were ransacked. Luis was nowhere to be seen. I imagined him out there acting for the guerrillas now; the serviceable language machine, struggling with a new set of propositions, a new set of questions and answers. I was shaking with fear, turning over in my imagination all the descriptions I had heard of Shining Path atrocities. Out of the corner of my eye I could see O'Rourke sitting upright, priestly; I could hear him praying the psalms in Latin.

One of the guerrillas eventually told him in Spanish to shut up; but he went on praying. Then the man came over and silenced him; he hit him in the mouth with the butt of his rifle.

All afternoon we sat as the guerrillas went about their sinister ministry of fear, turning out the huts, barking questions at the villagers, tormenting and beating those who had been singled out for whatever inscrutable reason as deserving a beating; we heard it all.

My parched tongue, congealed with blood, cleaved to the roof of my mouth; I had urinated and opened my bowels where I sat. I was certain of only one thing; only one thing occupied my mind now: the panic fear of death. My imagination was working on a repertoire of torture and butchery; I lived in my mind through every terrible form of death until I went blank with the sheer surfeit of terror.

Then I found myself praying against the terror; I cried out to God from the depths of my fear and despair and loneliness. I called on God, again and again and again, to deliver me, to hold me up, to save me. I could see no future, only a dark abyss of pain and violence; the total absence of a horizon of lived life. What would I not have done at that moment to secure even a glimmer of future beyond that day and night? Whom would I not have betrayed? Whom would I not have put in my place to be given back my life?

Then the thought dawned, with almost comical absurdity: I was going to be a martyr: *I*, Father Nicholas Mullen of the Society of Jesus, would enter the annals of the Church as a holy martyr, to be ranked alongside Edmund Campion, and John de Brebeuf, Isaac Jogues, and all the rest of them. My chest was heaving with the manic thought of such an absurd prospect! But where was the *grace* of acceptance? I felt nothing but an abyss of dread, and panic, and loneliness, and *non*acceptance.

At sunset two hurricane lamps were lit; there was a sound of low voices at the door, and Augusta came in.

We were roughly lifted from the floor and made to sit at the table while she settled herself opposite. She placed a bottle of pizco at her elbow, then she took out two cigarettes from her top pocket, putting one of them in my mouth and lighting it for me. Seeing that I had difficulty with my wrists she undid the binding. O'Rourke received no such consideration. That timid glimmer of hope was rising within me; perhaps Augusta had a spark of pity in her breast.

She sat for a long time looking at me, breathing deeply. Then she said, 'You see, Jesuit *gringo*, I warned you to stay away from the Eyebrow of the Jungle. This place is off limits to everybody except us and the dealers ... Now you've come trampling through and messed up these nice little people who produce the coca ...'

She lit her cigarette and took a swig from the bottle. She was looking steadily at O'Rourke. Eventually she said, 'So this is the famous Papa Rook! How do you do, Papa Rook!'

He spoke through broken teeth and bruised lips: '*Et ne nos inducas in tentationem* ...'

She leaned across the table and smacked him straight in the mouth. 'Don't *give* me that shit! Do you hear? I don't want to hear that Latin shit!'

I stole a glance at O'Rourke. His eyes were stony; he had strength and endurance; he was in another world; she did not exist for him.

'*Et ne nos inducas in tentationem* ...' he said once more.

She flinched, as if she would strike him again; then she seemed to change her mind. She put on her dark glasses; she relaxed and drew on her cigarette.

'We've got all night,' she murmured. 'We've got plenty of time ... I want to give you a chance ... *Fathers*.' She almost spat the word out. 'I want to give you the chance to *admit your errors*. We call it in our movement *rectification*, *thought* reform. Who knows, maybe I will give you back your lives.'

She spoke to her companions in a low voice. They put down their weapons; they sat on the floor, their backs to the grass wall. She took the pistol from her belt and placed it on the table before her. The grey-blue steel gleamed in the light of the hurricane lamps; I caught the harsh whiff of its oil lubricant. She took a long swig on the pizco bottle.

'I hear that your Pope is to spend two billion dollars,' she said eventually through the cigarette smoke; her voice was jaunty, conversational. 'Two billion dollars to evangelize

Latin America for the year 2000! Did I hear that correctly? We know what that's for . . . we know what his true aim is: it's to erect what our chairman, Abimael Guzman, called the reactionary shield. But we are going to eat the Church in Latin America for our dessert . . .'

She laughed huskily, blowing her smoke towards us: 'For our *dessert*! Our *pudding*!'

I could hear O'Rourke breathing deeply beside me; I could detect the whispered prayers coming off the tip of his tongue; I was praying too, a silent prayer that he would shut up and not antagonize her further.

But she was ignoring him now. I could tell that she was preparing to stoke up one of those diatribes she had tried on me in Iquitos.

'We know what the Catholic Church is up to,' she started, 'that's why you had your famous Second Vatican Council, so that you could find new ways of staying in business . . . We know what you're up to; we know why the Pope came down here preaching peace and blessing the weapons of genocide. He even had the nerve to go to Ayacucho, the home of our movement, and preach at us about evil never being the road to good. We've seen his plots in Poland, the Ukraine, in Russia, in China . . .'

Sitting at the table where so recently O'Rourke had harangued the Mekroti elders, she embarked on a one-way seminar. She was raking over Spanish Conquest history, the actions of the Dominicans and the Jesuits, the atrocities against the Inca Atahualpa, the Vatican conspiracies; the Liberation Theologians with their attempt to outflank and hi-jack true Marxism . . . And as her harangue expanded she took frequent swigs from her bottle and lit one cigarette after another.

Exhausted almost to collapse, I found it difficult to keep pace with her drift, until a new direction in her harangue brought me to my senses. She began to talk about death.

'Mao once said: We are ready to die; we dared the sun and the moon to bring a new day! The blood of martyrdom is the fire of purity. Are *you* prepared to die for your beliefs? Because if you are not, you are finished. There was a time when you Jesuits claimed all the martyrs; now you die like cats and dogs in the road! The martyrs of Latin America are our native peoples, thousands and millions of them; people like our Edith Lagos gunned down in Ayacucho where the Pope had the nerve to preach to us.'

She was looking at me steadily. 'Are *you* ready to die for your beliefs, Nicholas?' she said. 'Are *you*, Papa Rook?'

I was stunned. I could think only of the ruthless swiftness with which she had shot John through the head that afternoon.

She was glaring at us in silence, as if determined to have an answer. Then she said: 'Why don't you speak to me, Papa Rook? Did the cat get your tongue?' And she laughed huskily, amused by her own homely Americanism in that savage setting.

She turned and spoke to one of the soldiers. He rose at once from the floor; he straightened himself up and disappeared through the partition as if on his way to the chapel.

'We've got something ready for you two gentlemen,' she said, 'something to assess your suitability for rectification. Something to see what you're made of.'

She gave me another cigarette and lit it for me. 'Nicholas,' she said, 'you are a literary man, are you not? You've read George Orwell . . . You remember in *Nineteen Eighty-Four* how Winston faces his worst fear; when he must choose between submitting to that fear or sacrificing the woman he thinks he loves? That's a profound idea of Orwell's — that fear . . . It gets right down to the basics, the science of human nature itself . . . Did you wonder, when you were reading that book, about yourself? Did you ever wonder how *you* would cope? Did you think about your own secret fear? Your loyalty to the one you love?'

As she was still speaking, I heard O'Rourke gasp; it was a sound that sent a jolt of terror through me. Then I saw what he had seen. The guerrilla had returned silently; he was carrying our gold and silver ciborium, its consecrated Eucharistic hosts – the Real Presence of Christ. He had taken the lid off and we could see the pure white wafers against the gleam of the gilded interior.

Augusta took the cup in her hand and placed it on the table between us. I could hear O'Rourke whispering under his breath the hymn of Thomas Aquinas: '*Adoro Te Devote, Laetens Deitis'*

O Godhead here in hiding, I adore Thee.

She seemed to be waiting for him to finish, in an almost surreal demonstration of civility.

There was a moment of intense silence.

'Papa Rook,' she said quietly. 'I want you to listen to me carefully. These bits of white stuff in this cup, these little circles of white stuff; you think that they are the real substance of your Christ, your God. But you are mistaken. I'm telling you that they're just bits of old wafer; just stale old wafer.'

She took one of the wafers and bit into it, spitting it out almost immediately on the floor and stamping on it with her combat boot.

'Now I'm going to ask you to do something very simple here, Papa Rook,' she went on. 'I'm going to put one of these wafers down in front of you on the table and I'm going to ask you to spit on it. And after you've spat on it, I want you to say – "I deny that this is the body of Christ!"'

She let this sink in for a moment; then she said, 'If you do it as I ask you, Papa Rook, I'm going to spare your life . . . But if you don't, you're going to die tonight in the most painful way you could possibly imagine . . . Do you understand me? Accept the truth about these silly bits of white wafer; reject your magic superstitions: then you can live.'

With this, slowly, almost reverentially, she placed one of the hosts before him on the table.

My heart was pounding so hard in my chest that I thought

I would black out. I wanted to speak to O'Rourke; I wanted to plead with him, to tell him that it would be no sacrilege to do what she told him under such compulsion; all my scholastic training with its subtle principles of 'double effect', all my grounding in the casuistry of 'amphibology' and 'mental reservation' were at the tip of my tongue. And yet, so were the years of sacred taboo, the courageous example of our Jesuit predecessors in the face of torture: We *will* be true to Thee till *death*; we *will* . . . we *will* be true to Thee till *death*.

I could say nothing. I sat frozen, waiting to see what O'Rourke would do.

O'Rourke was moving; he was breathing deeply; he was lowering his huge head towards the table until it was no more than two inches from the host; he was saying, to himself, in quiet measured tones: '*Domine non sum dignus ut intres sub tectum meum; sed tantum dic verbo et sanabitur anima mea* [Lord I am not worthy that Thou shouldst enter under my roof; only say the word and my soul shall be healed].' He paused for a few moments more, then with a swift jerk downwards and a stab of his tongue he took the host straight into his mouth. Then he raised his head and shoulders once more. He was very still and silent.

Her cigarette dangling from her lips, Augusta began to clap; a slow hand clap. She laughed her wheezy smoker's laugh; she said, 'Oh, you're made of the tough stuff, Papa Rook, I can see that . . . You've got to be made of *very* tough stuff to do that! To throw away your life for a bit of stale old wafer!'

Now she was looking at me. She was scrutinizing my face through her dark glasses.

She was taking another host out of the ornate cup, raising it before her eyes as if she were about to invite me to the Eucharistic rite.

'Now. This is for you, Nicholas,' she said. 'I know that you're scared shitless. I can smell the fear coming off you.

246

You're not like Papa Rook; you're something different. You're gutless, and mediocre, and corrupt; the very best hope for our success . . . I'm going to place this wafer down before you; I want to see you spit on it; I want to hear you deny Christ, out loud; then I'm going to give you back your miserable life. I'm going to set you free so that you can drag the memory of your sacrilege and your lack of faith around with you for the rest of your days.'

She placed the host on the table.

Gazing at the circle of whiteness before me, I was enveloped by silence and stillness. Outside I could hear the rain and the wind in the trees; an abandoned village dog barking.

The instant seemed to expand into a vast moment of clarity and freedom, a panorama of associations and feelings connected with presence of God in the humble piece of bread before me. I found myself thinking of the 'clock-God' of my childhood; of the white circle of paper in my Mass games in the bedroom; of 'the most important day in my life', and Tom Daley walking ahead of me from the communion rail, slowly, gingerly, as if he carried in his mouth a small bird; I saw in that single moment each and every one of the thousands of Masses I had celebrated, bringing down God into that piece of bread, and taking him into my body . . . I thought of the church on Eastern Avenue, the Eucharistic hosts scattered and pissed upon. I was thinking of Jill, and all the hundreds of times I had 'had' her while my heart was shut against her. And I thought of the Mekroti's holy 'lama' – their path to the Goddess creator . . . I was gazing at the circle of whiteness: this Godhead here in hiding, this mystery of Faith, a mere thing, that I could take possession of; a mere vulnerable object, to be taken up, appropriated, exploited, abused, spat upon. What was at the heart of this mystery of the presence of God in such a weak and vulnerable object? Could I save both my life and my immortal soul by severing my outward actions from my innermost secret thoughts? Was there a difference between the words of my lips and the words in my heart?

The moment passed. I spat upon the host, just as I had been spiting on it for years. I said loudly, clearly, without inner or outer reservation: 'I deny this body of Christ'.

Then I began to weep.

CHAPTER 31

O'Rourke had been taken away as if to a fate that had been prepared for him in advance. Augusta had stayed behind with me a while, watching me in silence as she smoked a cigarette; I was pleading with her to tell me what was to happen to O'Rourke, begging her not to harm him.

Eventually she said, 'You'll see!'

Then she went out into the night.

Minutes later they came rushing in on me without warning, a band of young men I recognized as Chieske's friends. Holding me strongly by the arms they indicated with smiles and gestures that I had nothing to fear; then I was frogmarched out of the Gesu and through the rain and mud to the hut that Chieske had commandeered as his 'church'.

The remaining population of the village, it seemed, was huddled in its semi-darkness. On the mud-floored 'sanctuary', before the crude altar, a rudimentary cross had been erected a little higher than a man. A group of Chieske's cronies were gathered around, dressed in stolen items of our robes. A fire had been lit a little way from the altar and a Mekroti was busy stoking it with dry twigs and branches.

O'Rourke was standing in the centre of this 'sanctuary' facing the people. The guerrillas had gone, leaving me and O'Rourke and the Mekroti to our fate. Luis was nowhere to be seen.

I was just a few yards from O'Rourke and we exchanged looks. He was praying to himself and seemed calm, as if fully resigned to whatever masquerade was in store.

Chieske was moving to and fro around the altar muttering to himself and bowing and posturing with weird decorum, as if he were aping our rituals. Suddenly he stopped in front of O'Rourke and gazed into his eyes; O'Rourke looked back at him steadily and attentively, his face deathly white. Meanwhile the people had started up an incantation reminiscent of our plainchant.

Chieske now began to act out a dumb show, as if he were telling O'Rourke that there was much pleasure and comfort after death with an abundance of eating and drinking and sexual intercourse. And all this time O'Rourke continued to gaze at him impassively, nodding his assent to everything Chieske seemed to propose.

Held tightly by Chieske's young men on either side of me, I was thinking, absurdly, of an incident in those far-away days of the novitiate, and the weekly ritual known as 'the Ring' when we sat in a circle and told each other's faults under the cold eye of Father Rector. We were polite and carried ourselves with outward dignity, but the undercurrents of loathing were so savage that I expected physical violence to erupt at any moment. 'Brother Nicholas,' a companion of mine would say with a faintly ingratiating voice, 'often has a look of arrogance and pride; well . . . just an apparent air of that sort . . . at times.' All right, Brother Francis, I would be thinking, just you wait! On the nights after 'the Ring' the sound of our self-inflicted flagellations had a venom and a force that was diabolical.

The violence of Chieske's ceremony exploded with a suddenness and sickening brutality that sent my brain spinning into a black abyss.

When I came up out of that darkness I had retched up all over my chest; I was still being held, supported under my armpits by the young men on either side of me.

In the speckled gloom I could see the naked figure of O'Rourke, barely alive, wrists and feet sagging and skewered; battered and bleeding head motionless, limp; eyes like marble looking hopelessly into the darkness.

His great heaving torso was breaking into a sporadic death rattle, like an old man climbing a long steep flight of stairs.

Chieske was approaching the crucified figure of Rook; he was making many swift and elaborate signs of the cross and genuflections. He took up Rook's penis; he held it; then he lowered his head and took it straight into his mouth.

I was shrieking; I was howling from the depths of my lungs to the grass roof above me.

Chieske was turning to face the people, wild-eyed, his mouth full; his chin and chest one great beard of blood.

At that moment my guardians released me; they were rushing forward towards the body of Rook; his limbs were being hacked from his body, his fingers from his hands; his head was severed with one blow from his shoulders and tossed to the 'congregation'.

I felt a firm grasp on my arm pulling me backwards, away from the sanctuary; I turned, my fists ready to fight for my life.

It was Luis, he was pulling me away through the milling, screaming people; pulling me away to safety. Even before we reached the door a man came screaming past us carrying a foot on a stick.

Out in the open air we started to run; he was pulling me through the dark, heading for the river and the Mekroti dugouts.

EPILOGUE

A Dying Breed

'Tis sweeter far to me,
To walk together to the kirk
With a goodly company.

S.T. Coleridge [*The Rime of the Ancient Mariner*]

So, my old parish, Our Lady of Lourdes, took me back.

It's no New Jerusalem, my parish. The church stands on a roaring high road funnelling four lanes of unceasing traffic each way between the City and the factories of Dagenham, the dormitory suburbs, and the Tilbury docks. Our church is a pre-First World War warehouse of a building, standing high above the shopping parades, the betting shops, the supermarket, the used-car show room with its festoons of bunting; our two pubs – the Prospect and the Princess Alice; the public library and the Bingo hall. To the north of the high road is a jungle of residential streets and council estates, cramped terraced houses, concrete tower blocks. Most of the houses and buildings show signs of decay. Our streets are like graveyards for wrecked cars; it's difficult to park for rubbish skips and bumper-to-bumper rows of beaten-up Cortinas and Crestas and bruised Transit vans with coat-hanger aerials and patches of primer paint. The pavements and roads are unmended and seldom cleansed of garbage and dog shit; grass grows up in the pavement cracks, and I've even seen nettles and exotic wild flowers; the public urinals and telephone kiosks are smashed and unusable; young men with shorn heads prowl with Staffordshire bull terriers and Rottweilers. To the south there are grey vistas of industrial wasteland, disused factories, gasworks, a container-lorry depot. Beyond lies the river. To reach open fields in any direction would take a journey on foot of almost a day.

Some of my old parishioners still remember a time when London's docklands, now cleared and silent, were the centre of the world; when the sound of foghorns echoed across the winter sky, when seamen fought outside the pubs on a Saturday night, and funnels and mast-flags from the Middle East, the Far East, Africa, the Americas, inched slowly up and down the river on the southern horizon. My old parishioners look back on those days with a sense of puzzled nostalgia; they would not wish them back, but sometimes they think that an element of romance has disappeared from their lives.

They feel a bit like that about our church. On weekdays Our Lady of Lourdes is attended by the elderly; they come in for noonday Mass, off the high road, from the flats and the sheltered housing projects, from the library and the steaming warmth of Nan's Pantry café. Some of them are uneasy as if not quite knowing what to do with their hands and feet. They remember the early days of Monsignor Keenan when their church was like a public catacomb; when they looked up at the sanctuary with its reredos of plaster saints, its votive lamps and baroque candlesticks, the ornate silver tabernacle; the Lady Chapel with its forest of candles; the Monsignor and his curates bedecked in heavy copes and tasselled dalmatics, genuflecting and rising together with their backs to the congregation. They remember the cadence of the Latin, the Corpus Christi processions, the raised Eucharistic host encased in its monstrance like an emblazoned clock; they remember the Lenten missions with threats of hellfire and three-hour queues for confession; the old hymns, the Children of Mary, the Requiem Masses and the 'De Profundis'.

Now they look at a table surrounded by plain white walls; the ornate silver tabernacle replaced by a simple wooden box, discreetly situated in an alcove. Even the plaster statue of the Holy Mother has gone, its carved wood replacement relegated to the back of the church. Our people are no longer inclined to lose themselves in their innermost secret thoughts. Now all they see is each other, and me, for what we are.

The elderly have been susceptible to the changes, especially those disappearing dogmas about death – their daily meditation. I sometimes think they are indignant, although perhaps secretly grateful. They come up to me in the porch, like Mrs Minogue last Wednesday: 'Whatever happened . . .' That's how they start.

'Whatever happened to Purgatory?' she said.

'What about it, Mrs Minogue . . .?'

'You never mention it from the pulpit, Father.'

'Since *you* mention it, we don't have a pulpit any more, Mrs Minogue . . .'

'Which reminds me,' she went on, 'whatever happened to women covering their heads in the church?'

On Sunday my church fills up with people four times in the day; there are so many they have to stand in serried ranks at the back by the newspaper table and the pamphlet racks, and up in the abandoned choir and organ loft and along the aisles. It's the scope of their ages that hits me first: the screaming babies and obstreperous toddlers; the sullen, gauche prepubescents; teenagers dressed for the Day of Rest like New Age space travellers in studded leather, black leggings, and combat boots; young marrieds in golf shirts and freshly laundered jeans and day-glo trainers; the middle-aged in blazers and cardigans; the elderly in those shapeless coverall raincoats. There are Irish and British, Asians and Afro-Caribbeans, Vietnamese and Hong Kong Chinese, Italians, Poles, and Lithuanians, Spanish, and Filipinos, and a floating pilgrimage of unidentified polyglots passing through.

I stand at the altar facing them; we sing together, and pray together; we sit and stand and kneel and look at each other; we give each other the sign of peace; we take that little white bread wafer with a sip of red wine, in amnesty and mercy for the time being – which is the only time we have. They haven't come in from the streets to escape life out there; they come inside because they think it makes a difference.

I find it daunting looking out at all those faces: the adoring, the bored, the perplexed, the happy, the dreamers, the doubters, the jobless, the unloved, the sick, and the dying. I find it even more daunting when it comes to *saying* something.

I try to avoid generalizations; I don't talk about the soul, or infinity, or hell, or the Devil, or angels, or even heaven. I try to think and talk human, mortal.

Most of my congregation seem unaware that anything is changing, that anything is missing. Just being there, for the time being, seems enough. The elderly and the introverted sometimes look wary; but on the whole they're content that we're drifting away from those old dreams of paradise and hell; floating back into the midst of *this* Life.

Sometimes I go into the church late at night and sit in the darkness, looking up at the winking sanctuary lamp. I gaze at the wooden tabernacle, which stores those wafers of bread, and I wonder about the mystery of His presence, the mystery of faith. I can only suppose that He has as much right – as bread itself – to appear to us in the form of food. What better way (than the act of love!) to share, than by breaking bread and taking wine.

I suspect that His presence in the bread is a kind of language; like building the New Jerusalem, it's not a language I shall manage to learn in time; but sitting in the darkness I sometimes get an inkling of its meaning.

Scientists tell us that our universe of galaxies and stars, and chemical elements and physical laws, and life itself, was already determined from the very first moment of the Big Bang. They talk of 'fine tuning'; they say that had the values of the natural constants varied even slightly in one direction or another, our universe could not have been hospitable to life; no conscious human being could have existed to gaze out and back over the long odyssey we have travelled from the first great burst of energy.

I have a sense that He, too, known by so many names, has been travelling with us across those aeons of time and space; that His story is written in our brains and nerves, so that we are at home in this world, at home with each other; and at home with Him too.

He is engraved in us from the very beginning – sculpted in our faces and foreheads, resplendent in our eyes. I can no more ignore Him than I can ignore these hands. I can strain in every nerve and fibre to deny Him, but He is there, creator and giver of life: on my tongue and in my lips; in the shape and sound of my words; more present in me, and each other, than the food we eat and drink.

'Who do you say that I am?'

'You *are* us.'

And so; have I been transformed at last? Have I achieved that *metanoia*, that huge change of heart? Have I become chaste at last in my single ministry?

What do I know of the secrets, the hidden and unequal drives and compulsions, the unconscious yearnings, the unique and hereditary weaknesses, the fallenness, of my nature? My chastity does not consist in covering up my nakedness in sanctuary robes; my chastity is *His* nakedness; my nakedness in *Him*.

We priests, with our professions of chastity and celibacy, are sneered at as fools for God's sake; discovered in our failings and our lecheries, our broken vows and desertions, we are derided as hypocrites and liars.

What am I saying?

I never did imagine that my compulsions were the acts of a free 'moral agent', any more than I believed that they were attended by the glee of tempting demons and the weeping of guardian angels. But with the final passing of my soul, with the death of that control-freak operator homunculus in the head soul, I feel that I am being liberated back into my body: no longer a stranger to men and women; no longer a stranger to the world; no longer a stranger to Him. I am reworking the story of who and what I am, in the knowledge that He, and He alone, in the mystery of His own being, is nothing less than the unknowable fullness of *all* our stories.

And so, am I transformed? Born again?

Not so long ago I went to Farm Street church to attend a memorial service for Christian O'Rourke, John Williams, and Sister Anna. More than two hundred priests were gathered on the sanctuary. We priests were quite a sight in our white robes, more like a wedding, but we had all the marks of a dying breed; an average age of sixty, someone said: we're dying off faster than the new ones are coming in.

None of us looked concerned about being a dying breed. After all, we priests look death daily in the face, and somehow keep cheerful; not because we know something different, but because we have no other alternative.

We stood in a semicircle around the altar, noting each other's grey hairs and bald patches and sagging paunches, and we sang that canticle, 'Like the deer that yearns for running water'.

As the chalice passed around I was remembering the Mekroti, and all those other victims, tortured and destroyed throughout our history in the name of faith. And I was remembering all the martyrs of our Church, whose powerful longings sent them in search of souls, and torture and death, across the oceans, and mountains, and jungles, and Arctic wastes.

Looking at the dying breed around me, I understood that, at last, and by force of circumstance, I was acquiescing, reconsidering my hopes and lowering my vision.

I cannot pretend that this surrender hasn't involved a loss: the stifling, the lobotomizing, of that quest for soaring infinity; the death of those dreams of Divine encounter, face to face. But then, who is spared the choice between a humbling acceptance of our mortal limits, and the cruel wounds of our eternal strivings?

One afternoon I got in my car and drove out towards Ilford. I drove up to Eastern Avenue and parked outside that ugly little church, still locked. Then I walked on up towards Jill's.

I'd done this several times before.

I went into the park below the flats and walked beneath the great horse chestnut trees, the leaves now turning in autumn.

I saw them coming towards me, making the turn by the rain shelter. I left the path; I stood by a screen of hawthorn bushes – watching as from a hidden place

Jill was with a young man. She was wearing a tracksuit; but it did not hide the fact that she was pregnant. She was just the same, her body slightly taut with nervous tension, her long beautiful face animated with intelligence and humour.

He was good-looking, about thirty-five; he had long fair hair, and he was dressed in jeans and polo-neck sweater. They were laughing at something; she turned to kiss him, and he kissed her back – gently. And there was Dominic running a little way ahead, two years or so older; and Henry the Jack Russell terrier racing in circles.

As I stood behind that bush, my shoulders heaving with weeping, some compulsion like the force of gravity sent Henry running in a great loop, across the flowerbeds and the herbaceous borders, around the trees, out beyond the swings and iron see-saws then back in a straight unerring line to me.

There I was, standing behind the hawthorn bush like some municipal park voyeur; and there was Henry pawing and panting and yelping at me. Jill and her man had stopped; they were looking back. Then Dominic came running over; he came around the bush and saw me standing there.

He stopped in his tracks, his eyes astonished and filling with tears. I went down on my knees, and with a sudden rush he had his arms around me; he was kissing me in the neck and hugging me. When I disentangled myself I put my finger up to my lips. He was searching the surface of my face, my nose, my lips, my eyes. And I was telling him in silence, pleading with him, to keep our secret. Then he hugged me round the neck once more, and he was gone.

As I walked away towards the park gate and the road, I looked back just once: Jill and her man were continuing on up the path; and Dominic was jumping and skipping ahead of them, his mind already on other matters.

AUTHOR'S NOTE

My portrayal of the Mekroti people was inspired by two works of anthropology: *The Children of Aataentsic*, by Bruce Trigger (Montreal, 1976), and *Intimate Communications*, by Gilbert Herdt and Robert J. Stoller (New York, 1990).

The dialogues between O'Rourke and the Mekroti are typical of early contact exchanges reported in *Jesuit Relations and Allied Documents*, edited by Rueben Gold Thwaites (New York, 1952).

J.C.